MW01132738

"Because of his strange unconventional (ye[...]
scape of stories are, more often than not, the most disarming of any around."
— Stephanie Bryant Anderson, Up the Staircase

"At the intersection of the mundane and the surreal you'll find Bud Smith. Poetic, profane and bizarre, Smith's characters and the world he creates simultaneously attracts and repulses; just when you think you've got the characters pegged they do something wonderful like shitting in a box or disgusting like falling in love. Outrageous and frighteningly real, Bud Smith's writing is always beautifully written and wildly entertaining."
— Martha Grover, Author of One More for the People

"Bud Smith writes plainsong, blue-collar fiction with the best of them, but what makes his work stand out are the voices of his characters, which speak with the resonance that has become the squalid pathos of the American Dream and turns that corrupted aesthetic into a thing of terrible and heartbreaking beauty. The triumph of Tollbooth, is that he accomplishes this on every page of the book. You cannot afford not to read it if you want to understand where the literary state of the union stands."
— Paul Corman Roberts, author of (Neo)commuter

"I don't give a fuck about craft or nuance or any of that MFA homogenized bullshit. If a writer doesn't engage me from the first sentence with his or her voice, I will not invest my time in reading his or her words. There are so many books and there is so much life to live. I don't waste my time with mediocrity and pretension. I love Bud Smith's voice. He makes me laugh so hard I ache. That is the highest compliment I can pay a writer. I love his short stories and I love Tollbooth. My favorite sentences from Tollbooth sum up what I love most about Bud Smith: 'I don't care if you pay the toll,' I said, and I didn't. I've always been a restless punk rock romantic.' Word."
— Misti Rainwater-Lites, author of Bullshit Rodeo

"Bud Smith takes us on a gritty, hilarious ride with human insanity: 'Can I have a receipt?' blasts back from every car. Smith explores the dark forces that collide and coexist in all of us. The mundane is eerily depicted in the hell of a job that keeps base emotions at the surface and yet Tollbooth submerges us in the strangeness and humor that keep us getting out of bed each day. Don't miss this one! It's as disturbing as it is entertaining."
— Meg Tuite, author of Bound By Blue

3/1/14
#AWP

Tollbooth

Bud Smith

To Bonnie,
Much weird love
Bud Smith

First Edition

Book cover and art designed by Rae Buleri

Edited by Andrew "Ink" Feindt
Bobby Fischer
Keith Baird
Mark Brunetti

ISBN: 1482642174
EAN-13: 9781482642179

Published by Piscataway House Publications.
www.theidiommag.com

Manufactured in the United States of America

"I hate the smell of flowers."

—Rae Buleri

172

Shrieking tires startled me from my magazine: swimsuit girls kissing deep in tropical water. A yellow LeSabre, already smoking severely, was struck by a rusted out F-250 pickup truck. The impact shredded plastic, stripped away metal, sent the LeSabre careening out of control—pummeling into the tollbooth next to mine.

Debris whizzed into the window beside me. *Cling*. I flinched so hard I cut my head open striking it on the door handle. The floor felt electrified.

Black smoke all around. I jumped out of my booth as tires squealed again. The pickup thundered away from the LeSabre, ripping its own bumper and fender off. It almost got struck by another car as it zoomed away wildly through the lanes.

Stop pay toll.

The LeSabre had flames licking out from beneath the hood. I coughed in a fit as the wind sent the fumes at me. Cars snaked by in super slow motion: rubber necking as birthright, rolling through the toll without paying. It was fourth of July weekend.

"It's gonna blow up!" I heard an old woman yell out of a red station wagon, like we were in an action movie.

I ran to the LeSabre, the dashboard was engulfed. I pulled open the driver's side door. A woman fell out, her hair on fire, her once fair face now black. Orange dress, one pink flip flop. One bare foot. I beat the fire out with my palms, my shirt, her own dress. She moaned. I beat harder.

There was a little girl in a car seat, still in the back. Three years old. Blonde pigtails. I yanked at her, the car seat was still buckled in. She shrieked, clawing me as I unclipped her belt. I threw the car seat with her in it onto the road—skidding. The plastic was beginning to melt. I had no fingerprints on my left hand. All I could smell was burning hair, skin, plastic.

The little girl shrieked louder. And louder. The burnt woman wheezed. There were drivers outside their cars then, staring at me. I heard an ambulance. I heard a thousand car radios all at once. I heard horns in the distance because traffic was stopped. Someone else screamed, "It's gonna blow up!"

It was my second day on the job.

171

From inside, it was hard to gauge reality. Life was in constant jerking motions everywhere else, but in the booth, nothing happened. It never would.

If the magma of the earth spurted out like a misjudged ejaculation and birthed new islands for my heart to discover, I would've done the happy dance even though I was crowded into my tin can: where all I had was three point five feet of space one way, three point five feet of space the other way. I was boxed in, dealing with trauma and insanity between the invention of new crossword puzzles to solve, candy bars to ingest, girls to fantasize about.

There were untold hours of torture in my work day, I spent most of that time staring cross-eyed out the window at the toll booth next to mine, its siding still melted from that horrible fire, many years prior. Wanda Lewis. No one had ever fixed the damage. Would never fix it, either.

On the stainless steel wall above me, I'd hung a certificate resulting from that odd day, which the mayor had given me at an event in the public park, there'd been a band and a barbecue and everything.

The certificate said:

On this day July 16th, 2000, we'd like to acknowledge the bravery and spirit of Jimmy Saare, who put others above himself and inspired an entire community with his actions.

At first, that acknowledgement had done a lot for my sense of pride. But years later, I found my enthusiasm gone. No matter how often I looked up at the certificate, I couldn't imagine myself doing something that selfless ever again. I'd become a different person because of the mindless monotony of my "labor".

On bad days in the booth, I didn't even look up from my newspaper or seventeen-hundredth cup of coffee. I'd just hold my middle finger up in the air, aimed at them. I'd done the detail for many years, and after many years, I could do it in my sleep.

Early on, I figured out to wear earplugs so their horns wouldn't wake me.

I was stationed at mile marker 84.7 on the Garden State Parkway in a three lane plaza. Central coastal New Jersey: my proud home. Pine trees. Suburbia beside the Atlantic ocean. Strip malls. A half hour north of Atlantic City and its blinking Casinos. Approximately one hour south of New York City. It still felt like the middle of nowhere. Explain that.

I kept falling in love with the beauty queens who zipped by. Every time one of those foxes blew through my toll lane I'd blow a load, sooner or later.

Just after dawn, a red Honda Civic pulled up driven by a fat man, drinking a 64 oz coffee, eating a donut: chocolate with pink sprinkles. He steered with his knee, blasting, if you can believe it, polka. He asked what they all did, "How much is the toll?" Donut mash was stuck in his teeth like he'd been eating shit.

"Thirty-five cents," I said robotically, leaning out the window.

"I don't think I have it," he said. "Do you take credit?"

I shook my head, nah. The car behind started to lay on its horn. The fat man threw up his arms in disgust, angrily stuffed his styrofoam coffee cup into the holder in his center console, "I'm just gonna go, sorry. I don't have it."

"I don't care if you pay the toll," I said, and I didn't. I've always been a restless punk rock romantic.

The Civic pulled away, a digital camera mounted above snapped a license plate pic. He'd get a fifty-five dollar ticket. Not very fair, in my mind.

In quick succession more cars rambled up, each one of them shaking dollars. For each dollar, I handed two quarters, a dime, and a nickel. They asked, "Can I have a receipt?"

So I handed them receipts *when* requested.

"Can I have a receipt?"

"How much is the toll?"

"Can I have a receipt?"

"Can I have a receipt?"

"Can I have a receipt?"

It was the only real job I've ever had. I would've ran off in the night, vanishing forever, but I was too chicken. I'd fallen into a troublesome void. When I closed my eyes, I saw snow static. My life felt devoid of hope. "Can I have a receipt?" The world spun around me in a violent blur.

"How much for this toll, mister?" spoke a sweet voice, jarring me back.

I looked into her clear blue eyes. Blonde dreadlocks, driving a shitty collapsing American car instead of a bright, plastic Japanese or Chinese one. She had on a white dress covered in neon violets. I felt a rose blooming in my junkyard heart. What really turned me on about her was that she'd turned down her radio when she pulled up.

"Thirty-five cents," I said, as if speaking a revelation.

"I don't have it," she said. But in her eyes, I saw something that I hadn't seen in many of those motorists: life exactly what I was lacking.

"OK," I said, biting my lip, nodding with affirmation, " . . . just go."

"Will I get a ticket?" she asked. I wanted to cradle her, save her from the hordes.

"No," I said, "I'll make sure you don't."

"Tomorrow—I'll bring you the money, tomorrow," she said, staring at me, her car putting, threatening to stall out. The women I love most on this green and blue marble are the women who drive shitty cars.

"It's OK, you don't have to say that. Nobody brings money 'tomorrow.' Never have, and I don't blame them." A pickup behind her started to blare its death horn.

"WHAT'S THE HOLD UP?" someone yelled.

"Tomorrow, I'll be back," she said as she winked and started to pull away. "MY NAME IS BEE" she called louder than her misfiring engine, heading toward the horizon and the industrial slums of the north.

A Chevy pickup pulled up. The guy had a salt and pepper beard, was drinking a beer, that rested between his knees. Lynryd Skynryd exploded from the stereo. "What's the goddamn problem?"

"You," I informed, pointing for clarity.

"Yeah, no shit."

"Yeah, no shit."

"How much is the toll?"

"Thirty-five cents. Do you need a receipt?"

"Yeah, asshole. I need a receipt and I need the two minutes of my life that you just wasted."

"OK, well here's your receipt, and here's your change, and I'll be sure to use my third wish from the genie's magic lamp to return those two minutes."

When he pulled away, I made a manual override on the computer, snapping a photo of his license plate. The computer went *ding*. I stuck his change in my pocket.

I relaxed, thinking about the blonde with the dreadlocks. I sighed, "Bee."

Up on the wall someone had drawn a giant cock on my certificate. The cock was leaking goo across the pertinent information about my good deeds.

168

My shift ended. I cashed out the drawer, watching José come across the middle of the line of booths, dodging cars. I wasn't religious, but I prayed daily that he'd get hit by a truck or a runaway ambulance. Anything.

He was the one who'd drawn the dicks on my certificates. He would deny it if asked. So I never brought it up. I just kept going to Officetown and photocopying the original. Mostly though, I hated him for the bright outlook he had on the job. He hated me because he was stuck working night shift.

The side door of the booth opened, he squeezed in: his sweater perfectly ironed, his pants neatly pressed, his shoes magnificently shined. He even wore a scarf with the Parkway emblem on it.

I had a sweater with the parkway emblem on it too. We'd all gotten them the previous Christmas. My sweater was kinda sorta . . . unwearable. Two weeks prior, I found a mannequin behind the strip mall with the Great Wok of China restaurant. After putting the sweater on the mannequin, I took it out to the sandpits and unloaded a bunch of rounds into it. The gun belonged to my best friend Ted, who used to go turkey hunting with his dad. I'd stolen the gun because something made me want to carry one around in my pocket at all times.

"How you doing, James?" José said. I rolled my eyes. "Why do you do that, man?" he asked sharply, looking for a fight. I tried to move around him, but he blocked me with his big ass.

"You too good for this job?"

"No," I said. "I'm not too good for this job."

"Well then, what's your exact problem?"

"I just want to go home. Get out of my way," I said.

"People have it hard. You don't think I got it hard?"

"Get out of my way."

He shoved me and I fell backwards a little. Really, there is no where to go, just 3 and a half feet in any direction.

But then a rage washed over me. I shoved him into the side of the steel door, his head hit. He tried to swing his arm back, but there wasn't room. I knocked into him again, hitting his head even farther. I squeezed through the door, laughing. Giddy. Head buzzing.

In the main building, I scanned my time card. My boss, Larry said, "That guy is a real asshole, huh?"

"Yeah."

Larry's a good guy, he shouldn't be a boss.

"Real asshole," he laughed. "Every day he comes in here and says either you should be fired, or that Gale should be fired, and that he deserves the dayshift. I tell him that Gale has seniority and that you're a better worker. Boy that gets him sore!"

Gale was a senior citizen, wore those giant black cataract glasses. She'd worked in the Toll Plaza since almost before I was born. She was bat shit insane. Sometimes she gave seven dollars in change to a person who'd given her a dollar bill.

"José will just have to learn to love the darkness," Larry said, "because he's not getting the dayshift."

"Yeah!"

"Have a good night, Jimmy."

"You too."

166

On the way home, I stopped at Officetown. I was gonna make a new color photocopy of my heroic certificate. I didn't like having dicks drawn on my only source of personal pride.

Officetown was pretty useless to me otherwise. I just went for the copy center. I didn't even have an office. My bills piled up in old stacks causing little landslides. Sometimes, Ted Milo came over with his Rottweiler, Rommel. Later, I'd find that his beast had eaten one of my credit card statements. In turn, I'd get down on one knee, hugging his thick doomsday neck, saying, "Rommel, that was fantastic of you."

I wanted that dog to eat my whole life.

In Officetown, parents were picking up school supplies for their kids. Drones were faxing bullshit to the receivers of the bullshit. Everybody needed paper clips, rubber bands, hole punchers. Loose leaf paper. Staplers. A zillion different types of ballpoint pens. Notebooks to fill up with ideas to save the world.

I was there for a vital reason besides the certificate: Gena. The girl who worked in the copy center had taken over my dreams and my waking life. I used any excuse to go and see her.

I strolled up like Cool Hand Luke, "Hey, you're back," Gena said. She was leaning against the copy machine, long straight black hair. Sipping the last drops of a cherry coke.

I have a confession. Gena, I am in love with you. Every time

I'm on break, all I can think about is how much I'm in love with your mouth and how I want those bright green eyes to look up at me while you lick the evil and the disdain out of me. A sweet little fawn like you could save a guy like me: survivor of a shipwreck. Maybe you'll be my signal fire. Maybe that body of your's is a rescue crew all on its own. I have a vision of the two of us falling endlessly into a mountain of loose leaf paper, nude.

"Yeah, I'm back," I said nervously.

"Your order isn't in yet," she said, leaning on the counter towards me.

"Oh . . . damn," I muttered. I had a hard-on, and I really wished that she'd notice. I stood to the side a little bit. If it was for everyone else, I would've been embarrassed. But for Gena, I wasn't embarrassed. I was a goddamn wolf man for her—every day in my secret downstairs bathroom, a giant monster moon rising over my awkward lust.

"OK, well here is my home number again," I said. "Call me if the order comes in, OK?"

"You got it."

"My name's Jimmy."

"Yeah."

"Or just Jim," I underlined my name on the paper three times.

"I remember," she said, laughing, but not laughing at me. No, just laughing. A true gem of a girl. Her hair was pulled back in a ponytail. I would love to tug on that tail. She, she, she, oh—I wanted that shit. I wanted to strip off all of her clothes, all of her makeup, all all all. I wanted to slide into her, the wetness almost fictional and hear her moans like no-one has ever moaned on a porno set. She'd moan for the wolf man: satisfaction guaranteed or her money back.

The first time is free, Gena, but after that I'll have to charge you for my cock. I'm sorry, but it's too powerful to restrain, too wonderful to give out for free to checkout girls from office supply mega-stores.

"OK, well have a nice night," I said.

"Bye," she said as if we were strangers.

Gena, what's with the coldness? Don't you know that you are my number one jerk off fantasy?

After all, it was Gena who led me to place this order. I'd innocently been eating a slice in the pizzeria next door, when she strolled in with her tight black pants, and white sneakers probably made of cloud. Her dark hair fell onto unbelievable breasts swaying beneath the kind of face that cannot be denied. The perfect face. When she sat down nearby, all I could do was stare at the back of her head, let her strawberry body spray drift my way.

I couldn't even finish my pizza or the Fantá or the stupid garlic knots. When she left, her artful hips and legs and ass moving away from me, I followed slowly behind, leaving my trash on the table for the pizza people to care for. What was my next move? Follow her to her car? Assault her?

My plan may have been unknown to me, but it surely didn't involve anything sinister. The worst, maybe, would be making a fool of myself by asking her out on a date. But what did kids her age do? I wasn't that much older, maybe eight years . . . ten years max, but already I didn't know what the kids did. Did they still fuck and do dope? If they did all of those things, then maybe I had a chance. Maybe I could catch her on a horny, doped, drunken night; the odds in my favor.

Gena never looked back. I followed her across the entire parking lot.

She kept walking past all the cars, stepped around a pothole, onto the sidewalk, into Officetown. I followed her inside, went to the notebook aisle, gathered myself, if gathering was at all possible. I realized I'd left the pizzeria without paying. What an idiot I was. But, snowcaps on mountains were shrinking, spilling down rivers to fast waterfalls.

She appeared behind the counter in the copy center leaning seductively against the machine. She was in her work clothes then; a name tag pinned to her left tit.

I said her name to myself three times.

Gena. Gena. Gena.

I went to her counter, called her over from the copy machine. She flashed her eyes at me with speculation, came to me, twirling her hair and chewing a piece of pink bubble gum.

"How can I help you?" she cooed.

I almost jumped that counter tigerstyle and had my way with her on the copy machine, pumping out color copies of all our corresponding pink parts being beautiful together.

"Yeah, I need some help," I said instead of action.

"With what?" she said slow, her voice low and sexy, "what exactly can I help you with?"

"Oh . . ." I looked around at the poster sized advertisements on the wall behind her, the custom projects that Officetown made via special order.

I appeared utter zen, but there was a riot beneath my cool facade.

"I want to place an order," I said like James Dean, standing up straight, everything about me beginning to bloom like a mushroom cloud.

On my way out, I thought I saw a dead woman in aisle three.

She was sitting on one of those portable rolling ladders that the stock boys use. She was shaking her head at me, in complete disgust. Horn rimmed glasses. White sweater splattered with blood. Her leg was crushed.

I'd never shake her.

Thankfully, the dead woman didn't follow me out of the store.

165

There was a man in a silver Cadillac immune to the laws that governed the rest of the world. He appeared as a mirage up the highway traveling super sonically, darting through shadows, cutting sharply to avoid the other motorists who struggled in their low performance vehicles as if wading through glue.

The man in the silver car always had exact change. Everyone else had to slow down for the toll, he accelerated. His sunroof opened automatically, his hand appearing out of that opening. In his fingers, perfect coins. With a delicate flick of his wrist, he'd hook shot the change into the change basket.

Every time, as he zoomed away at high-speed, I'd sit there thinking about how absolutely dead-on his precision was. Looking down that highway at the fading thought of his reflection, his tail lights shrinking and his sunroof closing . . . I knew he wasn't thinking about anything behind him.

He was in flux. I was not.

I imagined that the things he passed through were either parts of my dream or parts of his dream that I was inside, or that we were just parts of someone else's dream and that none of it mattered—least of all how we are impressed by motions and precision and quality.

It was hard to gauge reality from inside the booth.

163

I went in to check my order, again. No Gena. Two of the stock boys were leaning against the shelves. They looked at me as I came down the aisle, unimpressed. I didn't command much of an impression. They kept on with their conversation, hoping that I would continue to shuffle past and keep my stupid question to myself.

"Beethoven was no way deaf, dude. Just no way," the tall blonde kid with the nose spike said to the stock boy with the missing arm.

"How you figure?"

"Back then they didn't have any of the devices to like, uh, prove that he was deaf."

"I'm not so sure about your logic," the armless kid said.

"And think about it, dude: if I was a kinda OK composer back then, back in the day, I would definitely try to work some kind of gimmick to try to get noticed. It's like how KISS dressed all in clown makeup to get music executives to notice."

"Awww shit."

"Beethoven could hear shit, he could hear all of it. Don't believe that vibration bull crap. That motherfucker had ears like a hawk."

I laughed like a creep, they turned to look, "You guys know if Gena is working tonight?"

"Nawww," said the nose spike historian, "she ain't here on

Thursdays or Tuesdays."

"Or Wednesdays or Fridays," the one armed boy said. "But she's so hot I wish she was here all the time. That girl has some tits, oh man, the kind to just suck on all day. Troy, you sucked them tits before, right?"

"Naw, I wish, oh I wish."

Silence.

"Yeah, I wish too," the stock boy with the missing limb said.

"But what about Tommy's party? I thought you sucked her tits at Tommy's party."

"Nawwwwwwwww, somebody else was sucking those tits at Tommy's party. But man, I would have loved it to be me sucking those tits at Tommy's party."

"Do you guys have a bathroom in this store?" I ask meekly.

Really, I just had to use the bathroom. I wasn't going to go in there to unleash some porno movie from my mind into a tissue or anything.

"Do you guys have a bathroom in this store?" I ask meekly.

"Not for the public," Troy said.

"Oh." I started to shuffle off, defeated.

"Dude you can use our bathroom," the stock boy with the missing arm yelled, punching the other kid in the shoulder, saying to him, "Don't be a dick."

He led me through several doors to a metal door tucked between piles of cardboard boxes that said PRIVATE. "Oh, yeah, and take it easy in there OK?" he requested, "I just had to clean this thing up yesterday."

I wanted to ask him so bad how he lost his arm. My guess woodchipper. Or . . . woodchipper—that's all I had.

I walked inside and sat down, there were magazines on a little table: I scanned through them. Foreign cars, import cars, import foreign custom cars, tailpipes that sounded like lawnmowers. Of course those shelf stocking idiots would drive little shitty cars, the kind that came through the tollbooth—sounding like chainsaws at their arrival and departure, a skateboard with an engine, a mouse sized joke for the race lane that made my head ring. I got so pissed that I wished I could do something cool like punch the mirror and knock holes in the wall. Why couldn't I do something like that?

I shifted my weight on the bowl, lifting my leg, pushing my

safety steel toe shoe into the little table. It stood on its side legs momentarily, before dropping back into position, wobbling.

I could definitely raise hell. I knocked the magazine table over. It crashed to some triumph. "Haaaaaa!" Then, I stood up and wiped. Fuck these kids. I was tired of taking everybody's shit. I threw the dirty paper in the sink; I didn't flush. I picked a few of the magazines, poised to chuck them into the back of the toilet tank, when a photograph slipped out from between them. It was my little sex machine, Gena. A prom photo of her that one of the kids had been whacking off to. The photo was crusted up.

These perverts. I decided that I had no choice but to walk out there and show the photo directly to their manager. It was the only honorable thing to do.

But instead, I took the photo, put it in my pocket, left the store as quick as possible.

161

I flipped on the switch, the cars came at me on parade. When they saw that the red X above my booth became a green O, the people were filled with such delight.

"Can I have a receipt?"

"Can I have a receipt?"

"How much is the toll?"

"Can I have a receipt?"

"Can I have a receipt?"

"Can I have a receipt?"

I was a stand-still robot with simple math skills who knew the change for a dollar.

A blue Ford Escort pulled up to the booth. I turned to face the driver, saw a clown head. Grease paint, bubblegum hair, blue stars for eyes. A yellow Joy Division T-shirt. There was a person with a stocking over his head in the passenger seat filming us with a camcorder. We were the stars of some epic showdown between good and evil. I wasn't sure who was good and who was evil.

"HEY, MOTHERFUCKER!! SEE HOW YOU LIKE THIS SHIT!!!" the clown screamed.

"Like what?" I said, like a dope.

"THIS!!!"

Laughing maniacally, the clown leaned forward and started to spray some kind of substance into the coin basket. It was bright yellow and growing. I made no attempts to stop him; I just gazed ahead in some haphazard triumph. Finally, a member of the populous had broken the spell. I wanted to give the kid a hug.

"YOU LIKE THIS??!!!" he demanded, twisting the can, sticking out his tongue to mock me, "YOU LIKE THIS, UNCLE SAM?!"

When he was done shooting the goop into the basket, he threw the can against the booth. It rolled under his tire as he peeled off in his blue car. A photo of the license plate came up on the screen, I hit delete.

I will save you, anarchist. I don't think you deserve the whipping of the state. I applaud you. I commend you.

I put on the red X, indicating that my lane was closed. I stepped out of the booth, picked up the crushed can. The print was still legible: "WONDASTUFT: QUADRUPLE EXPANDING MEGA FOAM SPRAY INSULATION FROM THE MAKERS OF CRACKZAP AND WINDOW GOOP."

The change basket was quickly becoming an impenetrable dome of plastic-like foam. Then, HOLY SHIT, a car was zooming at me. I tried to move my feet, almost fell over them. An orange Honda Civic doing at least forty-five through the toll; a red headed chick, window down. Change smashed against the booth—pennies and nickels sliding down into the foam, lost forever.

I went back in the booth, the red X steadfast, and stayed there until my lunch break. When I walked into the break room, I looked Larry in the eye. I knew that he didn't want to be there any more than I did. I nodded at him, put seventy cents in the machine, got a PayDay, opened it, took a bite, and chewed. Then, still looking at him, I said, "Hey, I don't know how it happened, but somebody shot Quadruple Expanding Spray Foam Insulation into my change basket."

"Huh?" he says.

"I wouldn't know," I explained, "but I think it's the same stuff that contractors use to seal up doors and windows."

"Oh shit."

"Yeah."

"Will change still go in?" he asked, scratching his head.

"Well for a little while . . . 'til it's solid," I explained.

"Then no?"

I took another bite. The wrapper made a joyous sound.

"Yeah, definitely not after solidification."

160

I called Ted from a pay phone. He was my only remaining friend. "It's been a while," I said into the phone. "What's new?"

Ted was at his desk at the DMV, where he worked, ate, and sometimes slept.

"Nothing," he admitted. "Gym. Paperwork. Kelly wants to go to get passports. We're talking about visiting Peru."

"Peru! Holy snap! I should be doing that. I should be going to Peru."

"Yeah, yeah—you should, really," he said. "You've literally never been anywhere."

"There's a world beyond the prison walls of New Jersey? Do they have tollbooths out there?" I scoffed. "Sorry, I haven't kept in too good of touch."

"Well I haven't either. It's just been this career, you know. I take it so serious," he joked. But it wasn't a joke. I pictured him in his clean dressed pants and button up shirt. Slim, smelling good, faithful to his wife. Ted is the kind of black guy that really has a tight head of hair at all times. Manicured to the nines. I admire him for it, for most things really.

I'm a mess. Every inch of me, interior and exterior.

"Rightfully so, that you take your job so serious," I said.

"I love being chained to this desk!" he said. "How's that booth working out for you, dreamer?"

"You know what I realized?" I said, yanking on the metal chord of the pay phone.

"What?" he asked, in his deep voice.

"We're both pathetic pussies."

"Not me. Buddy, I'm on my lunch break. I don't think I want to be belittled anymore than my desk job already belittles me."

"No, I'm serious," I said earnestly.

"OK, but I gotta go," he insisted. "I only got six more minutes here for break." I knew he was glancing at his heavy silver watch. "My Hot Pocket is getting cold."

"What kind?"

"Pepperoni," he said.

"N-n-n-nice," I laughed, "I need a favor before you hang up on me," I pressed.

"What?"

"I'm gonna give you a license plate number, Blue Ford Escort—I need you to figure out an address."

"Oh, this again, goddamn it," I heard him gather his paper and pen. He sighed, "alright, what's the plate number?"

159

Dear Kid with Clown Head,

I came home tonight to my empty house, and all I kept thinking about was how great it was for you to come across the great divide like that. My dinner tasted sweeter than any dinner I've ever eaten, and it's a fucking pepperoni Hot Pocket—so you go figure that one out! An old friend recommended it to me, and I thought, what the hey . . . so sick of tuna. But then I am so sick of a lot of things.

Don't worry about anything. This isn't a sinister letter or anything. You won't even get a ticket in the mail.

Oh, I forgot to mention who I am . . . I'm the guy from the tollbooth! I don't know how many tollbooths you fuck with, but if you think back, I was the really skinny guy with the green sweater on. I don't know if that helps. I look like a lot of people, and I act like a lot of people, not how you conduct yourself—OUTSIDE THE BOXXX!

I noticed something tonight. The tollbooth and the downstairs bathroom in my house are the same dimensions: three and a half feet by three and a half feet. The broom closet in the house I grew up in was the same exact size, too. Coincidence? Or is this how the universe reveals itself in its puzzles?

When I was eleven years old I used to sneak into the broom closet to jerk off to dirty photos. Now that I have grown up, I go into my downstairs bathroom and jerk off. I have this sick fantasy about this young girl that I know I will never get, but anyway . . . my point is that I work in that same tight spot, that three and a half by three and a half square, and I feel like a stupid prisoner of my own hard-ons and do-nothingisms. Ha! Maybe I need to see a therapist instead of writing some crazy kid with a clown head a letter of confession.

You're my hero! You've come out of the blue and attacked the very thing that has . . . I don't know where this is going. I'd like to burn down the tollbooth. That's probably my life's ambition.

I'm not a very brave person. But look, one more thing: I RUN THE TOLL BOOTH WHENEVER I PASS IT. I get tickets in the mail, and I pay them even though I work for the fucking system. Talk about a dizzying circle. I can't decide whether I want to be the wolf man or the milquetoast, but you got it all figured out. And this is even crazier, but I was fantasizing in my downstairs bathroom about that girl, that young chick I was telling you about earlier. Usually I am the star of my own fantasies, and I think for most people it's that way, right? Anyway, in this one, I was you! I was ME, don't get me wrong, but I went right up to her, myself dressed all in clown face, and kissed her semi-violently. I remember the grease smearing, which is gross, and that shit usually doesn't turn me on, but . . .

I found this picture of her the other day in a bathroom stall and pasted her head on this roller skate clad centerfold from a Hustler magazine. There I was, on the brink of cumming, when the phone started to ring. It just kept ringing, ringing, ringing . . .

Then, the front door opened.

"Honey, are you going to get that?"

Sarah, my wife.

"In a minute!"

Ohhhhhhhhhhhhh, I shot it. I shot it and it hurt. Some splattered the mirror. Wow. "Hey Jim! JIM, WHERE ARE YOU?" Sarah picked up the phone. I frantically cleaned up the cum. Then, I folded the picture, stuck it under the sink.

"JIMMMM, IT'S FOR YOU!"

And let me tell you, Mr. Clown Head, my head was spinning in so many ways. Sarah was pounding on the door, "IT'S UNCLE FRED!!"

"TELL HIM I'M NOT HOME!!"

"He can hear you saying that!"

"Oh well."

Kid with Clownhead, let me just make one little suggestion to you: don't get married. While you are at it, don't get your wife pregnant. Because that's what I did, and why I have no chance of ever, ever escaping the booth.

Sarah stood in the kitchen with her untrusting eyes, taking groceries out of that paper sack while I tried to pretend away the problem and hold back my lust for Gena and my lust to go to Officetown and retrieve my order.

Then, as if to twist the knife even deeper, my Sarah rubbed her belly, feeling the bulge. She had to sit down. From the chair, she said, "Gee, Jim. It won't be too long now."

Ain't that the shit?

Your Friend,
Jimmy Tollbooth

157

I wasn't always bald. It's shameful, yes, and I am embarrassed of it now—but when I was twenty-seven, I had a king size combover. Mammoth. I was almost completely bald on the top of my head, but I grew the remaining hair on the left side of my head, and brushed it up and over the top like a tidal wave.

I'd go to see Kimmy Simmons at her salon, she'd trim my eye brows and sideburns. I wouldn't let her mess with the top.

I'd read somewhere that the direction that people part their hair indicates how cool they are. I laughed at that idea, but still, I parted my hair the Superman way, not the Clark Kent way. Check for yourself: Clark Kent is to the right, Superman is to the left.

I had this spray glue. First, I'd spray my head, then gently, I'd place the wave of hair on the glue. When I checked the mirror, I knew I looked like shit. "At least I look better than if I was bald," I'd say, believing it.

I was engaged to Sarah at the time. We'd been together since the eleventh grade, and never once did she mention the fact that I was losing my hair.

I loved her for that. She loved me unconditionally. For most of our time together, I did the same.

Back then, I had a baseball cap that I wore everywhere. One month I never took it off, even to bed for sex with Sarah. I never took it off. She didn't say a word about the baseball cap, which I had personally embroidered at the mall:

ABOLISH
NJ TOLLS

There was a real sexy chick who worked at the embroidery stand. Sarah was just as hot, but that attention that she gave me just didn't seem to mean as much as the attention I received from girls who were new, who didn't love me with all of their hearts, who weren't prepared to stay with me until death dragged us away.

One day at the mall, I was hanging around Embroidery Stand Jill as she made me a new baseball cap. Flirting. She touched my arm, laughed at everything I said. She pushed a button, the automatic sewing machine pummeled thread into the baseball cap. She said, "What do you do anyway?"

"I work in a tollbooth on the Garden State Parkway."

"Oh my gawd! That's so funny!"

She wasn't very bright, but she was staring right at me with this look in her eye. It was a look that a girl gives a guy when she is thinking about how her arms would feel wrapped around his neck, his dick sinking in, her legs squeezing his back, as he kissed her neck.

"You would look pretty good without a hat on," she said. "You always wear a hat?"

"Yeah, pretty much."

I didn't want to get too far into that line of conversation, so I changed the subject. There was a T-shirt with a picture of two men smiling, one old, one young. The shirt read, "Thanks for Life Dad!"

"I lost my father to cancer," I said. "I wish I had a shirt like that with his picture on it."

She was quiet for a moment, trying to figure out what to say. It was then that I realized that the proposal I'd given Sarah was all concerning the legs I did not have to stand on in the world. I had lost my father as a small boy, I had just lost my mother, and needed someone to cling to.

Wouldn't it have been impossible for her to refuse me? I supposed this was her great dilemma too, something that she was thinking about while out looking for a wedding dress with the stranger she called a sister in the barren grid of lower Manhattan.

"Hey, do you get a lunch break?" I asked Jill.

She gave me an awkward look because she knew I was gonna ask her to come to lunch with me.

"No, no lunch break, plus I'm married," she said sourly.

The hat was done. She handed me the hat.

"You aren't married," I said. "Sorry for bothering you with the lunch offer. I didn't realize you were so high above me."

I took the hat from my head, revealing my expert comb over, "by the way, I'm not bald. I know that was what you were assuming."

"That's a comb over," she said.

"No comb over," I demanded, brushing the hair quickly with my hand, while the special hair glue held it steady. I tossed her a twenty dollar bill, didn't wait for the change. After all, she was a pathetic liar and needed the cash more than I did, because I was bathed in my virtue of truth and all.

156

I had three strands of hair left on the top of my head. Sometimes I would look at them in the mirror, inspecting them for
split ends. I'd treat those hairs with fine conditioners. I tried
to show them that I loved them so very dearly in case they could
spread a message and wake the ones sleeping below my scalp.

It was two days before the wedding. Sarah and I were getting
married in a little church by her sister's house, since she didn't
have a big family and all I really had was Ted. It wasn't going to be
a big wedding by any means, but our friends, mostly her friends,
would try their best to fake their way through the motions, whatever.

Sarah said, "I want to take you out tonight. I want to get you
real drunk and take advantage of you before I have to go to my
sister's."

And so my Sarah, my little bride to be, took me to the local
neighborhood bar, where we'd been time and time again. We sat
in a booth, letting the waitress take our order.

Sarah's long blonde hair fell across her shoulders. She kept
flashing smiles. Perfect teeth. I smiled and ran my mouth, com-
plimenting her. I was very much at the apex of my love for her
then. After a few drinks, when we were being all lovey dovey to
each other, the waitress said, "Thank god for a cute couple. Most
people who come in here look like they want to cut each other's
heads off."

"Well, we are getting married in two days, so I guess after that we'll want to cut each other's heads off."

The waitress walked off, Sarah said to me, "You know I love you, right?"

"Yeah, I know that." I stood up from the booth. "I've got to go to the bathroom."

Sarah looked nervous.

"Hey, babe, look," I said, "I'm sorry, I shouldn't have made that joke."

"I think we are gonna be a cute couple," she said. "Forever."

"I know we will be. That's why I want to marry you." I leaned over and I kissed her on the mouth. She grabbed my shoulders and held me there, over the table.

At that moment, the drinks came: two gin and tonics. I started to take my drink, but she grabbed my hand.

"It will still be here when you get back."

"Oh, so this is how it's gonna be." I smirked as I walked off to the bathroom, feeling vaguely drunk but not that bad considering that I hadn't had too big of a dinner on Sarah's request that we get nice and drunk, super drunk (me especially), so that she could take advantage of me. When I came back from the bathroom, Sarah was putting something in her purse.

"That was quick," she said.

"Most of the time, boys don't have to sit down or lift the lid."

I sat down at the table, and she looked away as if guilty.

"What were you doing, stealing silverware? Putting it in your purse?"

She laughed, "Me? No, of course not."

"Oh, because I thought I caught you in some kind of criminal act."

"No, I missed you, and I'm getting drunk, so . . . "

"So?"

"So maybe after this drink we'll get going."

"Already?"

"Yeah, I'm kinda getting in the mood. To . . . "

"Oh, in that case!" I said, tipping my drink back, gulping half of it down. She watched with intrigue—smiling broadly.

She smiled wider when I finished my drink, took hers and drank that too.

Halfway home, the last thing I remember was Sarah saying

"Jimmy, you know that I love you right?"

"Yeah babe," I slurred, amazed at how drunk I was already, "I know . . ."

"Good."

My head slammed into the headrest, the world was a tunnel closing in on itself. Then, as it happens occasionally, the world vanished.

When I opened my eyes, I was face down in a bedspread, but I couldn't remember whose bedspread it was, what my name was, who I was, where I was, why my mouth was so dry, or where my pants were (likewise, my shirt).

I suspected foul play.

My head throbbed viscously.

I grunted, rolled back over, "Sarah?"

I couldn't remember that she was gone. My balls itched, and my dick was hard. Where was my Sarah when I needed her?

I had to piss. I had to scratch my nuts. When I reached down there, my balls felt funny. They were cleanly shaven. I was drooling everywhere.

I looked at my nuts . . . yeah, cleanly shaven! I didn't remember doing that. While looking down, I also saw that my belly had been shaven of all of its fine black hair. My pubic hair was gone. So there I sat in bed, naked and without my natural defenses against the elements. That bitch!

I stood up out of bed, walked to the bathroom—the pain deadly. When I got to the toilet, there was a note taped to the lid. I lifted the lid, note and all, and pissed into the abyss of the porcelain pit.

When I finished, I closed the lid and grabbed hold of the note—surely some love letter from my beautiful wife to be.

Jimmy,

OK look, you know I love you right?

Well I do love you, from the bottom of my heart. I'm truly sorry about last night. But it was the only way that I could go through with the wedding. You are the perfect man for me and

I want to spend the rest of my life with you, but there is just no way that I could have walked down the aisle with a man with a comb over. It's just not how I pictured my special day.

I thought long and hard about how to confront you with this, but the truth is that I could come to no easy resolution, the only way was for me to take action. I am just so very sorry that that action was against you in the way that it was.

I hope that you can forgive me for what I have done to you. I had to drug your drink and shave your head while you were passed out . . .

I looked in the mirror and let out a little shriek. I was a monster! My head was clean shaven, two shades whiter than my already white as powder face, which I might add was also freshly shaven.

"Biff, Tom, Gregor!"

I had named my last three hairs after my three favorite literary characters. Biff Loman from Death of a Salesman, Tom Joad from The Grapes of Wrath, and Gregor Samsa from The Metamorphosis.

. . . I don't know how you feel about me now, after all of this deception, but I must let you know that it took me months to build up the courage to do it. Otherwise, I thought we had a great time last night and, I know you probably don't remember because you were passed out, but the sex was amazing. I had a little shaving party with you and then, well . . . oh my GOD! Also, I just want you to know that I think you are so sexy with your new haircut. I know that you will be mad at me for a while, but I hope you will forgive me by the time we exchange vows tomorrow.

Yours Truly,
Your wife in twenty something hours,
Sarah

PS. Attached you will find a page where you have signed a legal document agreeing not to call the wedding off, or else you will be liable for all of the costs.

Love again,
Sarah

The attached document said:

I, James Saare agree to let Sarah Culbert shave my head so that I will look my best for our wedding day which will join us in holy matrimony forever. I also agree to put the toilet seat down when I am done with it and to not go out to a strip club for my bachelor party or ever after that for any reason, because it would really hurt my beautiful wife, who is my life. I also agree to never look at another girl ever again or drink out of the milk carton with my bacteria laden lips.

<u>X JAMES SAARE</u>

It appeared to be signed in blood. Sitting down on the bed rereading the letter, I found the band aid on my forearm, confirming that, yes, the document was signed in blood . . . my blood.

155

The rear end of my Subaru was hurting—hanging low—its suspension crying. Everyday, I'd throw in handfuls of pennies and quarters, nickels, dimes and Susan B. Anthonys: the change that missed the basket, bouncing down onto the concrete outside the booth.

When the jug was full, I'd take it to the bank.

The manager had to help. He didn't like it the first time I'd brought him out to the car, pointed to the plastic vat of happy money. I said, "We need to get that out of the trunk and inside."

He shook his head in anger, "Sorry, buddy, not my job."

The girls who worked in the bank were hawt little things, though, watching us through the huge plate glass window.

"Come on, help lift this out. You don't want to look weak in front of the girls do you?" I conned.

He nudged me out of the way and pulled the change vat out of the trunk. I heard a wet pop, the sound of a piece of human anatomy being dislodged. While he grunted and hefted the bulk, the lowest rank teller opened up the bank door.

I went to the automatic change counting machine. I had a plastic beach shovel and a beach chair. I sat in the chair and shoveled the change into the mouth of the machine as it emitted clanks and hums.

During those trips to the bank, I was convinced I had the best job in the world. It was all I had to look forward to in life, really, that and seeing Gena.

I missed my hatchback Volkswagen though. A car that had been taken from me, by a cruel, unloving universe. That car would have fit so much more spare change than the Subaru. I'd have been rich.

155P

When I woke up in the morning the rain was torrential, so was Sarah. She was mad at me, but we didn't ever talk about what was wrong. So neither of us really ever knew.

She sat by the window, whispering one-sided questions to her pregnant belly, "Are you going to be a boy or a girl; a girl or a boy?" They were almost indecipherable whispers, but seemed amplified a hundred thousand decibels.

When she caught me looking, she stood, opening the thin curtains. The muted sun was just coming up, but no one could tell; our days were ambivalent.

"It's a pretty bad storm," she said, "maybe you . . ."

"It sounds like the end of the world out there, but I'll have work," I said.

"Bring an umbrella," she suggested, "Or call out, fuck it, right?"

I opened my mouth to speak, but she'd already left the room. The tea kettle was screaming. Or it was a pterodactyl crashing through the kitchen window to consume us in its thrashing jaws, whichever.

It was true, pregnant women do glow. It was true, Sarah had once rescued me from the bottomless pit. It was true, I'd replaced the lust in my balls for her with a lust for a trashy little whore who made photo copies in an office supply store. "I don't wanna grow up, I'm a Toys 'R Us Kid," I sang, swinging my feet out of bed, walking balls ass naked out of the room, " . . . there's a million toys at Toys 'R Us that I can play with . . . "

In the kitchen she sat staring at her steaming tea cup, waiting. I walked past, singing to her, pointing, "I don't wanna grow up, I'm a Toys 'R Us Kid, they got the best for so much less . . . you'll really flip your lid,"

I sauntered down the hallway, she laughed, "From bikes to trains to video games," she sang with me in unison, as I turned on the shower with a flick of the wrist. I hummed the song all while I washed, but there was nothing in that steam that held anything for me, so it was quick, routine. No deviations. Strictly business. Like a fool, I expected Sarah to come in the bathroom and climb in with me.

Before this thing happened to Sarah, this horrible tragedy, she was so good to me, so willing in bed, but not anymore. Flat tire. Broken window. All systems failure. Dried-up river bed. Bones of mythic creatures bleached by an unceasing sun. Sarah why did you ever get yourself pregnant on top of my dick like that?

When I came out, she was still at the table.

"I'm not talking to you, don't bother talking to me," she said playfully.

"I wasn't going to," I said, "but you know, you did just talk to me."

"Well, from *this* point on," she said, grinning sheepishly.

"That point?"

She made a motion of locking her mouth shut with a key. I went to the refrigerator. There was nothing for breakfast but eggs and toast and bacon and pancakes and cereal and sausage links and corned beef hash in the cupboard and coffee. I was starving. We were all starving. I didn't want any of it. I wanted it all—immediately.

"You hungry, babe? I thought I'd make you breakfast?" A ploy.

She opened her mouth as if to say something, then she threw the imaginary key inside. Swallowed. I hoped that key didn't hit my unborn namesake and cause a miscarriage.

I hoped.

I hoped. I closed the fridge.

"Look, I don't want to fight," I said. "I'm sorry, and I have a suggestion. I thought of a name for the baby." Her dark eyes brightened. I went down the hallway, got my baseball cap.

"Do you want to hear the name of the baby before I leave, or are you still going to be . . . "

She just shook her head, naaahhhhhh.

As I left, not a single raindrop was able to touch me.

Instead of driving to work, I drove downtown where I used to live. I stopped at the gas station, called work.

Larry answered, I could hear him slurping Raisin Bran at his desk, "Hey, I'm sorry to do this to you, but I'm feeling really sick today. I don't think I can come in."

"Oh, sick?"

"Yeah, not very good at all."

"Well not to call you out or anything, but if you are too sick to come to work, why is the caller ID showing a pay phone?"

I didn't say anything. Touché. What a chess player!

"OK, my car broke down. I'm sorry I lied . . ."

"Just stay home, OK," he said, then hung up. What a championship boss.

154

It was getting too dangerous for my porn collection: there was too much of it inside too small of a space. Sarah was a chick Sherlock Holmes. Her psychic abilities frightened me. It wouldn't be too long before she stumbled upon my stash and I wound up sleeping in Rommel's dog house beside his stinky ass. I had to act quick getting all of my Gena porn out of the little downstairs bathroom before it was too late.

I swung around the block, happy with my decision to play hooky from the booth. I deserved the day off. The driveway was empty, I pulled the Subaru in quick, almost clipping the seashell mailbox, skidding up right in front of my unusable garage.

The kid who mowed our lawn was walking down the street. As I stepped out of the car, he started asking, "Hey, Jim, grass looks crazy high . . . "

"Set it on fire," I said.

"What?"

"The lawn. The house. The world."

I walked to my porch, he said, brightly, "Will do!"

As I opened up the front door, Sarah was sitting at the kitchen table with all of the lights in the house off, just staring at me. She knew. I threw my car keys in the wooden cat organizer she'd glued together by the coffee pot.

"Can I help you?" I said.

"No," she said. "I don't need any help."

"Can you help me then? Where the hell is your car?"

"Took it in for brakes and oil and . . . I told you this. What do you need?" she drummed her fingers on the table. They sounded out my slow death march. She'd bitten the nails down to the cuticle. "Why are you home?" She looked at the clock directly above my head.

Once her hands had been well manicured. Bright colored nails, french tips. They were the hands of a thug now. She'd break my jaw most likely.

"I dunno," I said. "Every time I come home, you're just sitting there in that chair, and it's not because you're pregnant, it's because you're miserable."

"Miserable, who me?" she said faking shock.

I flipped the light on in the kitchen, "This place is drab! We need some sunshine!"

"It's raining out."

"More the reason!"

"Really, why are you home? Did you get fired?" she asked with some slight fear. I waited, let that fear brew in her, then grinned, shook my head; no you silly former cheerleader.

"I figured that maybe I could take my wife to breakfast, treat her to some eggs," I said. "If I can't talk her into an abortion, maybe at least some eggs and bacon."

"Treat me? Sure. I could go for breakfast."

So, I took her to breakfast. I made sure that it was an extra extra delicious breakfast, not even diner breakfast, but restaurant breakfast. We smiled at each other, feeling a slight tinge of the old love we had in our salad days, in our heydays. It was a place that overlooked the river, the waiter came to our table on light feet, obviously taken away by our deep, apparent love.

We ordered the deluxe mega lumberjack specials, with fresh squeezed orange juice. There is nothing that Sarah loves in the world as much as an orange. "Let's move to Florida," she often said. Fresh coffee! I demanded silverware that the sun could gleam off of even though there was no sun on that day.

She brought a fork of egg to her lips, bit. I raised a coffee mug in near tribute. So what? So what that my life was over and the hunger in her was a direct reflection of that? Look at this new hunger, eating for two. That little belly was stretching, and after the baby came, it would still be that big. After that, surely she'd be eating whole plates all by herself, but so what? So what.

She was not the girl who I had met in high school. She was a cheerleader then. I remembered ever so clearly the way that she used to cheer for my life.

When we finished the meal, the waiter brought us our check. I was so happy, realizing that I didn't really need this other young fantasy of mine, Gena. I didn't need to turn away from my wife. It might have been the coffee, all of the caffeine, and the fat of the meal, God knows, but as I sat there watching her, I thought: *baby, snookems, sweet thang, I'm a real fuck up and I love you.*

And shit and shit and shit! So what if you are a fucking stupid siren who sang a fake song to get me to crash my ship onto your rock? There have never been two people so perfectly screwed up for each other. We're just going through a dull patch. I'll get out of the tollbooth. We'll train the kid as a getaway driver. We'll start knocking over jewelry stores wearing werewolf masks, armed with AK-47s. It'll be perfect.

The bill came.

I placed the credit card down. The waiter took it lovingly, dancing like an elf all the way to the rear of the restaurant, whistling some elf song.

I signed the check and left him a handsome tip.

I looked at my wife. I was about to reach for her hand, to tell her something sincere, that I'd been a real asshole and that I did still love her, that I was sorry for the distance that had come between us. But love is a two way street.

"Hey can I ask you something?" she said.

"Yeah, what is it?"

"Well, thanks for the breakfast and all. It was good. All respect due for that delicious breakfast."

"But . . . "

She held up her finger, saying in sign language, one minute, hang on jackass. She revealed a picture, a very nice picture, of a black model with a large pink dildo in her ass and the face of an angelic white beauty—copy slut Gena.

"I found this in your pants pocket. I was doing your laundry. What the fuck is this?"

"That?"

"Is this what you want?" she hissed.

"That? Oh no!"

"In her ass!" she said, too loud.

"Quiet."

"You're disgusting."

"I'm sorry," I defended, "but it's all a mistake anyway."

"And that face looks familiar . . ."

"I think it's that Russian model, Frenza Larnalotzvia, but I can't be sure."

"Oh no, Dr. Frankenstein, you can be sure. You made this thing. What was her name?"

"I found that." I was hoping she hadn't found anymore of the mock ups. "I found it at work, in the break room. That José . . . ughh, I hate that guy. I guess I grabbed it without thinking. It was stupid, immature."

"The guy who draws dicks on your certificate?"

"That's him," I said, "So stupid."

"Well, it's stupid . . . yeah it's stupid."

I got up. She was still sitting. "Come on, I don't want to do this right here in the restaurant. If we go to the car, you can at least scream at me. It will make you feel better."

She was silent all the way to the car, silent when I turned the ignition, silent when I put it in gear, silent past the river, silent around the bend up by where the highway meets the bridge, silent past those old abandoned parking lots.

But then, as my luck was destined to fail, she became no longer silent.

"It would have made me feel a whole lot better if you just appreciated what I was going through for you," Sarah ranted, rightfully.

"I do appreciate it. Aside from the whole part where I wish it never happened, yeah I do appreciate it."

"You have something wrong with your brain. You are not supposed to tell your VERY PREGNANT wife that you wished she wasn't carrying YOUR KID! AND YOU DO IT ALL THE FUCKING TIME!!"

"I'm crazy, I'm sorry. But I'm trying to be honest."

"Honest? You're unreal. You lie and tell me that you aren't into porn, that this isn't yours, and I am supposed to be stupid and just say, No, it's totally OK for my husband to whack off to somebody else when he won't touch me."

"Calm down. It must be that José character at work. He seems like a real sleaze."

"Whatever."

"Whatever is right," I said.

"I think we need a little more honesty in our relationship."

"I think we need a little more trust in our relationship."

"I agree."

"I agree."

I pulled the car into the driveway, shut it off, got out, began walking to the front door. She was still sitting in the car. I began to unlock the front door, opened it. I turned to her, I expected to see her crying. Instead, there was a look of surprise on her face.

"Jimmy! Jimmy!" Sarah said.

"What?"

"I think my water just broke!"

My life flashed before my eyes.

"Seriously?"

The car door opened. "No, I was just screwing with you, you moron," she said it with warmth, the way two people could do only if they cared deep down. "I'm seven months. You've got a ways."

"Oh shit." I grabbed her arm, and we walked in as a giant hand would loop the curve of a tea cup handle.

"Sorry I got fat, but your fat cock did it to me," my bride said.

"I apologize for my fat cock."

"Am I too ugly now?"

"No."

"Well, will you lay down with me?"

"Now?" *Lay down* was code.

"Yeah. I need it," she said. "Bad."

"Holy shit, so do I."

We went upstairs, kissing madly on the stairs, knocking the photos off the wall of us at the prom; us on vacation at Niagara falls; us floating on orange pool rafts in Miami the previous summer.

We collapsed on the bed, I knocked the air out of her and she shrieked with laughter, "watch my belly, you klutz!"

"Shhhh," I slipped my tongue in her mouth and she ran her nails down my back. We rolled on our sides, eagerly tearing our clothes off. It'd been too long. Far too long.

"Touch me here," she said. Her breath smelled like fresh

mint. She rolled on top of me and we did it slow—with extremely synched rhythm, as only two people who've known each other for as long as we had could. Cries of wonder and happiness and grunts of release left our lungs and we couldn't do anything to stop them. A drop of sweat fell from her brow, landing in my eye. I didn't care.

My eyes rolled back in my head, her breasts swung over me. I was floating through the astral plane bathed in immortal vibrating pink light.

After—our breath hot and frantic, we rolled to the side, I clutched her from behind.

"That was like the old days."

"Yeah," I agreed.

"I loved the old days."

"Me too."

153

L   arry wanted to see me in his office, which was fine by me.
        Usually a trip to Larry's office meant some Girl Scout cook-
        ies that his daughter was selling, news on some adjustments
to the booths, some state money that was coming in—something
like that.

When I opened the door, Larry was sitting at his desk, reading a magazine: swimsuit girls kissing deep in tropical water. I
sat down, put my feet up on the edge of his desk. He didn't care.

"How you living, kid?"

"Not as good as you."

"Debatable," he said, cracking his bubblegum. "Look, I need
to talk to you about something very important." His eyes nar-
rowed, taking on a newfound sinister look. "We've known each
other for . . . what, how long have we worked together?"

"Eleven years."

"This whole time you've been in that same booth and things've
gone very smoothly."

"But now . . . "

He nodded, "But now, somebody has been blowing through
your toll lane, late at night on José's watch."

"Oh."

"I've been notified by the State that the only way to correct the
problem is to terminate the individual."

"José?"

"No, the motorist," he said, drumming his fingers on the desk. With his free hand, like a magic trick, he pulled a silver gleaming gun out of the top drawer. He slid it to me across his desk. "You ever shoot a gun?"

"I fired a gun once," I confessed, "But it was a turkey hunting gun. I shot up a mannequin."

"You could kill a thousand turkeys with this. You're the best we've got."

I wanted to stand up and back out of the office, but something made me reach for the gun. It seemed to hum with power in my hand—I recalled all the dreams of cowboys and Indians as a small boy in the field behind my house, where Ted and I would shoot the neighborhood kids in the blueberry bushes with sticks. We didn't have rifles and high grain to do the thing right, so we improvised.

It felt good to hold the true glow of death in my hands. The grip was wonderful and so was the smell of the gun oil. I knew I could shoot a terrorist from one hundred and ninety yards, the hostage wrapped up in his arms. I would get that terrorist right in the center of his skull. Laser dot aiming device? I didn't need that shit! I was American.

"It'll be a lime green Honda Civic. The tailpipe will make it sound like a lawnmower. After your shift is over, come in the break room and take a dinner break. I'll watch the booth personally, José won't be coming in tonight. He has the evening off. When you're done eating, come and relieve me in the booth, understood?"

"Perfectly," I said, sliding the gun in my pocket.

"The car comes every night between ten after ten and twenty after ten. It's been on a clockwork schedule every night of the workweek for the last seven months.

I nodded. So this was to be the new way.

I waited in the booth. It was the same routine at night, but much slower. I looked up at the wall, I hadn't bothered to hang a new certificate up there. It didn't matter anymore. The clock of life ticked down like torture. The gun sat on the little ledge. Every motorist who came to the window could have seen it if they really wanted to, if they stretched, but none of them were real people, they were all just ghosts of the highway—disassociated, in a trance between the streams of opposing headlights that danced over the median. The moon hung sweat-less and cold over the pines, still with humid air.

Those people must have felt like that moon as they sped along, the glass of their vehicle making an entirely new universe as they crossed through the space between blinks of millenniums in their God carriages. Their vehicles set themselves apart from the atmosphere of the sphere where they were said to live and rumored to have lives. Their stereos blocked out useless Earthly noise. Their seat belts cuddled them into immortality.

In an eggshell, in a bubble, in a sarcophagus on wheels, driving into a vortex, shifting through a new dimension, ripping a hole in the fabric of the galaxy without even blinking. That'd be nice.

The guy in the tollbooth breaks that fantasy, stops them like sheep, says, "You are not the moon, you're not the reflection of the moon on the ocean, you're not even a little wave in the water, you're just an asshole citizen. Heed all regulations. Slow down. Face this toll or face death."

Then, from afar, I heard the distant sound of a lawnmower.

There was me, the sheriff, and there was him, the outlaw Indian who'd been scalping all of the ladies of misplaced wagon trains. The vehicle soared towards me, I leaned out of the booth ever so slightly, aiming the gun into the oncoming headlights. I squeezed the trigger, the silver pistol recoiled. I laughed wildly, squeezed again, this time a wilder shot. A headlight burst.

I kept shooting as the green Civic came within the last fifty feet of the tollbooth. When the car passed I spun, squeezing off the final ten rounds at its tail lights. The tires flattened, the back window exploded. Swerving, the driver screamed as chocolate syrup blood sprayed from a hole in his neck. On his radio somebody was singing a very poppy hit song. He was dying to the rhythm of that song.

I watched unbelieving as the car went off the side of the parkway, into the darkness of the pines. I tossed the gun in the shadow of the booth, I counted to fifty in my head, then a hundred and fifty, my heart racing. What then?

Out the window I saw a dim light where the single headlight was reflecting off a pine tree. No one had seen anything. Still, I waited for police sirens. Headlights appeared on the highway. I

51

gasped.

It was a young guy, with an older woman, both looked annoyed, "Dude, how much is the toll?"

"Thirty-five cents."

He handed me a ten dollar bill, "I'm giving you a ten."

"I see that."

"Well don't try to be all smart and just give me change of a dollar."

I wondered if there were any rounds left in the gun. But, nervous, I gave him back the correct change.

"Dude," he said, "can I have a receipt?"

I handed him the receipt.

Up the highway, I saw a road department truck parked beside the car crashed in the woods. Two men were setting up flashing lights and road flares. I sat perfectly still, gulping. A few other men come out of the woods, carrying a large trash bag. It appeared to be industrial strength.

Another series of motorists zoomed through the exact change lane. The road crew loaded the bag into the back of one of the trucks, which left in slow official maneuvers up the highway. A quarter mile up was the service road entrance where the salt and the sand and the plow equipment and the road crew headquarters were located.

A few minutes later a tow truck came, hauling the vehicle out of the woods.

The flashers and road cones remained for perhaps twenty minutes and then those workers slowly packed it all away. In the center of this strange night, they were just trying to kill time until the time clock said that they were again free men. I saw a kid in a reflective vest yawning and stretching. It was somewhere close to three am.

At my next designated break I went into Larry's office, he was still reading the sexy chick magazine.

"Good work," he said.

"Thanks."

He smiled, "That asshole really had that coming."

I put the silver gun on his desk.

He smiled again, "You aren't done, there's one more person to take care of, who's been dodging the toll."

"Who?"

"Sarah," he said flatly.

He tossed me a fresh ammo clip from his filing cabinet. I caught it; there was no sense in denying Larry.

"Go home, get some sleep, kill your wife."

I nodded, walked down the hall to the vending machine, got a PayDay, munched on it as I drove my car out of the parking lot and to where Sarah waited. As I pulled into my driveway finishing the candy bar, I sighed, thinking that I would be sad when my wife was just a memory.

I stepped into the dark house. Sarah snored upstairs, she usually didn't snore. Since she'd become pregnant she'd started. I imagined that the baby was a snorer, that it was all its evil gremlin doing.

Gun in hand, I crept up the stairs, straightening some of the framed photos as I passed. Bedside, I aimed the gun in the darkness, preparing to fire at Sarah, but couldn't.

151

I drove around the random neighborhood in an ever broadening circle that neared the tollbooth. The rain was letting up, the sun threatening to peak through the comfort of the black clouds.

I turned on one street, surveying. Suddenly there was Gena, walking with a pink back pack. My sweet sweet tigress. I pulled beside her, as she turned, I saw it wasn't her.

"Sorry, I thought you were someone else."

Fear was on her young face. It was happening more and more. I was beginning to see Gena in everyone and everything.

Up the road, there were vacant lots, the pine trees and sugar sand removed. New construction. A foundation had already been poured. Small wooden stakes with neon ties flapped in the wind. Some concrete blocks were stacked in neat piles.

I stepped out of the Subaru onto the lot. I wondered how these builders had been able to lay the blocks so perfectly. I didn't know construction—I had no skill whatsoever, I didn't know how to do anything else besides hand out the change of a dollar.

I couldn't even be a fisherman, which, I assumed wasn't very hard. I couldn't even stand there at the edge of the surf with a fishing rod and catch a fish, I had no skill . . . I had dreams of being a fisherman, out on the vast sea, just me and the waves . . . but I had no skill.

That wasn't true, I had all kinds of skill. I looked up at the sky, trying to name some of those skills, any skill. Thinking even harder, so hard, so hard, what skills? But, then looking at the concrete blocks, I thought: why couldn't I learn how to do something like that? Set blocks? I could definitely learn that.

There was a tarp on the side of the property, I went to it, lifted it. All kinds of wood was beneath. Nails too. And Insulation. A box full of duct tape, surely the most important tool on any job site. I reached down, picked up the tape, so many people thought that it was called DUCK TAPE, but so many of those people were born looking like flipper babies. At least I knew that much about the construction trade, that duct tape was called DUCT TAPE and not DUCK TAPE!

I scooped the box up, carried it to my car. It's for securing ducts, dipshits!

This would be all I needed to build my new empire.

150

I called Ted from a pay phone outside Great Wok of China. He answered on the third ring. "It's Jimmy," I said.

"Why do you still say that, we've been friends since Kindergarten."

"My pre-school scores were better than yours. I didn't eat paste," I taunted.

"Still holding that over my head, I see. What's up? You want to do something?"

"Yeah," I said.

"Like what?"

"I'm at the Great Wok of China"

"Why did they ever name it that?"

"As opposed to the Great Wall of China? Wanna get lunch? Just come over here, quick too, I need your help with something," I said.

"With what?"

"You still have those do-it-yourself construction tapes?" I asked

"The home improvement ones you gave me?"

"Uh huh."

"Did you ever watch them?" I asked.

"Once."

"Perfect. Oh, and bring a level and a hammer with you."

"To the Chinese restaurant?"

"Yeah."

He sighed, "On my way."

149

My Subaru had eight sheets of plywood on the roof, about 20 ten foot lengths of 4x4 lumber on top of that. There was also a door and a window, all secured in place by miraculous wrappings of super-industrial strength duct tape. In the rear seat of the car were large rolls of insulation—unseen under that, two packages of roof shingles. In the trunk was a roll of tar paper, ten penny nails, heavy duty screw, silicone, caulk.

I was at a table by the gum-ball machine when Ted pulled up. I waved to him through the window as he parked. He took a good look at my car, shook his head, coming into the hot salty unease of the Chinese restaurant. I sat smiling and sipping green tea from a small wax cup.

"Amigo are you out of your mind. That Subaru is grossly overloaded. You can't just duck tape that much shit to the top." Ted is like a dad to me. He won't shut up with his wisdom and care for regulations. I need that, I suppose.

"It's not duck taped it's duct taped."

"Well, I think I would know a little more about the gross weight capacity of a vehicle, since I work at the DMV. What are you going to do with all that stuff?"

"Have a seat, we'll discuss it like gentlemen."

"Did you steal all of that?" Ted asked, quietly.

"No, it was a gift."

"From who?"

"From God."

"Out of your mind," Ted took a seat across from me. He said, "I really think that you should seriously consider talking to someone."

"I'm talking to you."

"Not that kind of talking. I mean, like a professional. A shrink. I think you might need some medicine. Ya know, Jim. You just seem plain off to me. Off."

I ignored him. "I don't know . . . I had a dream last night that I shot somebody for driving through the tollbooth without paying . . ."

He was looking up at the lunch specials, squinting, "Yeah, get a psychiatrist."

I always ignored him when he said that I needed psychiatric help. "I have a plan, a necessary plan."

"Concerning . . . ?"

"We're going to build an escape from our boring stupid lives."

"I don't have a boring stupid life."

"I disagree."

A Chinese woman came out of the kitchen, sweating and carrying a large tray. Two lunch specials for us.

"I got you the boneless spare ribs, Dr. Jung," I informed.

"I love boneless spare ribs," Ted said with delight.

"You probably have never tried anything else off of a Chinese food menu in your life."

"That's not true. I just know what I like."

"Well I have the same problem, as you can see."

"The middle of the road is fine with me," Ted said.

"I don't like being married." I said, "and I know that you don't either. If I wasn't a coward, I'd leave."

"I'm happy."

"You're fatter than you used to be. I'm balder, we can't be that happy."

I put some of my ribs into my mouth, began to slowly crush them in my werewolf fangs. I slurped my tea.

"I have a plan," I said, manic.

"I have a plan too," he explained, "I'm trying to get promoted at the DMV, to get my own office, a pretty secretary who wears nice perfume and colorful skirts."

"Hold it right there!"

I held up the Chinese food place mat, showing the drawings explaining Chinese Horoscopes, "You know what this says? I'm a boar and I should avoid rabbits."

"Sarah is a Rabbit?"

"According to this," I said point blankly, shaking the place mat in front of his face.

"OK," he said, leaning forward, "just a short stay in a nice facility? The Mayweather, out by the cranberry bog. Please, think about it. They'll listen to you, they'll talk to you about your problems . . . it'll help."

"Do you have a pen?"

"No, no pen," he said, patting himself anyway. "No pen."

There was a tea cup full of crayons next to a coloring book with Chinese cartoons of dragons. In a frenzy, I scooped up the red and blue and green crayons and I began to draw my detailed plans on the back of the place mat.

"What are you doing now?"

"You'll see."

First I drew the far walls, and then the near walls, then the door, adding the windows. I carefully scrawled detailed dimensions, like any good architect would.

Munching on his egg roll, Ted asked, "And why are you off in the middle of the week anyway?"

"I might be quitting my job," I said as I slowly drew the roof. "If all of this works out, I might quit my job."

"Might! You can't quit your job, you have a kid on the way. This is exactly what I mean!"

"Enough idle chit chat, check this out."

I slid the drawing to him across the table.

"There you go, there are the blueprints."

"For what?" he asked.

"Our hideout."

148

Sarah had vivid nightmares about car crashes. She would often wake me—hysterical. A reoccurring object of her night terrors was my old car, a diesel Volkswagen Rabbit, that I'd named Diesel Cottontail as a teenager.

Usually in Sarah's nightmares, Diesel Cottontail would strike into her while she was walking or riding her sea green bicycle. She would lose a limb, pinned between other cars, telephone poles, brick walls.

For the most part, it was Sarah's leg that was lost. It'd vanish in a swarm of black bees.

Waking, she would grip onto her leg underneath the sheets as she thrashed in terror. I'd stroke the sweaty hair from her brow and comfort her the best I could, as she wept, saying, "that car . . . that car . . . that car."

When she was calmer, I'd bring her a glass of ice cold water, she'd fish a tablet out of her top drawer beside the bed, take it down with a gulp.

"Everything's alright now," I used to say. "That was a long time. That car is gone, and is never coming back."

147

Dolly, Sarah's mom, was dead. She visited me from time to time, just to make me squirm. That's when I knew I was doing bad. She'd come dressed in the clothes she'd wore on the day she died and harassed me venomously.

"You're a real piece of work," she said, materializing in the booth at my shoulder. "Utter scum," she hocked ectoplasm at my feet.

Dolly grew up in Long Island, lived through hardships there, moved to New Jersey with Sarah in her womb. She'd raised my Sarah alone while working as an ER nurse. Dolly had done the best she could. It was my fault she was dead.

The first time she appeared to me from beyond the grave, it was in an Atlantic City bathroom mirror on the night of my bachelor party. I was washing my hands in the sink, they smelled like the insides of a stripper.

She'd materialized in the bathroom mirror, flips of jet black hair and her horn rimmed glasses, "Look at you! Pathetic!" Dolly snarled, "Pathetic!"

Then she vanished. Just a brief little insult, then gone.

Behind me in the tollbooth, Dolly whispered, "Jim, I'm not gonna make this easy for you."

I turned to look at her, all that was there was on the silver wall was my certificate with more dicks drawn on it.

145

Sarah killed her mother and she did it with my car. Diesel Cottontail. I was out of town, on a school trip. Dolly, who wasn't much of a driver herself, was teaching Sarah how to drive. I'd been real cool with the idea. Excited even. Sarah the driver! I remember sitting on the yellow bus as we pushed west, hoping she'd get a real badass car with a big back seat, so we could screw with more comfort.

Their driver's lesson, hadn't gone so well. I still have the article from the paper:

PARALLEL PARKING
DEATH RULED ACCIDENTAL
Examiner- Staff
Toms River, New Jersey

Authorities say 16-year old girl, Sarah Culbert, who accidentally ended her mother's life by backing a car over her in the midst of a driving lesson will not face any criminal charges.

The Ocean County Prosecutor's Office Crash Examiner Unit and the Investigation Unit reviewed the circumstances and ruled no malice was involved in the incident.

The incident happened around 2:00 pm on the 300 block of Buleri Avenue in the parking lot of the Wilbur Buleri public park. Children who were playing a basketball game were noted as eye witnesses, one of their mothers, Ira Grosse, also a neighbor and friend of the deceased placed the initial 911 call.

Dorothy Culbert, 41, was teaching her daughter, Sarah, how to parallel park the vehicle, instructing from outside the car.

The girl who was operating a Volkswagen Rabbit, had the vehicle in reverse and may have inadvertently stepped on the gas rather than the brake.

The car backed into Culbert, pinning her underneath. She was pronounced dead at the scene.

"This is a very tragic accident, our thoughts and prayers go out to the Culbert family during this difficult time."
RICHARD ROE- OCEAN COUNTY PROSECUTOR

I could understand why Sarah hated cars, it was just a shame that she had to hate the one car that I ever loved.

144

Dolly's coffin was lowered slowly into the wet earth, each pallbearer gripping onto a satin sash while one of the nameless cousins played Danny Boy on the fiddle with wobbly uneven strokes.

I wasn't there, funerals weren't my thing. My father in his copper urn on the mantel was all the ceremonial death I ever needed from this life. It was a shame though that the contents of that urn hadn't been able to teach me what was right and wrong.

I had no concept of what giving respect was, either. Blame the ashes. My mother didn't have the capacity to explain anything. She'd shut down after my dad's death.

When Sarah's mother died, she'd done the opposite, becoming vivid and dislodged. Frantic.

Sarah was seventeen at the cemetery, crying into her teenage hands, avoiding eye contact with her mother's casket. Black dress. Trembling knees. I was in the opposite of a suit, at home parked outside the garage, spray painting my Volkswagen. The wind kept whistling, the blue paint catching the breeze and blowing back at me. Ted skidding up on his BMX, said, "You look like a smurf."

I didn't say anything.

"You still have that car?" he asked, surprised, "it was used in a murder . . . don't the cops confiscate it for evidence?"

"Go away, man," I said. "I'm not in the mood to joke around."

"I wasn't joking . . ."

There were tears forming in my eyes. One welled up and rolled down my cheek. Ted watched the tear roll and shake on my jawline as the breeze blew. When the tear fell, it screamed down to the earth and made a sound like a bomb going off when it struck the blue tarp I'd covered the driveway with.

I recall him flinching, jumping almost.

"It's gonna be alright," he said.

I went into the house. Sat on the couch. Staining the cushions blue.

I talked to Sarah on the telephone the night that she tried to kill herself. She was in the guest room at her aunt's house. Two days had passed since the funeral. I tried my hardest to make her laugh. It wasn't easy. We talked about going to see a movie. There was a dog barking outside her door. She said she hated the dog more than anything in the world. She said that she missed me. She wanted to hold me. I suggested we go see Weekend At Bernie's II. She was deathly silent. "Really, Weekend At Bernie's II?" she asked in disgust.

"Yeah."

"Sure, sure, whatever. Anything. I just want to see you."

"The feeling is more than mutual."

She said goodbye. Then, she went into the bathroom, turned on the sink. She turned on the shower. She ate every single pill in her aunt's medicine cabinet, laid down in the bathtub with the shower raining down her. She contemplated drinking Drano, like Kurt Vonnegut's mother had done. She'd just read Slaughter House Five because it was on the banned books list. She closed her eyes.

One of the nameless cousins found her.

She was doing time in the Mayweather Home. I went to visit her there: seventh floor. At first she was in a ward where you weren't allowed to sit. She laid in the bed staring up at the florescent lights. As visiting hours allowed, I stood next to the bed. They'd let me come for two and a half hours. I'd stand the whole time, leaning against the wall next to her bed, she would say nothing. Not even when I said, "Supposedly, there are secret passages underneath this place. Al Capone used them to get away from the G men. Did you know that?"

That went on for three days.

The fourth day, she said, "go away."

So I went away.

I fell in love with her when she was there in that home. She was brought down to my level. I don't think it's possible to love someone who is high above you or far below you. You might be drawn to them, you might feel affection or admiration of some kind, but not real love.

When I came to see Sarah again, she'd been moved into her own room. I wasn't allowed to be anywhere near it except during visiting hours, it was OK for me to sit with her. We sat in the communal area and played checkers. We watched a VHS of Romeo and Juliet because "I have a book report and I don't think I can bring myself to read anything," she said.

She didn't know that Juliet drank poison at the end. I said, "I'm bored, can we shut this off?" somewhere around the middle.

"I wanna see what happens . . ."

"They get away."

"Oh, alright," she said.

The next time I came, we went down to the basketball court. We didn't play. We sat Indian style on the green grass and watched some of the other patients dribble around the court awkwardly, tossing the ball up at the rim, ricocheting off wildly into the pine trees.

She looked at me, "I want to stay with you. I don't wanna go back to my aunt's house. She doesn't want me there anyway."

"Of course," I said, holding her hand on the cool grass. "You can move in," I said.

It was my mother's house, but she didn't care. We were gonna graduate high school in two months.

Across the lawn was my blue car. The murder car—Diesel Cottontail.

"Is that your car?"

"Yeah," I said.

She was very quiet.

"I painted it," I said.

"I see that."

"It's not orange anymore."

Sarah let go of my hand.

144A

Sarah sat on a plaid couch in the rec room, shell shocked of course, but her lips were no longer thin and blue. There was some life to her eyes.

She looked up at me, "Thank god you're back," she said. There was a sign on the wall that said ABSOLUTELY NO TOUCHING ALLOWED. I sat on a plastic chair across from her, we held hands, hidden on the seat beside our thighs.

She was wearing a pink sweater with a kitten on it. A hand me down from her aunt. She was so upset about the sweater. She said, "They took my cassettes, and I'm in this fucking ridiculous sweater and I'm supposed to write down how I feel in this journal . . . they take it every night and read it. I'm in this fucking kitten sweater and I . . ."

I leaned over, grabbed her. She started crying. We hugged hard on the couch.

A big guy with a beard came walking over, "YOU'VE GOTTA LEAVE."

I didn't let go, he physically pulled me off Sarah. I was basically thrown head first out of the place.

I got in Diesel Cottontail and drove to the county mall.

Two hours later, I was back at the Mayweather. The guard said, "you're not allowed back."

I gave the desk girl a plastic bag for Sarah. It had something in it for her. A hooded sweatshirt. Black. Three wolves howling at the moon. It was supposed to be good luck. It had a secret "stash pocket" sewn into it. It was faux fur lined and you couldn't tell. That's why it was so expensive, the last of my paycheck. I slipped a cassette into the stash pocket for her.

Nirvana In Utero.

It'd just come out. I hadn't even listened to it yet. The people at the home never found the cassette. Sarah couldn't listen to it there but she told me that when she laid in her bed at night she clutched into it, imagining that when she got out, we'd listen to it together. It kept her going.

When we got married, our song was "All Apologies".

143

After she was released, Sarah rode her bike everywhere. Even though I'd painted it from orange to blue, she wouldn't ride in Diesel Cottontail anymore. But, good things came out of those bad events. We were drawn closer, our love got heavier than death itself. The crux of our relationship was my car. It had been a good thing to me, a good transport, I had lost my virginity in it. She wanted nothing more than for me to set it on fire.

Instead, we went for long bike rides to the abandoned railroad trestle, jumping off of it not quite certain if we were going to die or live. We took chisels to the concrete wall of the dam, carving our names in it. When we came out of the sandpits there was a cop parked there. We hid in the honey suckles for hours, filling our mouths like humming birds would. Sarah and I rode away down the wildest hills to where the electric lines hummed over nothing but our youth dissolving everything else in a throbbing pink bonfire.

Sarah said her favorite song was "Moving in Stereo" by the Cars.

"That song where the girl comes out of the pool in slow motion? What was that movie?"

"Fast Times at Ridgemont High," she said, "But I loved that song for so long. I only saw the movie last year."

I said my lucky number was 77.

She said, "That's the year I was born."

"Best year ever."

We waded out into the cold, brown Cedar Creek, determined to prove that we would live forever. When we climbed out we had a leech on each shoulder. We clawed them off, tossing them into the mud. "We should follow the train tracks until we find a dead body," she said, finally capable of joking around again. I said, "They're always in the blueberry bushes."

"Shoes knocked right off 'em."

We fell in deep love at other people's parties, on couches completely alone surrounded by a hundred thousand wayward kids.

She liked to cut the cores out of apples and smoke weed at sunset while the bats flew around the apartment complex and our laughs echoed off the gutters.

"I wanna learn how to play the piano, build me a piano, Jimmy."

I found her a Casio with a blown out speaker on bulk trash day. For a little while she tried to play it, but never learned any chords. She tried to sing too. She had the most beautiful shaky voice and used to finger those chords while we drank bottle after bottle of Seagrams gin in my mother's basement. She was a true angel, "I'm all alone in the world but I had you to save me."

Underneath the water tower we both felt like the full moon was in our eyes even though it was hidden behind rain clouds holding out for morning. She spread out a blanket and let me climb on top of her. I knew that it wouldn't have happened if not for the circumstances of the previous months. A piece of glass pushed into my knee while I pushed inside of her. We were eighteen.

Right then my wisdom felt light as a feather, the wind came up out of nowhere. I'd wanted nothing more than to be eighteen forever underneath that water tower—inside Sarah for the first time. That glass in my knee, even.

We took our flea market junk heap bikes down steep hills. I hit a brick, flipped—broke my arm. That's how I became a bicycle casualty.

But she kneeled like such a princess never should, kissing my cast, signing her name, a heart, an arrow, a swear about forever. I Imagined my broken bone. I imagined all of her broken brain circuits misaligned after her mother's funeral.

I should've been taking college classes, but I didn't want to leave Sarah.

"Even if the future doesn't mean as much money, I don't care," I said, "as long as I have you I won't need money."

"That's fine," she said.

We were the ones in the back of the movie theater, back as far as we could get, the worst showing of the worst film, empty seats, but she was a cheerleader and liked to be enthusiastic about her boyfriend in the darkness. For every fuck she carved another notch into my cast, when it came off it looked like havoc, all those notches.

She wrapped her arms around me the day the cast came off and I carried her for miles.

I dumped gin into her until she finally climbed inside the Rabbit for the first time since the tragedy, "It's silly, it's just a car . . . "

We drove Diesel Cottontail out onto the frozen bay. It used to get cold enough to do that in Jersey.

I killed the ignition, and we sat in the darkness, snow falling. We sang to the radio, making up our own words. She told me that she thought it was all worth it, "to be here with you." I didn't see how she could mean it, but she meant it. She put her head on my shoulder.

We fell asleep—woke to the reflection of the sun off of the ice. That was the day the bay thawed. The ice had been cracking for some time, no one thought about it. Ted drove his dirt bike out that afternoon and lost it into the water below, he nearly drowned.

The ocean takes a lot.

142C

Sarah was pregnant and driving through town. She still suffered from the occasional nightmare about my old car. The white noise machine I'd bought was no help.

I was happy she'd surrendered and slid back into the driver's seat after so many years of absence, for convenience sake. She didn't like the thought of being on a bicycle with our baby inside her. I didn't have the heart to tell her that more in utero babies are killed by lightning strikes than by bicycles.

Ahead, traffic was frozen on main-street.

There'd been a horrible wreck by Dinosaur Liquor.

I got a phone call at work. She'd pulled into a plaza, ringing me up from the pay phone outside Fried Paradise. "Oh good, you're still alive," she said with relief.

"Yeah, still kicking," I said.

"I see an ambulance on route 9. Traffic's gridlocked. I got worried. But you're fine. You're fine." Love is relief. Love is doubt. Love is a car crash that can't kill you. Love is kissing a wound that will not close so that you both survive the night. "OK, I'll talk to you later then," she said.

"Wait," I said, "Don't go. Tell me a story."

"A story?" she said. I could hear her light through the telephone line, "Well, let me think of one . . . "

"How about that story about the girl who loved oranges?"

"Oh, well that's an easy one," she said. "There was once a little girl from New Jersey who was very sad because her daddy was gone. He'd flown the coop—"

" . . . go on."

"She would sometimes get letters from him from different parts of the country. Tiny letters. Gifts too. She remembered the first time that she got a package in the mail from the daddy."

"What was it?"

"It was a wooden box, little—3 by 3."

"What was in it?"

"Citrus," she said. "He sent her oranges and it was the first time she'd ever seen one before and she thought it was a ball. She asked her mom to play catch with her and the balls that her daddy had sent her. But her mom just cried and cried." She sighed, "The next day, she peeled one of the oranges for her and the girl ate it her playhouse, hiding. It was the best thing that the girl had ever eaten. Sweet citrus."

"I meant the story about when I took you to the orange grove on vacation in Florida," I said.

"Well, there's many stories from the girl who loves oranges about oranges," Sarah said. I sighed. "For instance, the next time my daddy sent me a box of oranges, I was three years older. I'd told him in a letter how much I liked the first box. The second box of oranges were dry and bitter. Nothing like the first. There were worms in the second orange I tried to eat. After that, they sat on the table, unloved—until the fruit became green and fuzzy white with mold beginning to rot in the heat. Then we threw them out. That was the last time I ever had contact with him."

"Shhhhit," I said.

"When I see an ambulance, I like to hear from you."

It was nice to know that people wanted you alive.

"I'm OK," I said. "I'm not going anywhere. Me equals strong as ox. Or cock-a-roach. Same thing, maybe."

"Good," she said. I heard sirens scream by in the background. "I need you, warts and all." The line went dead before she could say she loved me. We'd been through many wars together. We'd been blown apart by land mines. We'd been machine gunned down out of the sky in Apache helicopters. We'd ducked under barbed wire and crawled through the mud and filth and hate. We sometimes forgot to say I love you. But, wars will do that to you.

I went in the break room and took all of José's food out of the refrigerator. All of it. I walked it around back, shook it out into the weeds for the raccoons and deer to eat.

When the rain let up an hour later, at least half of the town had heard about Kimmy Simmons.

She'd just finished cutting the mayor's daughter's hair in Jake Annopolis's International Hairport next to Food Universe. Kimmy had brushed the girl off, took the modest tip, realized that she had a soda in her car and decided to walk out and get it.

She dropped her car keys in a little puddle trying to get in her car. As she bent down to pick them up, a car rounded the corner by the gas station, hit the curb in front of the antique store. Kimmy heard this far off, was putting the key in the lock when the driver came into collision with the telephone pole. She turned towards the sound, one headlight still lit was aimed at her, she was between her own vehicle and the open door when the car hit her.

A Volkswagen Golf, not quite a Diesel Rabbit like Sarah's nightmares. It was sky blue. It had a bike rack. When it struck the telephone pole the bike rack was damaged, when the car struck Kimmy Simmons' Cavalier, pinning her, a bike flew backwards off of the roof of the car, it hit a red Oldsmobile, splintering the windshield.

Kimmy Simmons lost her leg.

Sarah nearly went back into the Mayweather. The details were so surreal and close to her nightmares.

Kimmy Simmons got a prosthetic leg, but still cuts hair in the strip mall even though she got a settlement too big to imagine. The driver was drunk, of course.

How could somebody that beautiful and that good get struck down over a bottle of Diet Coke and still come out of it smiling, cutting hair, wanting nothing but to be near all of the friends who she was guaranteed to see everyday because they all had hair and it never stopped growing.

142B

Often, I looked at Sarah's little orange bottles of pills. Lithium for a time. Then Prozac. Paxil after that.

Alone, I studied the small plastic containers in our empty house. Safe, except for the dripping faucet that I didn't know how to fix. I shook the bottles, enjoying the sound of a baby rattle without the trouble. It calmed me.

I wondered if those little suckers would help me. Newspapers stuffed into wet sneakers sucking up the water. A shot of whiskey in a cup of lukewarm coffee. Soap flakes in the garden to keep aphids away from the roses. Miracle cures. We had no roses.

Would medicine improve me? Would it solve my complex problems within my standard issue wrinkle free, stain free, set it and forget it life? Would my worry vanish like lemmings toppling off a cliff into the thrashing waves some four billion feet below the surf breaking on sharp dark obsidian?

At times, my life and my thoughts got so heavy, I snuck away and thought that I'd have to eat a handful of Sarah's pills just to keep from sinking completely and unmercifully into the swamp of my skull.

But I never did.

In a way, her pills were part of the reality of our love. I was afraid to get help, to see a therapist. I thought it would be like giving up.

I'd sometimes open the lid of her pills and look in for a long time. But that was as far as it went. If I went and got help, I feared that I'd lose her, because I'd lose myself.

Our lives were games of chess. We didn't know how to play chess.

142A

T ed knew a spot for our hideout, "It's down towards the river," he said. "Sometimes I walk Rommel there. It's down a secluded hidden trail just wide enough to fit your car."

He seemed totally numb to the whole idea. While, I parked the Subaru in an area of unknown beauty—the dark woods behind the neighborhood. There, I could hear the cars on the highway, and somehow still see the river.

"It's nice out here," he said. "Maybe your idea isn't so bad."

Slowly, I looked up at the trees and down towards the river. What a place to hide away. I began to rip off the duct tape, pulling the boards down from their resting place. "We'll get this all hooked up and then you'll have a place to come and hang out, get away from our wives."

"We built clubhouses when I was a kid," Ted said, kicking a pinecone into the woods, "It might be a lot of fun."

By the time the sun was falling we had what resembled a shack leaning against the space between two trees. We stood back, expecting the whole thing to collapse. We'd set all of the plywood walls, cut an opening for our front door. All it would take was another day or so to hang the door and the window, and then a little time to do the roof, I picked up a large rock and smashed it against the closest wall, a massive echo shot thorough the woods,

"I can't believe it didn't fall down!"

"I have clubhouse experience! I've done this before," Ted said.

"And I'm totally proud of you!" It was my first clubhouse. My dad hadn't been the kind of guy that actually did things with his kid. I was more proud of the fort than my own home.

"OK, this whole thing has been tons of fun, but I have to go, Kelly will have dinner ready soon."

"I'm staying here tonight," I said.

"Here?"

"Yeah," I said, "I have a sleeping bag and everything."

"Why?"

"Because I want to. Plus, I'm fighting with Sarah."

" . . . If you need somewhere to crash."

"No, I don't need somewhere to crash."

"Well, that's fucked up."

"You're wife doesn't want a guest anyway."

" . . . You're probably right," he admitted. "Go home, it can't be that bad."

"Sound advice."

He began to walk back up the path to where his minivan was parked, "Call me tomorrow, maybe you and Sarah can come over and watch a DVD with me and Kelly."

"Sounds good."

All I could think was: is Ted completely out of his mind? Doesn't he know that no matter what, I'd be there after work, finishing the roof of our fortress?

141

Again, I didn't go to work. All day, I labored on the construction of my fortress.

When I was finished, I couldn't believe my eyes. What a wonderful place. I decided it was a better home than the where my wife and I lived. So, hey why not move out into the woods with the other stupid animals?

I'd live in a shack by the river with the sounds of the dinosaurs on the highway, and only half a mile from the toll plaza, I would be two miles closer to work. That meant four miles a day saved in gas, twenty eight miles a week. Surely that was enough money saved for what I would have to pay my wife in alimony. Because it was obvious to me that first night that I slept there, that I had to make this change. The air of the woods made me feel like I was nine years old again, on a Cub Scout camp out, even though I was never a scout, something else my father forbade.

But the fact remained that I needed my clothes, and oh, oh yeah, my savings account passbook. A million other things too. My international passport just in case.

As much as I wanted to cut all connections off from my wife, I had to go home and I had to see her. I knew that she would be there, just sitting at the kitchen table, waiting.

I opened the door, the telephone was ringing, as if it knew I was coming and it had to react quickly in order to interrupt some murder scene between me and my wife.

For sure Sarah wanted to kill me.

I went into the kitchen. She waited like a lioness, staring at me. Behind her, our phone tolled out its belled doom. "Answer that," I commanded. She tore it off the hook, "Hello," she said agitated. Then, cupping the receiver with her hand, she scowled at me. "It's some girl. Some young girl. Some young girl asking for you."

"Huh?"

I snatched the phone from her, "Hello?"

"Jim? It's Gena from Officetown."

"Oh, hey. How are you?"

I cupped the phone, looking at my wife, "It's nothing, no one." She looked pissed. She had every right to be.

"Jim, you there?" Gena asked.

"Yeah."

"Um, I was just calling to tell you that your order's in. You can come and pick it up if you want, I mean, of course you want it, I mean, you should, like come now, and like get it."

"Oh great." get it? get it? get it?

"Have a nice night." get it? get it? get it?

"OK, you too." I hung up the phone. get it? get it?

"Who was that? She sounded nice?" Sarah mocked.

Suddenly all the bravery I had before entering my house had vanished. It was just like old times, the thought of leaving Sarah was like some myth that had been whispered over the years but couldn't become truth.

"Where were you?" she hissed.

Thinking quick, "At Ted's. I got drunk."

"Me too," she said, "got drunk, anyway."

"Yeah, I bet."

"How could you do that, just not come home?"

"I don't know."

"And then this call, from this girl?"

"That girl . . ."

"Who is she?"

"She's just some fat ass who works at the office supply store."

"Officetown?"

"I think that's what that place is called." She studied me for a moment and I felt like screaming. Where had the certainty gone?

Was I leaving my wife and moving into the shack in the middle of the woods? The idea had vanished into the wind. It would be impossible for me to live out there, with no electricity, no running water and no . . . and holy shit, I'm so helpless.

"Ted is having some real big problems with his wife."

"Like you?"

"Not quite, she left home. She's going to divorce him."

"Oh I have an idea of why a girl would want to leave her husband . . ."

"You see, their marriage isn't as strong as ours."

"Is he alright?" She was turning. Falling.

"No, not at all, I think he might be suicidal."

"Suicidal?" Sarah looked at the floor. "Oh my god."

"Yeah, I came home to get some things and to apologize for disappearing on you, but it's just that my oldest friend in my life is going through hell."

"Well . . ."

"Well, are you going to be all right here tonight by yourself."

I sat closer to her, she studied me, studied, and I didn't know I had it in me to be such an actor. I let her study me.

"You should go to your friend, I'll be fine," she said softly.

"You don't mind?"

"Friends are important."

"Yes they are, and you are my best friend, you know that right?" Really, she still was.

"Well I have had my doubts lately," Sarah said.

"Don't be cold to me, baby."

We hugged. She started to cry, so emotional these days.

"Teddie needs to get real fucking drunk, talk about old times, the usual, get it all out."

"OK."

"I'm gonna get some things together."

"OK." I started up the stairs, "Do you want coffee?"

"Yeah, I'll put it on," my Sarah said.

I grabbed a few shirts, a few pairs of pants. I freaked out when I couldn't find my bank book. I realized that I was in the middle of a mental breakdown with nothing to do but run with it. When I came back down the stairs she was putting the coffee grinds into the filter.

"What did you order from that store?"

"Nothing."

"You ordered nothing?"

"Larry had me order some supplies for the office and they came in."

"You do things in the office now?"

"Well I do have a baby on the way. Gotta try to climb the ladder. That booth sucks."

"That's great, that you want to better yourself."

"Us," I said, "it's for us."

"Do you want dinner?" she was almost smiling then.

"Look, I don't really have time, I'm really worried about Teddie. I should go."

I went to her, kissed her lips.

"Tell him that if he needs someone else to talk to he can always call here."

"He knows that."

Casually I walked to the car, casually placed my clothes inside. Casually started it. Sarah stood on the porch, loving me, waving goodbye while the bugs of the night were singing their song. I casually lowered my window, casually waved to my wife, she blew me a kiss, I caught it, brought it to my chest—a prized possession from a prize of a woman. She practically melted right there on the front porch.

I backed out of our driveway.

When I was far enough away from the house I stomped on the pedal like the true werewolf I was and I made my way madman style toward my own fury. She went back to the table and believed that our love was stronger than anything, and that only good things were coming.

140A

The one armed kid was at the register, sipping an orange juice in a paper jug. "Is Gena here?" I asked.

He shook his head and then retrieved my order, placed it in a bag. Special Orders are prepaid. "Oh, I thought . . . never mind." He shrugged.

I hung around in the notebook aisle for a moment, stalling, then disgusted with myself, I left the store.

But, out there, under the shimmering light, there she was, waiting by my car. She watched me as I walked towards my Subaru.

"I was on break," Gena offered.

"I got my order." I said, holding up the bag. She was smaller than I remembered; short, but just as hot. The glow of the light made it worse to be there with her. Why would she be out here waiting for me if she didn't want to get closer to me?

Closer to me?

Was she some sicko?

"This may seem kind of weird," she said looking away, "me being here waiting for you, but I dunno."

"I was hoping something like this would happen," I confided.

"Why?" She looked at me, as only a girl who knows exactly who she is can look at another person. "And what do you think this is?"

"I'm not sure. I was just gonna get in my car and go home."

"I was getting a slice over there," she pointed at the pizzeria, "It's good, real good. You should try it."

"Yeah, one day."

For a second, I thought that she wanted nothing more than to be pushed against the car, her skirt hiked, her blouse ripped by my hands, that Gena wanted the impact of another body—badly wanted it. There wasn't an ounce of innocence in her eyes, but also awkwardness, the kind that someone projects just before suggesting something obscene.

She wanted obscenity. No problem, in my mind we'd fucked in thin air, in the dark recesses of countless dark spaces. I'd imagined her mouth and her neck, every fragrance of her. The way she'd look ass up, head down. Knee high socks. Converse All-Stars, nothing else.

"My break is almost up, Jim," Gena said, leaning back against my Subaru. "I have five more minutes. Are you busy? Do you want to sit with me. This car have air conditioning? It's so hot tonight."

"Yeah, of course," I said. We got in. I was trying to be smooth. I whacked my head hard ducking in. I played it off like it didn't happen, starting the engine, flipping on the AC. "It will take a few minutes to kick in, but . . ."

"No, that's better already, plus I didn't want anybody to see me out there, might look weird."

"Fraternizing with the patrons."

"You got it." She turned to me, "You're pretty funny, and not like, immature about it or anything."

"Uh huh," then I thought about how old she was, and what the words, *not immature* meant, it meant that she definitely wanted my not so immature cock in her immature pussy, that was a definite! How could the universe be so in tune?

"You don't think I'm weird do you?" she asked, "That I'd want to talk to you outside of the store . . ." She was playing with her hair, her lips super moist. A small green stone in her earring caught the light, "I'm not a stalker or anything."

"Never said you were."

"I dunno, you just seem so intense. You come into the store and you place this order, and every time I see you, I dunno, all I can do is wonder what makes you tick."

"Me? Oh nothing." What makes me tick? Do I tick, oh I guess I am now. Tocking. Momma take my pulse, I am ripping off the cobwebs chomping them in my werewolf fangs in the middle of silver lit field beneath the cursed moon.

The night was a disaster. It couldn't have worked out any better or any worse than getting her young flesh in the car.

When Gena broke the silence, being brave, I couldn't believe my luck, "Hey, do you want to come to a party with me later?" she cooed.

"Tonight?"

"Yeah."

"I think that would be cool."

Cool! Do kids still talk like that? FUCK!! Cool one daddy-o, now she knew I was born before punk rock was invented.

"Cool." She said. "It's gonna be a really big party. This girl I know."

"Oh?"

"Yeah, lots of cool people. It would be real great if you came."

"Well I'm coming."

"I'll be off at ten," she said. "Can you pick me up here?"

"Yeah."

She opened the car door, stepped out, then leaned back in, "Oh, and do you mind getting some beer for the party, nobody is old enough yet to get it. I'm nineteen. Beat, huh?"

"Yeah, beat. Nineteen," I said, "beat."

"You don't mind, do you?"

Get the beer, sonofabitch. Figures.

"No, not at all," I said. She smiled, blew me a small kiss goodbye. She walked away, blushing, shaking that ass. At the doors to Officetown, she looked back again, waved goodbye one last time. What the fuck was going on? Had I slipped into an accidental tear in the fabric of the universe. Was I occupying some alternate dimension where things worked out?

139B

I skipped around Dinosaur Liquor like a genuine lunatic, pushing the cart aggressively, throwing in case after case of beer. I wondered what kind of beer the modern underage drinker preferred. Soon I had so many cases that it seemed like some kind of backwards joke. It'd be smarter to economize, with two kegs.

It was Saturday night, it'd be a huge party. These kids knew how to party, or so I assumed.

"Not sure what I need totally," I told the guy behind the counter, reading the sci-fi fanzine. "Let's start with two kegs."

"Well it's getting late," he warned, "after ten I can't sell any hard alcohol."

A law of some kind, I had heard it whispered at some earlier point in my existence, but now wanted to scream in his face, "Don't you know, all of the rules are off. Tonight is the night that all nights have lead up to. Rules used to exist, they don't matter anymore."

I knew, the world would not understand the importance.

"No hard alcohol after ten? I better get cracking." I stuffed bottle after random bottle into my cart. Gin. Whiskey. Vodka. More Gin, because I like Gin. Tonic. Coca-Cola. Rum, Coconut rum for the girls. Wine coolers for the girls and margarita mix for the girls, for the girls, to loosen whatever tightness they had wrapped around the tightness of their young bodies, or old bodies if there happened to be a stray mother present who also wanted to party her old heart out. Tequila. Peppermint Schnapps. Let this be a huge festival of a party, attended by every dripping wet friend of Gena. We'll all just forget about our baby mama dramas and tollbooth dilemmas.

The geek at the counter did not look impressed with all my purchasing power. He rang it all up, frowning.

We both knew that while I was having the time of my life he would be home, masturbating to a still shot of princess Leia dressed in that golden outfit, while Jabba the Hutt drooled over her.

He looked me in the eye.

"Five hundred and eighteen dollars and seven cents." he said.

"Peanuts," I replied.

On that twisted night I was having an out of body experience, thinking that perhaps by the end of it, the whole world would be over and none of this would matter, wouldn't matter with the bank or my wife, or myself or the police. Ha! The universe was so in tune! How could all of this be something going wrong? And if it was, why was I so happy about it?

Thank God for all of my savings, all of those trunks full of lost commuter coins! All of those salvaged coins were fistfuls of hope.

I slid him my credit card, as would have any true lover.

139A

The parking lot was the loneliest place in the world. I waited there, alone, eating a 99 cent value menu cheeseburger from Burgerland.

I kept gazing into the bright florescent lights of Officetown for some movement in the store. No one came. The clock said 10:27. No one came. She'd said ten.

I put the cheeseburger wrapper in the bag, wiped my face with the napkin. I wanted to look good when she comes to the car. Quickly I checked my face in the mirror, I'd decided not to shave, even though I had purchased a razor and some shaving cream in the drugstore. I'd also purchased some cologne with a cowboy on the bottle.

I was going with stubble, always a good choice, I assumed. Assuming that young girls found stubble attractive, did they? In that bathroom at Burgerland, I had a small panic attack, looking in the mirror, thinking: do I shave or don't I shave?

Then I had a brainstorm.

I walked back out of the bathroom, to the teenage girl behind the counter. I decided to ask her, as she leaned in a chair against the wall, in her purple and yellow uniform, her straight blonde hair pulled behind in a long ponytail. She was dangerously skinny. She did not eat at her place of employment. She had the same look that I have on my face in the booth: desire for death.

"Excuse me," I said, startling her.

"Yeah." She jumped out of her chair, thinking that I had left the place and that she was safe until the front doors opened again. I'd been a while in the bathroom, trying on my new clothes and doing the best I could to wash up with the antibacterial pump soap that they stock. Suddenly here I'd appeared, as would an apparition. It made her heart thump.

"I have a weird question for you," I said.

"Well, I'm not alone, there are other people here."

"No, not that kind of weird. I'm not dangerous."

"Oh, OK." She fixed her hat, slumped her shoulders, relaxed. As she squinted, it made me realize that she needed glasses and refused to wear them, worrying they would ruin her looks. "You remind me of my track coach," she said.

"Coach, huh . . ." I smiled, said, "look, I have a date tonight with a much younger girl."

"How much younger?" she said, intrigued.

"Your age I guess, how old are you?"

"Seventeen."

"Well she is like nineteen or twenty I think."

"You think I look nineteen? That is so hot."

"I can't be sure under a certain age, kids grow up fast."

"How old are you?"

"Twenty four," I said.

"Yeah?" she didn't believe that.

"Anyway, maybe my question is weird, but I'm gonna ask it anyway, because, well because I don't have anybody else to ask. Uhhhhhhh, do you think a young girl, your age, would think stubble is good, or should I shave. For my date."

The doors opened and a family stormed in like a herd of hippos.

"You shouldn't shave," she said. "You look hot."

I look hot?

Of course I look hot!

"Thanks," I said.

"Have fun on your date."

The hippos smashed past me to devour whatever they could. The girl at the counter braced herself.

The Officetown doors opened, it was that one armed kid again.

He was talking on his cell phone as he walked towards route 9. I assumed he was going to catch the bus, which ran irregularly all up and down that strange sweep of highway. But, when he reached the bus stop, he bent, supporting the cellphone with his shoulder, pulled up a yellow bike that I hadn't seen. He entered a combination, removed the chain, placed the chain back on the bike frame, stood the bike up, hopped on, still on the cellphone, still supporting it with his shoulder. Like some mad daredevil, he jumped the bike over the curb, taking his free hand off the handlebars. He pedaled hands-free across three lanes of highway traffic, cars screeching their brakes, peeling out, almost smashing into each other, while he shot across the opposing lanes of traffic! AMAZING! Then, he was gone, disappearing out of the realm of streetlights, into the last of the undeveloped land on the whole stretch from Philadelphia to the Atlantic Ocean.

My mouth hung open.

There was a knock on the window, it was Gena, she was standing there, smiling and waving.

I opened up.

"Did you see that? It was . . ."

"That's Tony, he's out of his mind. All his friends are like that, 'specially Brian."

"Yeah, crazy kids for sure," I said as she climbed in the Subaru. "Hey, I got some beer, and other stuff for the party." I motioned towards the backseat.

"Oh my God! Look at all of this stuff!"

"Well there's more, I couldn't fit it all in here, some of it I had to put in the trunk."

"WOW!!" She leaned in, kissed my cheek, "this is gonna be the craziest party ever!"

138

We drove down dark roads. The summer homes along the lagoons were unoccupied because the weather report had predicted a rainy weekend. It was all some mystic error by way of misfiring crystal balls. The moon was out. The stars throbbed. It was a night of beauty.

I had the window down, the cattails swayed. I could feel the darkness of the sea. I could smell the salt and sense the far unknown. I could have caught a bullet with my teeth and spit it back at any target, dead on.

Suddenly out of the darkness, a pop of purple light exploded against the black sky. My eyes grew wide.

"They got fireworks!" Gena yelled, jumping in her seat.

Another one went off, it was hot pink, filling the space between the moon and the sea of stars that hung white: cast dice over the blanket of infinite choices—pick one of those dice and run with whatever magic number it gives you in this lottery of happiness or misery.

Gena clutched my hand, I grabbed back. Slowly, I began to be aware of a burning that was happening in the spot where her lips had touched my cheek. My hand was burnt too. She was a muse who'd come and tapped an uninspired man on the shoulder, saying, "Wake up—your life is almost halfway over."

The radio wasn't on—there was just the sound of her breath, the buzz and hum of the electricity in her body. As we passed under the power lines, they also buzzed and sang, but not equal to her. Even the tree frogs and the bugs screamed in the grasses and cattails, responding to Gena. They were growing larger, growing louder. Was the world ending?

"Over there!" more fireworks, green and fresh, burning the sky and ridding all the old film of filth that'd clouded my eyes and my judgment. The things dwelling in the shelter of the darkness, in the hidden spots, were looking up, with fear, green fire. They hid deeper.

I stomped the gas.

There couldn't have been a more perfect of an entrance for us. Piercing light, exotic minerals, empty houses: some of them small mansions—flashing for an instant the color of the fireworks, a green beast there, a pink beast there. Far ahead, the first traces of the bay could be seen, and on it, there was the house, all lit up, every window full of gold light.

"They have a band!" she said, realizing, the first strains of music drifting in the window on the wind.

I pushed the pedal the rest of the way down.

137

W e parked something obscene like three blocks away from the house. Every single spot up was taken by Honda Civics of varying color.

At the front door, there were fifteen kids standing around passing a joint. When they saw me coming, one of them ate it.

"Relax," I said. "I'm just here for the party."

"Yeah," Gena said, "He's cool."

"Oh Fuck! If I knew I wouldn't have eaten that."

"But the moral of the story is that you never know," another kid added.

"Until it's too late!" another girl said. Someone began to roll another joint.

We went up the steps, "This is my friend Jadie's sweet sixteen party," she said. "She's a really close friend, even though she's so young."

We couldn't find Jadie anywhere, but kids who knew Gena kept coming out of all kinds of different hallways, "Have you seen Jadie?"

"No, have you seen Jadie?"

"No I haven't. Is she here?"

"It's her party," A girl said, "She better be here."

"Well have you seen her?"

"No."

We walked into the kitchen where some guys were standing

around playing beer pong, except they didn't have any beer, they were basically playing Hawaiian Punch pong.

"We only had a six pack, and we ran out of that at like four o' clock."

"Gena, what's up?" This kid flashed her a look.

"Hey, what's up?"

"Nothing much, is this your dad?" he asked.

"No, you idiot, it's my good friend Jimmy, don't be an asshole or he'll probably kick your ass."

"Whatever, bitch." He introduced himself to me as Anderson, and he was nice enough. So no harm done on the outlandish question about me being Gena's father. What a joker, probably the class clown of the eleventh grade.

I told the guys that I had two kegs of beer in the car, and if they went down and carried the kegs into the house they could help themselves to as much beer as they wanted. "Dude, that's awesome."

Anderson pulled me aside, "Just so you know, I've got a lil coke, and you're welcome to a line or two. Just don't tell anyone else."

"Sure."

They couldn't get booze. I remembered all too well about the cop hanging out on the side of Dinosaur Liquor, praying and hoping by the light of a cross on a nearby church that he'd have some young kid coming around trying to buy beer, some underage punk, so the cop could take the beer and go back behind the bowling alley—guzzle that down with his party funnel.

Gena went looking for Jadie, I walked back outside with the guys. They weren't that smart, that much was obvious, but it didn't matter, as long as they didn't mind carrying the beer into the house, I didn't care.

I opened up the trunk, pulling the paper bags of alcohol out. They hefted the kegs.

It was fine by me.

136

little while later, Jadie showed up. She was this tiny mouse of a girl. She almost fainted, so excited about her party. She was throwing a sweet sixteen party for herself even though her birthday wasn't until November . . . four months away. All because this would be the only weekend her parents weren't around. "Oh my God you guys! This is so great!!"

Some local hip hop act performed on the back deck. The entourage had .22's that they were firing up in the air, here and there, whenever the mood struck them. So a lot of kids were in the back watching. But we were in the kitchen, I was doing shots with all of my new friends while Gena sat on my lap.

Jadie's eyes were wide as she explained all she had to go through in order to get back to the shore for her party, "It was crazy, my mom and dad went away for the weekend to Monte Carlo, and they dropped me off at my aunt's house. I had to tie all the bed sheets together and climb down from the window. It was so scandalous!!"

"Sounds it," I said.

"I took the bus here, and this really weird guy was moaning in his sleep, so the driver turned around to look, and yell, or whatever and he hit this kid on a bike, I saw the whole thing but nobody else noticed, and because I wanted to get home for the party, I didn't say anything, I didn't want to have to wait for the police to come and fill out an accident report or anything. Oh my God, I hope that kid is alright!"

Already we were all wasted.

"He'll be fine," Gena said.

To us, at that moment, the world was beautiful and nothing could go wrong.

Then, I saw a very familiar face. One I hadn't thought about in a long time. Allison Lewis. The little girl who had been in the car seat on the fourth of July during that horrible accident. She was seventeen and looked otherworldly. Beauty beyond Gena. Allison looked pure, seemed to glow with a gentle white light. She didn't notice me as she sipped her peach wine cooler. I was glad. I still had unsettling dreams of her mother burning.

At the house party, there was an indoor jacuzzi, so of course, all of the kids were crowding around it, climbing in and sucking faces with each other. I was doing shots with Gena in the kitchen. She looked like she was on the threshold of good and evil. I wanted to get her in one of the bedrooms, because I had a feeling, and I knew that the feeling was right, that it was then or never with her. After that night, her interest in me would be gone. Never to be recaptured. She said, "This is great," as she touched my wrist, smiling. I moved her off my lap. I was loaded, almost falling over. I went to the bedrooms, they were all occupied. Annoyed, I went back to the jacuzzi. The gunshots on the back porch were subsiding, whether the rappers were out of ammo or their set was drawing to a close, I didn't know. There was a young couple in the hot tub. The girl had her shirt off, he was sucking on her tits, "Oh I'm sorry to interrupt."

She covered up.

"Do you guys know Anderson? Well he is giving away free coke to anybody who wants it." They got out of the hot tub as fast as they possibly could. I went back to the kitchen. Gena seemed to have caught a second wind, she was sipping a beer from a plastic cup. I took her hand, led her into the back room, where we took off our clothes, at least down to our underwear, climbing into the warm swirling bubbling water.

Gena came quickly to me in the water. Swimming like a mermaid princess, her dark hair flowing all around her in the bath of chemicals. She was willing, so willing. I thought for sure that I was sleeping, in the middle of some cruel dream, where I'd wake in bed with my Sarah, as she snored, her bloated belly beside me, ready to explode like a bomb, but not a pleasant one full of fireworks.

Gena brought her lips to my neck, and her palm to my chest. I kissed her again on the mouth. Unreal, the things that went into that kiss, the movement behind it. She was open for me, warm. Her soft tongue found all of the pleasant places of my mouth and seemed to dance in there. It was trying to rip answers from me, secrets. I bit her lips to keep those secrets.

I brought my hand tightly around her ass, hoisting her so she sat with me, belly to belly, crotch to crotch, her breasts pressed against my heart. I pulled back her hair, and kissed all down her neck, she seemed to be having the time of her life, then as if by some miracle, her hips began to swivel in the water, grinding against me, and she let out the first gasp, a tiny moan.

Fuck yeah.

The flashing hot white static in my mind was gone. Instead, vast serenity was laid out long and never ending before me. Then, I began to pull at her panties, wanting them off, she pushed away, "No," she said, "whoa . . . not now."

"Alright."

Suddenly she'd become very pale. Very pale and very quiet. I knew what was coming. I moved away from her in the water.

Luckily, she was facing the other way when she ceased to be a beauty queen and became a cruel fountain of vomit. A cease and desist order was slapped on my hot tub romance advances.

I hopped quickly out of the water.

She puked again, this time into the spa.

Not good. Revolting horror. Floaters.

There was a knock on the door. I moved even farther away, flinching. "The cops are here," someone said.

"The cops are here?" she slurred.

"The cops are here!" I shouted, pulling my dry clothes over my wet body. Tricky work.

Oh shit. Instinctually I went for the window, missing a shoe. Outside on the pebbles, I looked back into the darkness for Gena, but she was not following, "Come on."

I heard her groan like Frankenstein's monster.

Through the garden, I ran, stomping on innocent flowers. Others, kids, were running in the wrong direction. There was the blue and red flash of the police lights. I got in my car, peeling out, almost driving headlong into the marsh along the road.

A cop was in the street in my rearview, shining a flashlight on my car. But, I was out of there. Free.

135

I slid into bed next to Sarah.

"Is everything alright?" she asked—alert.

"Yeah, everything's fine—she came back," meaning, Ted's wife. Kelly was magically back from the place where fed up wives vanish and wait for relationship reboots.

"Oh, good. Why do you smell like vomit?"

"He got me drunk."

"Poor thing," Sarah said, "can I get you something? Pepto? Ginger Ale?"

"I'm gonna lay on my side facing the other way," I said.

When I rolled over. The bed was spinning. I laid there wishing it would stop. Closed my eyes. I could feel Sarah next to me shifting.

"I know why she would come back," she said.

"Yeah?"

"You can't help who you love and they can't help it either. It's a great weight. A great dilemma."

She put her arms around me from behind.

The bed stopped spinning. I felt fine.

131

I stepped through even more rain, ducking inside the building for shelter. Larry was there at his desk.

"Ah, you again," he said. "Everything OK?"

"Yeah."

"Alright, well if you want, go open the third lane. If not, that's fine too."

"I want to," I said. Then, I walked back out into the rain, carrying my change drawer. The basket was still filled solid with Quadruple Expanding Spray Foam. I smiled, broadly.

The rain was almost typhoon strength. Not very many cars were on the parkway, they were all afraid of the rain, the high wind. Cowards.

I flicked the switch, the light came on: green. I sat down at my stool, no cars came. Then, a red Saab, "How much is the toll?"

I opened up my paper sack and took my order out of it.

It was a small personalized stamp, it read:

Help me I'm trapped in this

Spider Web of a Toll Booth.

I punched this in red ink on the back of the receipts. I did a hundred receipts before a car showed up. "Can I have a receipt?"

I nodded, handed it over.

Help me I'm trapped in this spider web of a tollbooth.

Help me I'm trapped in this spider web of a tollbooth.

Help me I'm trapped in this spider web of a tollbooth.

At break, I walked back into the building, went to the vending machine, bought a PayDay. I sat on the bench next to the pay phone, gloomy, my jaw aching. When I was done chewing, I picked up the phone and moved my fingers, and then moved my achy jaw.

Sarah picks up on the first ring.

"You sitting by the phone?"

"No, well . . . yeah."

"What the hell do you want to call the kid?"

"It's gonna be a girl," she said, "I can tell by the way she kicks"

"Good, I hope it's a girl."

"Why?"

"My dad didn't show me any tricks to raise a boy."

"True," she said, "so what would you name our little girl?"

"Gena," I said.

"I like that," my Sarah said, her voice clear. I could feel her light through the telephone connection. It felt good.

Just then: the rain stopped.

131B

As I opened the door to my hideout, my fortress, I found that someone had gone and done something terrible. All my pictures of Gena had been removed from the walls and from the hiding spot in the secret drawer, which, to the thieves discredit, was the only drawer in the entire room. I couldn't even begin to explain my anger.

I ran out the front door, kicking dead leaves around. Out of nowhere came the sound of a dog barking and a human trying to tell the dog to calm down, to no avail. Then, a cat hissed. What the hell could be coming up that path? I froze.

Ted appeared down the trail, "I thought I saw your car go past me, I was walking the dog, and the cat, I got a hunch that you would be here. Nice fort! I guess you didn't need my help after all."

I got right up in his face, Rommel barking like crazy, the cat shrinking back in worry. "Listen to me, I am gonna ask you a question and you better tell me the truth or I'm gonna to have to murder you!"

He tugged Rommel's chain. Bubblegum, the cat hissed. "What is it, psycho?" Ted said.

"Did you steal some pictures out of my shrine."

"Nope," he was straight faced, true blue.

"I believe you," I said, backing off.

"Did you just say shrine? Man . . . you haven't been yourself lately."

"Ted, what's the deal with this?" I pointed straight at the cat, "why are you walking a cat?"

"Bubblegum needs walks too. Kelly has me walk them both. Usually I walk them individually, but I was lazy tonight, I thought that I'd consolidate the affair. They fight like assholes."

"Like cats and dogs."

Ted was squinting and pointing, "What the hell is that?"

"What?"

I looked too.

It was a skull, painted very sloppily with orange paint, it had two opposing lightning bolts for its eyes, rows of jagged monster teeth. Where the nose should have been, there was a vagina. The vagina had a nail through it, the nail was also through a very large and hairy spider.

Written was as follows:

"SKULLFUCKERS."

Ted nodded, "Amigo, the Skullfuckers definitely stole your porno."

131A

I took Bubblegum's leash, walking her. Ted followed behind with Rommel, named rather originally after the German WWII tank general, I mean really, have some goddamn originality. Ted was faceless. Ted was safe. He was the only dependable person in my universe.

If it wasn't for his friendship, I'd be flying over the moon. Cuckoo for Cocopuffs.

"This one time I was walking the dog back here . . ." he said, "and I was ambushed, somebody was throwing rocks, hit me right here in this tooth, look!"

"Oh holy shit, they really chipped it!"

"You don't remember me telling you about that when it happened?"

"No." The trail got narrower and overgrown. We kept walking. He took me to the general area where the rock attack happened, no evidence, no sign of the Skullfuckers: the most ruthless, cut throat gang of killers on the eastern seaboard.

Bubblegum started to go, "MOW! MOW!" She was tired, and didn't want to walk anymore. So I had to pick her up in my arms, carry her, cradled like a baby. Rommel looked up at his master, wanting also to be hefted, sitting in protest. Ted tugged on his choker chain, "let's go . . ." We kept walking.

Then, as baffling as it was, we found a small house, roughly one fifth the size of a real house. Thoroughly modern. It was baby blue. Modern accommodations. A paver patio, complete with a picnic table. There was a sign that said:

ANOTHER GREAT JOB COMPLETED by
D R MASTERSON, Custom Carpentry.

Another sign, mounted on a nearby tree read as follows, THIS IS THE LAIR OF THE SKULLFUCKERS: DO NOT ENTER!!!

A similar skull was drawn on the sign.

"Holy hell," Ted said. "This thing is a clubhouse? It's nicer than my house!"

Rommel was excited, he wanted to sniff everything. I put the kitty down, tied her to a branch and went to the front door, tried the handle. It was locked. The lights were all out. I tried the nearest window, that too was locked.

"This place is really professional," Ted said.

I went around to the rear of the clubhouse, there was a back door. No dice there either.

"Yo dude!" Ted called, "I found the spare key." I went around front, Ted was already inside, with his dog, "It was under the mat."

"Figures, anybody with money is usually careless."

The interior of the clubhouse was fully furnished. Ted flipped on a switch, a ceiling fan sprang to life. Recessed halogens bathed the room in warm relaxing light. Ted let go of Rommel's leash, the dog headed down a hallway that lead to another room. It was a bedroom with a TV and a computer, countless video game systems. Ted turned the TV on, Mickey Mouse appeared laughing. Quickly we learned that it was satellite. We were disgusted, since neither of us had satellite and both wanted it very badly. I took the controller from him, shut it off.

Ted screamed with laughter, leaving the room. Down the hallway we found a small kitchen and a bathroom. Opening the refrigerator he exclaimed, very detective like, "Kids . . ."

"Yeah, I know." I shouted back, "Kids play here. It's their clubhouse. HOW DID IT TAKE YOU THAT LONG TO FIGURE THAT OUT?"

"The fridge was full of candy, ice cream, sodas, juice boxes. The cupboards are jammed with marshmallows, Kool aid, Reese's Pieces."

I was looking through the piles of DVD's, they were all things that ten-year olds would be interested in: cartoons, monster movies, pro wrestling, not a single iota of porno. I scattered the movies on the floor. Then started to open up the dresser drawers, dumping clothes all over the floor.

Rommel must have thought that I was playing a game, he jumped on the pile, began to tear the corduroy pants, basketball shorts, swim suits. I let him play, what did I care?

But seriously, where was that stack of pornography?

Gena was somewhere in the room. I flipped up the mattress, nothing.

"HEY, YOU BETTER GET OUT HERE. I JUST FOUND SOMETHING!!"

Ted was calling from a small garage where BMX's were parked neatly, where a baseball and a baseball bat rested, where thirty cans of Pepsi were still scattered around, the little kid version of a beerbash. Pixie stick dust was out on a table where it had been snorted, as would coke by their mommies and daddies.

"Look at this," Ted said, pointing to the wall where Gena was pasted, in all of her different incarnations. The kids had been throwing darts at her. Darts protruded from her simulated flesh.

Written on the wall:
SKULLFUCKERS SAY,
GIRLS HAVE COOTIES

"Girls have cooties?" Ted asked, "Are they serious?"

"They must be second graders, this is ridiculous."

I started to gather the pictures off of the walls, the hole punches in Gena's flesh were horrific. Ted took a look, "Hey, this is all the same girl!"

"Yeah, I know her."

"Know her? You've been stalking her?"

"No, not exactly." I said, "Just . . ."

"You cheating on Sarah?"

"No, almost, but not quite."

I was folding the pictures, placing them in my pocket, Ted said, "You oughta be happy to have Sarah, you dummy."

I ignored Ted, began to scrawl out a note.

Dear Skullfuckers,

 I am surprised to see that you have dared to steal from me, as I am the ghost of an evil demonic werewolf, whose spirit still roams these woods after being cursed to it by an ancient curse. I know all of your names and where you live and also, being that my brother is in the FBI and the CIA, he is very knowledgeable about the gang violence crimes your gang has conducted in these woods, ie. the chipping of a tooth with rocks, plots to blow up your school, plots to blow up a church, plots to assassinate high ranking government officials, it was all right there, on the hard drive of your com puter, which I scanned with my supernatural evil werewolf powers and sent via telepathy to him in his top secret CIA/FBI base head quarters located in the Lost City of Atlantis, (whoops, I wasn't supposed to mention that, now you might have to be turned in, regardless). But all points aside, it's in your best interest to vacate these haunted woods forever, or else you will be prosecuted by the government or other wise just plain old ripped to shreds by my evil monster fangs and claws. Assholes.

Sincerely,
Evil Demonic Werewolf

PS- The girl who you were throwing darts at, the girl you accused of having cooties, well, she doesn't have cooties. She is beautiful, and perfect and the best thing that ever happened to me aside from my Sarah. You little freaks are lucky I don't burn down your stupid clubhouse that one of your daddies had to build for you.

 Somehow Rommel and Bubblegum were tired enough to sit on the sofa that me and Ted carried back down the trail. "I think they are really finally getting to really like each other despite how different they are to each other."

 That renewed my hope.

 "If this dog can get along with this cat, why can't you work things out with Sarah?"

 "We don't talk."

"So, talk. Just fucking talk."

We placed the sofa in my fortress.

The next day I returned with the photographs. I set the pile of photographs on the couch and contemplated hanging them up on the wall, but I couldn't do it.

My heart felt frozen. My eyes stared ahead blankly. I left the fortress. When I got back to the Subaru, I couldn't believe it, I'd been crying without even realizing it. My hands shook as I tried to drive the car home. When I closed my eyes all I saw was snow static. The radio was just a deathly ground hum echoing through my brain. I had to pull over and collect myself. That hadn't happened in a long time.

130

Sarah walked in, sooner than I expected. Those days I expected her to never come back. I was the prototypical uncommunicative, unsupportive husband. She should have poisoned me in my sleep. That's what I deserved.

I came prancing down the hallway wearing my black ski mask. She doesn't say a word about the ski mask, just gives me that *what the fuck is wrong with you?* look.

She had more groceries, she loved to buy new things so that she could throw the old things away. It's a very common thing with the living organisms of the planet, complex or single celled, we all feel a great accomplishment in replenishment and likewise, destruction. Even when things are not spoiled, it's a great relief for us to dispose of them, before the effect of spoilage sets in. Good riddance. As fast as those things were replaced, they're becoming things that needed to be replaced themselves.

It's never going to end.

We were all becoming useless. Somewhere on a swing set, a third grader was getting an idea about how to make a little more space for himself on this blue globe, and that idea involves one of the old spoiled dinosaurs being slashed apart in their sleep.

Sarah unpacked soup cans.

I said, "Don't worry," from inside my black ski mask.

She shrugged.

"Did it ever occur to you that my face just might be cold?"

"It's not cold out, darling," Sarah said.

"Sarah, no use in being worried. I'm a revolutionary now." I rifled through the kitchen drawer next to the dishwasher, "Hey, did you move the duct tape?"

"No."

"Fuck."

"Use zip ties, they work better on hostages, it's what the cops use," Sarah said flatly.

"I take no prisoners," I said.

"Babe, what is the duct tape doing in the corn on the cob holder drawer?"

"Bah, you're whacked," she said. "I got you new yogurt anyway," she said. She was tossing the leftover yogurts from a week before into the trash can.

If we cannot create, let us destroy.

I walked out onto the driveway. The neighborhood was the same as it ever is. I knelt at my front license plate, putting duct tape over it. "NEIGHBORHOOD WATCH!" a voice yelled out in the street. A whistle was blown, "HALT!" Another whistle. I jumped up, A man was standing in the middle of the street with a funny looking dog, cowering behind him.

"Citizen's arrest!" he yells.

The light went on in my immediate neighbor's window.

I pulled the ski mask off of my face, "I live here." I said.

"Oh . . ." He drops the whistle from his lips, says, "I thought you were a hooligan."

"Nope."

He laughed, hurt, ashamed, egg on his face. He remembered me then. The husband of the hot chick on the block, the one that everybody watched. He'd seen me come out and get the paper sometimes, he'd seen me walk to my car. He knew everything about me, he was bored and surveillance is part of his way of dealing with it.

All of my neighbor's are like that, all of your neighbor's are like that. They know everything about you.

At his error, he looked embarrassed, but also let down.

He wished that I was a burglar attacking the house, because it would be great for him and his stupid dog, they would be what most bored people want to be, heroes.

People got so bored that they either start hoping for something bad to happen to break the monotony. Or they got so bored that they went and did something bad to break the monotony.

He pointed to his own house, "I was getting some home renovation done, I hope all of the construction noise wasn't too loud."

"Didn't hear any of it."

He had a sign on his front lawn that I didn't notice. It said, ANOTHER GREAT JOB COMPLETED by D.R MASTERSON, Custom Carpentry.

I scanned the block. There were signs like that in front of three other of my neighboring neighbors neighborhood dwellings. They were all in competition. I could care less.

"I see that Sarah is preggers. Congrats!"

"Yeah."

"We are planing on having kids in the fall."

"Good for you."

"There just hasn't been anytime with Molly finishing her masters and me—"

"Hey, who the fuck are you again?"

"Excuse me," he says.

"You've got this air about you that I don't appreciate. This annoying air of competition. Hey. . . do you guys have a pool?" I ask him.

"No, we don't have a pool," he said.

"Oh, because we were planning on putting in an Olympic size swimming pool."

"Olympic size?"

"Or larger."

"I bet."

"With a grotto—one of those waterfall caves, very sensual."

"Funny that you say that, we were planning on having two swimming pools installed," he says.

Disgusted, I held my hand up, pointed at myself, "Let me ask you a question . . . why would you fuck around with your lunatic neighbor as he's wearing a ski mask?"

He comes to his senses. "Your lawn looks great," he says. "I never got your name."

"I don't give my name out, sleep tight," I said.

"You too."

The window opened on the side of my next door neighbor's house. A face was up there that I'd never seen before, just glaring at me, saying nothing. Then, the window closed and the hand attached to the face shuts off the light.

The neighbor with the dog walked into his front door. I did the same. Sarah is on her hands and knees in front of the refrigerator, discarding old fruit.

"Hey, what are you doing? I need that stuff," I said.

"It's almost rotten," she defends.

"So?"

"So I'm throwing it out. I have new fruit and new vegetables, which you won't eat either—next week I'll be throwing that out too."

I reach in the trash can and start to pull the things out.

"Jim . . ." She stood up, annoyed, hitting her knee on the cabinet, getting even more annoyed. "Whatever."

"Yeah, whatever."

She disappeared down the hallway as I harvested the rotten fruit and vegetables as if they were diamonds.

129

As I walked in, Larry said, "Listen, there was an incident last night."

"Incident?"

"José was attacked." Larry looked worried, "He had his nose broken."

"Didn't see that one coming."

"Somebody pegged him in the face. Hard. And yeah, just between you and me, he got what he deserved, but regardless . . ."

José's father had been a tollbooth collector upstate before retiring after thirty one years of service. His grandfather had collected dividends on a multitude of bridges, ferry boats and at the mouths of a few keynote tunnels. His great grandfather was a tax collector in Spain appointed by the Queen herself.

Collecting tolls was in José's blood, and nothing made him more irritated than to look at someone like myself who didn't take the position seriously, and not only that, but held the day-shift when he had to work through darkness over the second shift.

"What did they throw at him?"

"Produce," he snickered. And if you knew José, you'd understand why his own boss would snicker at some random lunatic pelting him with fruits and vegetables.

I laughed too.

"A head of cabbage," Larry said, busted out—caught himself, "a few rotten tomatoes and a pineapple. The pineapple did the brunt of the damage."

"Holy shit."

"The best part is that the heaver paid the toll, so we didn't get a photo of the plates or anything. The guy had on a ski mask."

"Where's José now?"

"Home. Left hours ago. When the cops came, José wanted them to dust for fingerprints off of the remnants, case in point, the pineapple. To his dismay that had to point out that it was impossible."

"Too fucking funny."

"Don't be surprised if you hear from the police. They think there might be a link between the vandalism to your booth last week and what happened to José."

"It's possible," I said.

"Did that guy have on a ski mask?"

"No," I said about Kid with Clownhead. "But I didn't get a good look at the driver. It was a girl."

"Oh, well José says this was a guy."

"I don't know."

"Be careful out there," Larry said. He reached under his desk, pulling out a baseball catcher's mask. "Do me a favor, wear this today."

I slip it on, "Feel better now?" I ask.

"The world is full of lunatics," he said. "Secret lunatics."

I headed out to the booth. Gale was there reading a magazine in her booth, also in a catcher's mask.

Later that day, Gale grabs my shoulder as I am coming out of the break room. She says, "Jimmy, I want to tell you something."

"What?"

"I don't feel safe."

"It'll be alright, Gale," I said.

"Somebody is trying to kill me."

"Nobody is trying to kill you."

"I have been receiving threatening letters."

"Junk mail."

"What happened last night made me think about things differently."

"Nothing bad is going to happen."

"Someone slipped this under my door last week."

This is what the note says:

Toll Whore,

Resign or Die.

Signed
> Your Secret Un-admirer

Originally I'd felt bad about José's broken nose from my pine-apple launch. But reading Gale's note, I beamed with pride. I'd done the right thing. I was a hero.
Again.

127

I came home, stopping at the mailbox. I tried to open it but it wouldn't open. I pulled harder on the door. When it ripped off the hinges, I saw the entire mailbox full of quadruple expanding spray foam.

OK.

"Did you get the mail?" I asked Sarah.

"There wasn't any mail today, too much rain."

"Oh . . ."

"But this was on the front step." She hands me an envelope, it has this message inside:

Dear Tollbooth Jimmy,
You are a waste of sperm. And, I'm totally gonna fuck that Gena chick and film it.

Your Arch Nemesis
Kid with Clown head

125

It was a hazy heat wave day. I'd lost myself totally and completely in the booth. There was no real me outside of it, and even in it, I was no more than a robot on low voltage. That was the big day of the cooter X-ray. The vagina vault scaneroo. Sarah said, "You stay home today, come with me, you should be there."

A car pulled up to the booth. The woman inside was young and beautiful with blonde dreadlocks. She wore a light blue dress and actually had real flowers in her hair. The car was shit brown and looked like it had been through a world war—a slide off a mountain, tumbling and crunching all the way, knocking into jagged outcroppings of rock. Its brakes were singing. Its busted windshield a delicate maze of fine cracks.

"Hey, I'm back!" she said.

"What?"

"I'm the girl who said she would be back to pay the toll, remember?"

"Everyone says they'll be back to pay the toll."

"WELL, HERE I AM!" she exclaimed.

"Lady, no one ever comes back—who are you? Are you feeling all right?"

"I'M BEE!!"

A truck behind her laid on its horn. All it takes is thirty seconds of pause in the procession and everyone has to start freaking the fuck out. Gonna be late, gonna be late, gonna gonna gonna BE

LATE FOR WORK!!! Cattle out on the promenade. Bee smiled. What a wonderful mood this woman was in, she palmed me a five dollar bill, "I don't need any change or anything."

"No?"

"I think when people help you out, you should help them out."

"COME ON, MOVE IT!!!" screamed the truck driver behind her.

I stuck my head out of the booth and looked at the truck driver. Nothing changes, these faces and vehicles are all interchangeable. The only thing that will surprise you is kindness. I looked at her again, at the flowers in her hair, and at the vehicle, at how it smoked and smelled like something plastic was on fire.

"You have a big heart, and a shitty car, maybe you should save it and get a new car," I said.

"Hey can I ask you something. Do you want to go to Iceland? I'm going to Iceland. You should come!"

I shook my head, "I can't go to Iceland."

"Why?"

"It's just not possible," I said.

"YOU'RE WRONG, ANYTHING IS POSSIBLE!!!" Then she started to slowly pull ahead.

"That car won't make it to . . . anywhere . . ."

"I LOVE MY CAR!!! IT'LL MAKE IT EVERYWHERE!!!" she said as she pulled away. "BYE BYE TOLL BOOTH MAN, I LOVE YOU!!!! KEEP UP THE GREAT WORK!"

Great work? Was I really doing great work?

The truck pulled up.

"How much is the toll?" the guy demanded gruffly.

"Thirty-five cents." A giant green sign hung next to my face and it said believe it or not, THIRTY FIVE CENTS. He handed me a dollar.

"Hey, can I ask you if I am doing a good job here, what do you think, am I doing a good job in this booth for you, the commuter?"

"No, you're doing a horrible fucking job. If you were Japanese I'm sure you would have fallen on your sword in shame." He peeled away. His bumper sticker said. GO FUCK YOURSELF.

The world in nature is set at polar opposite points by which it spins.

124

The path led into the dark woods. I passed beneath the water tower. Sights along the nature tour: deer skeletons, a pentagram painted on a tree, a mattress somebody had lit on fire—mostly just springs. My destination was my little hide out. I opened up the plywood door, stepped inside

I'd taken Gena to the public library, ran her through the copy machine. Printout after lovely print out, her face pasted on a revolving door of different porno models. The walls of the entire hideout were plastered with her. Every square inch.

Gena superimposed on a red head's body with her snatch exposed, as she leaned over a desk, in sexy fish nets. Well, slop slop slop and some glue all over her, Gena you are my little toy Frankenstein Monster gal and I will put your severed head wherever I see fit.

I sat down on the old pink couch.

She was gone from Officetown. I'd been back three times and hadn't seen her. She was dead. I just knew it.

Even though her vomit fountained outward to derail my romantic advances in that hot tub, I was still fixated on her.

Gena pasted everywhere. I lean over, breathing heavy, eyes closed, forgetting where I am for a brief moment. It was an awkward moment of near black out and total euphoria.

I look at my watch, late again. Then, a rock smashed against the fort. One of the pictures fell off the wall.

"HEY COME OUT OF THERE YOU FREAK!"

I wait to hear more rocks, none came. I opened the door a crack, a rock smashed against the edge of it. I pull back inside, looking all around at Gena in various materializations. My princess, do you have any powers of saving grace that I don't know about? Things that slipped your mind to tell me? Because if you do, holy shit, now is the time to help me out.

More rocks. Knock after knock. How many of them were there? How many rocks? No way of knowing. Then I start to notice that my Genas on the east side were beginning to breath a veil of smoke. That ol' familiar smell of fire. I was being smoked out.

The fortress was going up in flames.

There was nothing to do but open the door. I knew that's what they wanted. But, oh well.

One. Two. Three. I knocked the door open, charged shoulder down—straight ahead. A rock caught me on the crown of my head, but I kept going like a madman. I grabbed the nearest rock thrower, squeezed him so hard—slamming him to the ground, a little guy. His baseball cap covered head smacks on rocks and root knots. He screams out. Something breaks, maybe a rib. I stand up, it's a little kid. I mean little. Maybe third grade.

Then, scanning around, there are five more of kids, other than the two who were already running off, their little tiny Nike's disappearing off in the pine trees. More rocks come at me, I dodge one. Another catches me on the hand, my knuckle bleeds bad. I scream threats at them. More rocks come.

The little kid I tackled is whaling, "THAT'S OUR CLUB-HOUSE, YOU LOSER!!"

A rock smashed me in the collar bone. I spun around almost falling over. Then, well . . . I don't care if these are little kids or what, nobody fucks with me and gets away with it. Or maybe they had up til then. I grab another kid and knock him over, he yells, falls in the dust, I grab another one, he has long hair like a girl, blonde, in a rat tail, I yank that rat tail, "YAHHHHHHHH-HHHH!!!" throw him against the fort. They'd truly set fire to the thing, the pukes.

I grab one of their bikes, break it against a tree. The handlebar bell goes ding. Playing cards in the spokes go flying out.

I scream, "I'M GONNA RIP ALL OF YOU TO DOOMED SHREDS . . ." A big rock whipped into my stomach. I didn't feel it, some hollow sting.

They'd woken up a werewolf, look out.

I chased down a kid who liked to munch Oreos and slop pudding into his fat privileged mouth, I pulled him back by his 2XL shirt, "ARE YOU CRAZY!" I scream at him, pointing at the fortress fire that had become a full blown blaze, "YOU COULD HAVE KILLED ME!!"

"DON'T HURT ME, DON'T. . ."

I threw him down. He picks up a stick, comes at me with it, AH-HHHHHRGHHHH, I grab his hand, pull the stick from his grip and I beat him—beat him, so hard with that stick. He squeals. I release everything I shouldn't on those weak little boys. Then, I break the stick over my knee. I back up, looking at all of the damage. One of the children got up slowly, just to fall back over.

I picked up the bicycle again. I threw it onto the bonfire havoc of the blaze.

I ran up the path, start my car—drove away, the plume of black smoke rising and stirring in the grey sky. I'd said goodbye to another sector of youth.

Back in the tollbooth, my head was a broken record. It spun while I tried to serve the citizens. They blasted radios, fumbled with change, "How much is the toll? Can I have a receipt with that?" I kept drawing back to the epic battle. To the rock wounds. To the attack fire. To the bikes, the twisted wheels, the burning crinkling epitaphs of porn star Gena and her disappearing lusts as they vanished into ash.

I could see a little of the plume from the booth, a quarter mile into the pines off the parkway.

I may be a pathetic pervert, but I'm not gonna let the little kiddies of the world rock me to death without a fight. My heart came up in my chest, and I feel so alive, I felt so very very alive.

Goodbye to you Gena: I don't need you anymore. I'm glad that you burnt in that fire. Those photos were just a cop out.

I didn't see her at Officetown anymore, if I had, I might have kidnapped her. "Where we going?" she'd ask. I'd respond like Cool Hand Luke, "We're going to go jump into a volcano and make love on the way down, parachutes on our backs."

Suddenly, Sarah appeared at the tollbooth, in all of her faded glory. A rider on an awkward storm. Her mouth was wet and open, a tangle of her hair stuck in her teeth. She smiled at me.

"Hey," she said.

"What's up baby?"

"Check this out, boy."

She handed me the sonogram.

I gazed at the body within her body. I couldn't believe what I was looking at. The cars behind Sarah start to lay on the horn, "I better go," she says.

She leans over and kisses me, I kiss back. I grab her hand, "See you at the house," she says.

"Hold on Sarah," I say.

"I'll see you at the house."

"Wait."

"What is it?"

"Baby . . . thirty five cents, baby."

She gives me this deadly look, so deadly. You viper. You killer.

"Sarah, for the toll!"

123

At break, I go see Larry.

"What's going on?" I ask.

"Nothing. Hey look, I brought these in, my kid is in little league and they have a fund raiser happening." He points to a box of candy bars, "I know you like PayDay's, there are some in there, and I dunno, I figured if you were gonna buy one from the vending machine, maybe you would just get one from me instead. Help the kid out."

"Yeah, sure."

I sat down at his desk, he looked a little surprised, I never sat down, no one ever sits down. Something is up and he knows it.

"I like Fifth Avenue bars the best to be honest with you."

"Yeah they're good, but . . ." He looked through the box, "Nah, no Fifth Avenue bars, sorry. What's on your mind kid? I can tell somethings cooking."

"Look, I have a little thing I wanted to talk about. It's personal and I try not to bring personal things to work, but, well here goes." I get a flash in my head and it really throws me for a loop. I am picturing the sonogram of my unborn daughter with a copy of Gena's face glued to it, it swims there in the pic.

"Larry I'm going to have to resign."

"Really?"

"Yeah."

"I don't like the sound of this."

"I have a kid on the way, and I can't stay in the toll booth anymore."

"You've thought this over?"

"Yeah."

"Just do me a favor Jimmy, sleep on it OK?"

"I will, right after break, in the toll booth."

I stand up and start to walk out, "Hey Jim, hold on." I turn. He throws a PayDay at me, I catch it. "That ones on me."

120

"Can I have a receipt?"
"Help me I am trapped in this spiderweb of a tollbooth."
"Can I have a receipt?"
"Help me I am trapped in this spiderweb of a tollbooth."
"Can I have a receipt?"
"Help me I am trapped in this spiderweb of a tollbooth."
"Can I have a receipt?"
"Help me I am trapped in this spiderweb of a tollbooth."
"Can I have a receipt?"
"Help me I am trapped in this spiderweb of a tollbooth."
"Can I have a receipt?"
"Help me I am trapped in this spiderweb of a tollbooth."
"Can I have a receipt?"
"Help me I am trapped in this spiderweb of a tollbooth."
"Can I have a receipt?"
"Help me I am trapped in this spiderweb of a tollbooth."
"Can I have a receipt?"
"Help me I am trapped in this spiderweb of a tollbooth."
"Can I have a receipt?"
"Help me I am trapped in this spiderweb of a tollbooth."
"Can I have a receipt?"
"Help me I am trapped in this spiderweb of a tollbooth."
"Can I have a receipt?"
"Help me I am trapped in this spiderweb of a tollbooth."

"Can I have a receipt?"
"Help me I am trapped in this spiderweb of a tollbooth."
"Can I have a receipt?"
"Help me I am trapped in this spiderweb of a tollbooth."
"Can I have a receipt?"
"Help me I am trapped in this spiderweb of a tollbooth."
"Can I have a receipt?"
"Help me I am trapped in this spiderweb of a tollbooth."
"Can I have a receipt?"
"Help me I am trapped in this spiderweb of a tollbooth."
"Can I have a receipt?"
"Help me I am trapped in this spiderweb of a tollbooth."
"Can I have a receipt?"
"Help me I am trapped in this spiderweb of a tollbooth."
"Can I have a receipt?"
"Help me I am trapped in this spiderweb of a tollbooth."
"Can I have a receipt?"
"Help me I am trapped in this spiderweb of a tollbooth."
"Can I have a receipt?"
"Help me I am trapped in this spiderweb of a tollbooth."
"Can I have a receipt?"
"Help me I am trapped in this spiderweb of a tollbooth."
"Can I have a receipt?"
"Help me I am trapped in this spiderweb of a tollbooth."
"Can I have a receipt?"
"Help me I am trapped in this spiderweb of a tollbooth."
"Can I have a receipt?"
"Help me I am trapped in this spiderweb of a tollbooth."
"Can I have a receipt?"
"Help me I am trapped in this spiderweb of a tollbooth."
"Can I have a receipt?"
"Help me I am trapped in this spiderweb of a tollbooth."
"Can I have a receipt?"
"Help me I am trapped in this spiderweb of a tollbooth."
"Can I have a receipt?"
"Help me I am trapped in this spiderweb of a tollbooth."
"Can I have a receipt?"
"Help me I am trapped in this spiderweb of a tollbooth."

117A

A cream Oldsmobile driven by an elderly woman arrived at the booth. Her mouth hung slack. She wore huge cataract glasses. "He's Got the Whole World in His Hat" was on the 8-track player.

"Hello," I said.

She stared straight ahead.

"Hello!"

She just gazed down the highway, oblivious. Everyone behind her was late for work. They were going to have to slaughter her just up the road. I'd watch on in amusement.

"HELLO!!!"

She turned her head, "Oh." As she smiled, she went to get something out of her bag, but fumbled.

"The toll is thirty-five cents," I said. "And I can give you all the receipts you want."

"So sweet."

Behind her, they were late for everything. Late for picking up their brother . . . He was getting out of prison in five minutes and would have to kill somebody for a ride. They were late for the train, the show, the truth, the blood, the hope, the utter wine of Heaven—an emergency they'd never see the likes of again. HORN HORN HORN HORN HORN HORN HORN HORN HORN.

"FUCKING MOVE IT," They screamed through their wind-shields, "IF YOU DO NOT MOVE THAT CAR, I'LL DIE IN THIS

LINE, MY HEART IS EXPLODING."

Advice for the road: chill the fuck out, ya'll.

"Oh," she said, finding what she was looking for in her purse, "here it is." She held a black VHS tape. "You're Jimmy Saare, right?" Only she pronounced my name wrong.

"Yeah," I admit.

She flashes yellow rabbit teeth. Lay off the tea grandma.

"I see it on your name tag, but I couldn't be sure."

LATE LATE LATE LATE.

"Yeah that's me," I confirm again, reaching out for the tape.

"You promise?" She clutches it to her breast cautiously.

"Uh huh."

"Then this is yours."

She finally hands me the tape with shaky hands.

"It's from a nice clown fellow. He said you'd love it. I know you will. He is a good clown, that fellow."

"Yeah."

Then she drives through the toll.

And so do the ten cars behind her, all in piggy back. They are all wolves and they are going after her, to rip her apart, run her off the road, into ditches where she will burn, will burn till there is no more to burn.

117

When I come home from work, my beautiful Sarah was sitting at the kitchen table—an ashtray in front of her. "I brought you an orange," I said.

"Here comes my man" she said, snuffing out her cigarette. The fruit was peeled, naked in my hand. I had abandoned the rinds out on the lawn by the seashell mailbox.

On the way home, I'd stopped and bought a single orange from a lonely fruit stand. I placed half of the orange on the table for her. "You're home early," she cooed.

"You're pregnant," I added helpfully.

"You're a sleuth."

"A what?" I sat down, the chair creaked. I leaned forward, elbows on the table, looking at her closely.

"Just like a detective—Hercule Perot." Sarah said, "All you need is a magnifying glass and a pencil thin mustache."

"You got one growing in, there," I said, leaning farther, tracing it on her face gently.

"My hormones are venom," she remarked, placing the slivers of citrus in her mouth, smiling. She had a soft spot for oranges. "What are you looking at?"

"You," I said. "Your mustache. You still look beautiful."

"I feel like a B-42 bomber."

"Understandable."

"Let's go to the bar and get wrecked, please."

"You wanna?" I asked.

"Delbert, I'd give anything for a drink." She finished the rest of the orange, greedy, "like the old days. You giving me all your paycheck in quarters to play songs on the jukebox."

"You'd just play Bruce Springsteen."

"Who else is there?" she said. "Boy, give me the rest of that orange. I need all the juice I can get."

"They don't serve pregnant chicks anywhere nice."

"I don't wanna go anywhere nice."

I handed the orange right over. I watched Sarah eat it slowly. She made an art of it. Sucking the slivers into her mouth. She was happy with me watching her. With my interest.

"How do you get so dirty in a tollbooth?"

"Soot hanging in the air, my love. It makes a healthy boy sick. Filthy. Delirious."

Sarah made the sign of the cross, "bless you and the weight that you carry. Go take a shower. I'll make you a hero's dinner."

"Eh?"

"Pork chops. Mushrooms. Marinating. Fridge. Nice?"

"Beyond nice," I said.

I went into the bathroom. I turned the shower on, climbed in, waiting in the corner for the walls to sweat and the steam to gather like a shroud of lovable fog. Without thinking, I'd locked the bathroom door. Sarah came, using a butter knife to unlock the door. We had child safety locks, already ahead of the game.

Through the steam, Sarah opened the sliding glass door, watched me soap up.

"I'm coming in there," she said, taking off her socks, pulling her pink tank top over her head.

"OK, then," I said, washing my hair, the little that I had left needed to be super super squeaky clean. Then she undid her bra, her breasts spilled out. One flopped to the left, the other flopped to the right. They are twice the size they used to be. One advantage.

She took the bar of soap and slowly started to wash me. My chest. My shoulders, my arms. She looked at me, studied my eyes, as if I was a new person that she was curious about. The water got very hot. The steam obscured her briefly. She washed my upper back, coming closer. Her belly rubbed against mine. I started to get hard. She leaned in and said "My baby, my sweet one . . . I will blow you a kiss and if you catch it, then I will know that this is forever."

She began to slowly lather me up below the belt.

"Do you like that?"

"Much," I said, shuddering. I turned away, washing the soap from my groin.

Sarah got down on her knees in the warm water, looking up at me the whole time. Sucking slow.

After, I washed her, kissed her neck. She leaned against the wall, as I rubbed her until she came, too. She looked up at me with wonder, as if to mean I know that guy, where has he been? As we toweled each other off, she finally said it, "What happened to us?"

"A lot of stuff happened to us?"

"I wish we could talk, but we can't. We're not those kind of people."

I smelled the coconut shampoo I'd used in her hair, and thought briefly about taking her to Tahiti. I knew that she would cry soon. It was how it always was.

When she looked up at me with clear eyes, and her grip on my back became loose, I understood: we didn't have much longer together.

116

VHS. I slid the plastic thing into the mouth of the other plastic thing. The two reacted, making a fuzzy warbled picture appear on the TV. At first there was just static—then the film cut to a shot going haywire, "Is it on?"

A face looked into the camera, blurry but gaining focus. A young kid wearing a giant prop mustache that hung from a pair of silver studded rhinestone glasses. I recognized the Joy Division T shirt right away.

"So what are we gonna do today?"

The camera was handed to the mustache boy, he centered it right on the original camera man, who shrugged. He only has one arm, wearing a Ninja Turtles mask, Michelangelo, the orange nunchuck turtle. "Let's make a music video."

"What song?"

"Something real crappy, it will be funnier," the one armed kid, Tony said.

"Nahhhh, this camera idea sucks, I'm bored already."

The screen goes blank.

Some more violent snow fuzz static. A music video, it started with some song that I don't know. There were edited scenes of these two fluffy kitty cats fighting and fucking and jumping all around a house. It must be footage filmed over the course of weeks. Then there is a break down in the song and mice are tossed at the cats in slow motion, the cats reacting to the tosses with dread pounces.

Suddenly the camera pointed out a car window in motion, vehicles zipped by.

"Dude, this guy is a total loser."

"No shit."

"He works in a tollbooth!"

"LOSER!"

"But his wife is so fucking hot!" he said.

The camera was then focused through the front windshield.

"OK, get this."

"I'm getting this."

The car pulls up. Then, there I was, on camera. I look like a zombie, too thin, bags under my eyes.

Kid with Clownhead screams, "YOU LIKE THAT UNCLE SAM!!!" as he douses the toll bucket with quadruple expanding foam, laughing, driving away.

The static comes back.

After a moment, he appeared, terroristically delivering demands, this is what he said:

"Jimmy Tollbooth. I have all kinds of fucked up footage of you. I was in the woods when you beat up those little kids. I was at that sweet sixteen party. Meet me at Trixy's marina, tonight, ten o clock. On the far west dock, in front of the boat that says "Nice Piece of Bass". Bring this tape with you."

And as soon as I popped the tape out of the VCR, Sarah walked through the front door.

"You still live here?"she said, smuggly.

"You still live here?" I ask back, "Did you have that baby yet?" She is smoking a cigarette, carrying two bags of groceries.

"Nahhhh," she said. "No baby, but lots of canned goods."

"Nothing that can melt?"

"Nothing that can melt."

"Then, forget that for now, come with me."

I get off the couch, walk to her, surprising her. I take the paper bags, set them down. Then, I snatched the cigarette from her lips, putting it into mine, puffing as I walked out into the driveway.

"Come on, Sarah!"

"Where?"

We walk passed the car, to the street. The neighbor had a basketball net and a basketball conveniently sitting there on his front lawn.

I scooped up the ball, dribbled clumsily. Sarah snickered. I set up way off in three point land. From another zip code. squared off—leapt for a jump shot. For once in my life, the ball released from my fingers in a perfect arc.

The ball hit the rim, teetered, fell in. Magically, it rolled right back to me.

"Nice shot," Sarah said.

"It felt good."

She came over. We started to play Horse. I won, but couldn't believe it. We used to play basketball all the time, when we were just getting to know each other and she lived in the apartment with her mother, across the street from the ignored basketball court. I'd never won before.

"Let's play it H-O-A-R-S-E," Sarah commanded.

"OK."

This time it comes down to the last shot, but Sarah wins. I kiss her. She pecks back, her lips cold.

114

When I was seventeen, I had Diesel Cottontail in full effect. The world was a race track. Sticky tires. Suicide steering wheel. An air freshener with a topless blonde. Eight track player. All I had was the Squeeze 8 track Argybargy that'd been left in the Volks when I bought it.

I zipped around town, my life soundtracked by *Pulling Mussels From a Shell* on an infinite loop.

My first girlfriend, Kate, had said, "You can't take me out on a second date unless you get a car." My BMX wasn't good enough. We couldn't do it on the handlebars. "I wanna park," Kate said.

No problem. I practically ran to the bank. I picked her up in that tiny orange car, not even registered yet. On Make-out Hill, I lost my virginity in the back seat. I vowed to never separate from Diesel Cottontail.

No matter how small the back seat, I would do all my fucking there: for the rest of my life.

Then I met Sarah, we screwed around like absolute acrobatic sexual professionals in the small confines of my car until her mother's unexpected and tragic death.

I gave Diesel Cottontail a fresh coat of paint, orange becoming powder blue . . . There was a lag of much time until happiness resumed. On a rainy Thursday in May, we laid down again in the backseat, squished like contortionists.

All was well.

Sarah said to me some months after the funeral—as she dribbled a basketball on the court behind the Fried Paradise, "I really like you, but I don't like your car."

"My car?" How superficial could one person be? "You don't even have a car."

She just shrugged, dribbling the basketball. She was a natural. So good, I couldn't believe that she didn't want to try out for the school basketball team. She was a shoe in. Honestly the best basketball player I'd ever seen, shot for shot. We'd done a lot of grieving on the basketball court behind Fried Paradise. We'd worked out our pain with Around the World. Games of 21. One on one until the sun fell and the street lights came on, it didn't matter. We didn't have guardians. Hers were gone. My mother was a careless drunk, numb on painkillers. My dad was on the mantel in a copper urn.

Me and Sarah would play until the moon was high and our clothes were soaked in sweat. Then we'd go down to the creek and jump in. The insects and tree frogs screaming.

Her father had left many years before. The reason? God knows. How can you figure something like that out? All I know is that Sarah's mother used to be very beautiful and when I first met her, she was sitting at the kitchen table, smoking. I thought to myself, maybe this will be what Sarah will look like when she is an older lady. That wasn't such a bad thing. I thought of myself as an old man with grey hair, sitting beside her at a table.

But looking back at the whole thing, I suppose I understand why the father hadn't been sitting at the table with Sarah's mother. Because I didn't want to be with Sarah when the tables were turned and she was becoming more and more like her mother.

As Sarah was becoming more and more like an aging photo of her mother I was becoming more and more like the father that Sarah had never had. The abandoner.

Those days, it was difficult to hang out at my mom's house, we spent a lot of time behind Fried Paradise, seeking solace at the basketball court. She'd even shoot alone for hours and hours when I wasn't around, hanging with Ted and Ray while I sometimes unloaded trucks at Food Universe where I was a stock boy for the summer.

After I saw *White Man Can't Jump*, I had the fantasy of taking her to the city and making a lot of dough putting her up in two on two basketball games. She was supernatural behind the three point line. No on would suspect.

I came to her one day in my diesel, she was shooting alone, making all of the shots. Effort out the window,

I had Ted in the car with me, this was the first time that two of them would meet.

"She's the best basketball player I know," I told Ted, he didn't believe it for a second.

"Oh, good for a girl. Are you trying out for the school team?" he asked.

"No," she said. "I don't play for free."

"Oh?" Ted said.

"You can't beat her," I warned him. "She's too good."

"I bet you three hundred dollars," he said to her, then smirked at me.

"Well, she doesn't have three hundred dollars," I said.

"How would you know?" Sarah asked me, annoyed.

"Well do you?" She hadn't gotten a job after she got out of the Mayweather. All she did was play basketball and Bubble Bubble on Nintendo in my mom's dark basement, listening to Nirvana, Mazzy Star, Ziggy Stardust and the Spiders from Mars.

"No," she finally said, turning red, "I don't have the money."

She pulled me aside, "I can beat him."

"I think so too," I agreed.

"Put up the money," she said.

"I don't have it."

"What about your car," she insisted, biting her lip. She looked so happy. So into it. I hadn't seen her this way since before her mother's funeral.

I nodded, "Hey Ted, will you play for my car?"

"One on one, for the car?"

"Uh huh."

"OK," he said, shrugging.

They were playing to 21. Sarah weaving all around Ted Milo, making him look like his Air Jordan's were stuck in glue. She dribbled between her legs, pull up: fade away jump shot, nothing but net. "Swoosh!" I yelled, already counting the money in my head.

Ted was alright, he got around her, missed an easy layup but got his own rebound and tapped it in.

I booed.

Sarah hit a three pointer. Another three pointer.

Ted said, "Jesus." Sweat appeared on his brow. He took his over shirt off. He was just in his wife beater. Sarah hadn't even broken a sweat.

She was going to crush him. It was obvious.

Then, he stole the ball from her, sank a shot. I noticed defeat in her even though she was eight points in the lead. If you can believe it, Sarah just gave up, letting him win. She wasn't trying to block shots, she wasn't doing any of her pyrotechnics.

She'd planned it that way. All of it. It was her way of getting rid of my car. Losing. All she'd have to do was lose.

That is how much she hated my car.

Ted drove Diesel Cottontail around for two months before crashing it into a telephone pole over by the cranberry bog. He was drunk. I'd gotten him drunk in the sand pits. He was always the worst drunk driver, lacking that crucial modern skill.

My car stayed for a long time under a tarp on the side of his father's garage, wrecked, unconsolable, becoming a home to spiders and centipedes and a few mice.

I bought a Nissan, but the Nissan was nothing to my liking. Sarah had picked it out, if you hadn't already gone and guessed that. Later, she took the Nissan, I bought a used Subaru. Even later, after her pregnancy, we traded the Nissan in for a minivan, buying a car seat for the baby in the same afternoon.

At the store, I caught her staring at the portable basketball hoops. "You want one for the driveway?" I asked.

"I don't play for free," she said.

I snickered, "I won't play you at all anymore. You're diabolical. You cheat." She slapped me hard on the back. We both laughed.

109

At Trixy's marina, I pulled inside the gate as if my Subaru was controlling itself. I slouched back, rolling, unconnected. The boats that mattered were in the dark lulling water, the rest of them up on concrete blocks.

I suspected a trap.

I went down the gravel path, looping around the sleeping boats, going lower towards the west docks.

Backlit by the distant lights of the bridge like carnival bulbs wavering on ominous water was his figure.

"You're late," the kid said, stepping towards me. The clown make-up was not coating his face. I sighed with relief. It was one less thing to worry about. Without it, he was just a skinny high school kid, carrying no overtones of evil.

"Sorry," I said. "I'm usually late."

"It's cool," he said, leaning against a piling.

"Give me the tapes," I said.

"Nope."

"Give me the tapes," I repeated.

"Nope."

It was useless.

"But I'll leave you alone if you help me with something."

I hesitated. "What?"

"In a minute we're gonna go out on this boat, you and me."

"No."

"You afraid of the water? Don't be stupid."

The kid had a knife in his hand, nothing to be too worried about, just a little utility razor. Slowly he began to cut the line securing a twenty six foot boat that said S'ALL GOOD. With the line cut, the boat did nothing spectacular. It just sat there.

The kid went up the pier, began to cut the line of a black boat, named RACEWAVE.

When its line was free, RACEWAVE bobbed in the water, not fully understanding that it could make a break for it if it wanted. You know, get out there in the big waves, to live the real life, with the sharks and the killer whales, beyond the little choppers of this bay and the tyranny of its owner.

"OK, now how bout some help?" he said.

He tossed me my own knife, and as if under some trance I began to cut the lines with him. We sliced many ropes, and then the tide was beginning to go out, a thing of perfect timing, "The tide is going out," I said.

"I planned it like that."

Of course he did!

A planner! We had a planner in our midst. We walked farther down the pier, cutting the last two of the boats. When this task was complete, there were seventeen dark vessels slowly bumping and making motions out towards the green and orange lights of the Seaside bridge.

He hopped into the last boat, it said NICE PIECE OF BASS. "OK, come on Jim, let's go."

I jumped in.

He started the boat, it came to life in a low guttural growl.

"It's a nice night for a boat ride, look up there, it's a werewolf moon."

"Yeah, full moon all right. The water is all lit up."

I leaned back in my seat, looking at the back of his head. He was a fine captain. Must have sailed all seven seas and such.

"Where are we going?"

"A little farther."

When we were near the middle of the bay he opened up a compartment and retrieved a jug of gasoline.

"Lemme guess, you're gonna set the boat on fire."

"Uh huh."

"Why?"

"Because it'll look real badass."

He started to dump gas all in the interior of the boat, making large pools of it in the lower recesses.

"You got heavy shoes on?" he asked.

"Why?

"You can't swim in heavy shoes. Take them off."

This was the first time I'd noticed that the kid wasn't wearing shoes. He had on those slippers that people wore into public pools.

"Seriously," he said, "I don't want you to drown."

We were in the middle of the bay, he increased the throttle on the boat, stood up on the captain's chair.

"Don't sweat it, this is practically my own boat, it's my uncle's—asshole deserves to have his boat sunk." He took out a flare gun from his swimming trunks.

"Yo, dude, grab that life saver. I can't swim very well," the kid said.

"You should plan your pranks more accordingly then."

"I did, that's why you're here. You're my lifeguard. But don't get any ideas bout drowning me, this is being filmed too."

I pulled out a floaty O that would save any hapless victim of the potentially deadly watery depths—Davy Jones' locker. We clipped on the life vests and stood higher, poised to jump off our seats. "This is fucking ill."

"Yeah, OK." He aimed the gun at the floor, "When I pull the trigger, you better be ready to jump."

"Brilliant plan."

"OK, on 3 . . . 2 . . . 1!"

He fired the gun. We both jumped.

The boat became incandescent.

105

I came up from the water. I'd lost the life ring. I doggie paddled, kicking my Nikes off in the smelly bay water. It was no joke, the idea of them weighing me down. I was no championship swimmer either.

I could hear the kid gargling, gulping.

I swam towards that sound.

"Where's the ring?"

It could have been floating anywhere. The kid really needed it. I swam in a random direction, found it, some miracle. I tossed it to him and he came permanently above the water.

The boat was speeding diabolically away from us, a funeral pyre on the black water beneath the werewolf moon.

"The boat's gonna hit the bridge!" I said.

"That's the idea," he said, out of breath.

"Holy shit!"

He paddled towards me. I took hold of the ring too. We swam together back to the marina.

"He's nuts," the kid said.

"Who?" I didn't get it.

"Brian."

"Who's Brian?"

"The one filming this, from the top of the bridge. He's out of his mind."

Just then, the boat struck the base of the bridge, its engine making a cry like a strangled dinosaur as the fiberglass splintered and broke away. The fire popped upwards in sparks towards the camera man in his clown paint, on the bridge above.

"This is going to be a great movie."

"What?"

"He's making it right now."

"You kids are fucking whacked!" I dunked his head under the water. He swallowed a mouth full of bay water, came up choking.

"I always wanted to be in a movie," the kid says, stone cold serious.

"Congratulations," I mutter.

"You never wanted to be famous?"

"No, I never wanted to be famous," I shout.

He turns to me, grinning, "I would do anything," he says.

As we got closer, we had to swim around the boats being taken out by high tide. On the dock, I walked dripping wet to my Subaru. The kid sprinted for the woods, gone.

I watched the fire on the water, it was dealing with itself. No need to call the fire department.

102

E very night before I went to bed, I had to smoke two cigarettes. If I didn't smoke those two cigarettes, I'd lay there
in bed, wide awake, looking up at the ceiling: listening to
Sarah's breath become more steady as her sinews let up in their
rigid holding against gravity.

Sometimes, I'd lay there and think about how she had found
me, walking to my locker in the hallway. She'd said, "Hi, I'm Sarah, you're cute."

"Oh." Gulp.

"I just wanted you to know that."

And that night, I went out with Ted and Ray to the abandoned
sand pits, where we routinely shot bee bee guns and drank beer.
We had cases of beer buried in the sand, just in case some of the
dirt bikers wandered over to our area. It was a better idea to hide
these things that we wanted to preserve.

"I'm gonna ask out that hot cheerleader," I said to Ted, "Sarah."

"Wasn't she runner up for homecoming queen?"

"Yeah . . ."

"Well, go for it," Ted said.

Other nights, I used to go out to the dark living room and just
sit, in front of the television, smoking my two cigarettes for the
evening, before going off into the void.

The TV said that the planet Pluto was not a planet anymore.

It'd been demoted from a planet, to something lesser. Oh well. I shut the TV off. I thought about going away. If Pluto could do it, I could too.

On that couch I felt like I could just sink into it and disappear forever. It was big and blue, very fluffy. It felt very possible that I was just gonna fall right into it, never be seen again. Like deep sea diving. Like a magician with a smoke bomb. Like a lizard changing the color of his own skin to make himself completely unrecognizable to his prey and to those who preyed on him.

I reached for the ashtray, and well, it's just that, there wasn't an ashtray there anymore. Just a little note that said:

Jim, I don't think it's a good idea to smoke in the house anymore, what with the baby on the way and all. I've moved your ashtray into the garage. Best— Sarah

Into the garage!

The evil bitch.

I wanted to go into the room and shake her from her sleep. But I didn't.

There is no reason for me to be different than the rest of the men in the world who have been strong armed by their spouses, pushed by guilt and unneeded responsibility out into the places where men are left alone to brood.

Into the garage.

Into the garage, among the piles of boxes that cannot be contained in the attic, among the misplaced things of domestication, old clothes on their way to the donation sites, never making it. Old dishes on their way to the dump. If I was any kind of a man, I would have this whole place as my own anyway, working on cars in there, covered in grease and oil. But since I wasn't a man, my wife had claimed it as a dumping ground.

I ashed my cigarette on the concrete floor beside all of the boxes, wondering what was inside them. How could we really have that much shit that we don't even want in our house? A thin path cut to the center through the boxes piled all the way to the ceiling. It was just enough space for me to squeeze in shoulder to shoulder with the boxes, that was it. The garage doors were completely obscured.

I looked through a box full of papers, old dishes and cups. I opened another box, with Christmas sweaters in it. I opened another box, a chicken lamp.

"Useless crap."

I walked back into the house opening the garage from outside. I was greeted by an impossible wall of geometric cardboard locked in tight. The garage door disappeared up and over the pile, and I stood there with my cigarette hanging out of the corner of my mouth. "What I am getting myself into?"

Out on the street, one of the nameless neighbors walked past with his labradoodle, a stupid tan fluffy dog. A new breed, the old breeds were being overwritten, replaced. But these new breeds suck. The neighbor waved, said, "Nice night."

I reached up and pulled on one of the boxes, it smashed down onto the concrete driveway. The neighbor stopped, observing me. I picked the box up, walked it to the curb, dropped it with a crack onto the asphalt beside the my seashell mailbox. I hate that seashell mailbox.

"Spring cleaning?" he asked.

"You got it."

His dog sniffed the box. I walked back to the mouth of the garage, grabbed another box, walked it back to the edge of the road.

"Are you throwing all of those boxes away?" he asked.

"Yup."

"Oh boy! Anything good?"

"Nothing good"

"Mind if I look?"

"Yeah, check it out."

I lugged box after box, as he sifted through them. "You're really gonna throw this chicken lamp away?"

"Take the goddamn chicken lamp."

"No, I've already got enough lamps. I'm gonna tell John about it."

John was the neighbor in the peach house. They had volleyball games and barbecues. Sarah attended them, I avoided them.

"Hey, Jim, do you need a hand truck?" He was being a friendly suburbanite. I said, "sure."

He walked the dog home. His garage opened with epic precision. His garage was empty, clean swept concrete, rakes and shovels neatly hanging on the wall via hooks. There was a soft light spotlighting the hand truck—the only object in the garage that wasn't neatly hanging on a hook.

He'd been waiting his whole life to show me how superior his garage was.

Smiling and whistling, he pushed the hand truck over to my side of the street.

"Good luck," he said.

I'd moved enough of the boxes in my garage so that I could stand in the middle and jump into them, causing a massive collapse to happen outward onto the driveway. This brought me great delight. I was then able to move the boxes with expert speed, thanks to the loaner hand truck.

Soon the pile of boxes got so high in the street that I couldn't see the rest of the neighborhood from my driveway. Such satisfaction. I always wanted to live in my own little world away from the prying eyes of those assholes.

I sat on the front step, continuing to smoke, tapping my foot to some melody that I have sporadically invented in my head.

It took me three more cigarettes and another hour to clean out the rest of the boxes. My house then had it's own protective castle wall on either side of the driveway.

I pushed the hand truck back across the street, leaving it at the entrance to my neighbor's sealed tight garage. His floodlight came on, but the house remained quiet and sleeping. The dog was a giant pussy, didn't even wake, or bark, or anything.

100

While I ate frosted corn stars, Sarah came out of the bedroom, looking nice, bright eyed, hair back in a ponytail. Her pink sweat pants said "I USED TO BE HOT STUFF" on the ass. At least she had a sense of humor about the whole thing.

"Did you sleep good?" she asked.

"Like a fucking rock."

At the kitchen sink, she reached into the cupboard for a coffee cup. I'd made coffee earlier, then stood out in the empty garage, uncharacteristically smoking a cigarette in the morning! All the while sipping that coffee and humming a song. It was a change of our morning routine, but it felt right. I'd ashed right onto the bare concrete floor. After all it was my garage now. I figured once I had a big enough pile of ashes I could just take a big broom and sweep all those devilish ashes right out into the driveway.

Of course, I had no broom.

Sarah, looked out the window, noticed that she couldn't see anything because of all the boxes blocking the view.

"I cleaned out the garage."

"Wow."

"A lot of shit in there."

"It's all out?"

I nodded, crunching corn stars in my jaws, slurping milk off my spoon. A hero husband, reluctant to boast, but let's face it, I was a hero and . . .

"I don't believe you," she went to the garage, opened the door. Yeah, it was empty.

"Wow," she said again, "I'm very proud of you."

I shrugged.

"I'm sorry I left you that bitchy note about having to smoke out there."

"I'm used to it. No bother."

She opened the front door, "It's really a lot of boxes, looks like twice as many out here! You did all this yourself?"

"Last night."

She got me a cup of coffee, kissed my cheek, sat down at the table.

That was all it took to get her to completely love me again.

98

The cars were coming slow and steady at the booth. For fun, I went extra slow, so the line backed up. All it took was an extra ten seconds of change dispensing to disrupt the flow of traffic. I felt godlike.

I was positioned at the first booth, to the far left. The three center booths were EZ Pass. Billy was in the farthest booth.

He retired the previous year, but when I got to work one morning, there he was, temporarily filling in for Gale. Billy was pulling a one day pop there with me, delaying a fishing trip as a favor to Larry.

I was happy to see my old friend.

He had the walkie talkies.

So we decided to proceed with the old games.

He called me in the middle of rush hour.

"Wild Hawk, come in."

"This is Wild Hawk. Go ahead Billy Goat."

"Seeking the go ahead on shutdown."

"Go ahead Goat."

"Commencing shutdown in ten, nine, eight, seven, six, five, four, three, two, one . . ."

The light above his toll went from green to red. The line of cars in his lane were stranded. They sat there for a moment, stunned. Then those drivers began the dangerous mission of crossing the EZ pass lanes, dodging drivers zooming along at breakneck speed despite the fact that they need to be going fifteen miles an hour to have the passing register. A major jam up began to form as everyone crossed from Billy's lane into my lane. I slowed down dispensing change even farther, working at an amazingly clipped pace.

Billy was a mastermind, he taught me everything I knew about the booth and I loved him for it.

But, boy oh boy, how I hated those drivers.

As the drivers who were in Billy's lane began to arrive at my window, the conversation changed from "Can I get a receipt?" "Sure thing." To: "What's the deal with you assholes closing these lanes?"

"We are out to get you," I said, blank faced, "would you like a receipt?"

"What!"

I handed out receipts unwarranted. Then, I got on the walkie talkie, "OK—Bill, let's do it."

Despite the impossible line I had—all of the motorists who'd just crossed over, I turned on my red light.

One driver looked at me with horror and anger, and blame. I felt nothing.

"I'm closed," I said. "Sorry."

"No!"

"Lane four is open."

"I JUST CROSSED FROM LANE FOUR!"

"That's life, dude," I said, walking out of my booth, into the safety of the building.

Billy is braver than I am, he stood out there, trying to look like he cared. Then, to perfect the horror, a car began to smoke. Then, smoked more and more, then overheated. Oh damn! Poor commuters. Leave them to sit in idle for ten minutes and surely someone was going to have their piece of shit die right in everybody else's way.

Billy closed his lane for real, the smoking car becoming a car fire. I watch out of the window and I feel nothing. A car fire. I might as well be watching a rerun of *Cheers*.

When Billy came inside the building we both sat by the vending machine eating candy bars. Larry walked down the hall, "What are you two assholes doing?"

"Chillin," Billy said, smiling, a peanut stuck in his beard.

"Walkie talkies treating you good again?"

"You know it, boss!"

We had all been a team long ago, back before EZ Pass. But that was so long ago. And the past is just the past.

Fire trucks, police cars, ambulances (even though no one is hurt) all showed up blocking the EZ pass lanes, halting everyone from illegally going through those lanes and just eating the tickets. Everyone was doomed: late for work, furious. All of them inconsolable except for me and Billy and Larry.

"I'm glad that Gale has the flu, it's good to have the old gang back together."

"I hope she's too sick to come back tomorrow," I said.

"Me too," Billy agreed.

The next day, Gale came back: she couldn't understand why we are all so blue at seeing her. The booth felt even more confining.

My elbows kept hitting the things closing in on me.

In the evening, after work, Ted came by the house. He was taking Rommel for an extended walk. We came into the kitchen, sitting at my counter drinking old coffee out of the pot from the morning. Rommel roamed down the hall sniffing at dust bunnies.

I followed him down there, opening the door to the spare room. "Hungry buddy?" I asked, stupidly. I opened up my file cabinet, took out the original certificate from the mayor documenting my bravery on the fourth of July many years prior. The Rottweiler sat on his haunches as I dangled the certificate over his head. Drool fell. He huffed. He licked his chops.

"Hey, what are you doing to my dog down there?" Ted called.

"Nothing," I said, dropping the certificate down.

Rommel snatched it out of the air, ate it like it was made of pure bacon.

91

There was a young girl in a soccer uniform outside Dinosaur Liquor shaking a can beside the concrete brontosaurus. She smiled at me. Her face was busted up, but otherwise, a very nice specimen. She waved politely and held out the can.

"We're trying to raise money for a soccer match, we want to go to Europe to compete in a tournament this summer."

"Europeans are too good at soccer, forget it."

"Oh come on," she said, "just give me some money."

"You remind me of my wife," I said, "I already gave her everything I ever had, that was twelve years ago."

"Ewwww, you creep."

"Tramp."

"Asshole."

"Yeah, you're just like Sarah."

Inside, the same sci-fi geek clerk was behind the counter, "And he's back," he said to me. I was surprised that anybody had remembered me.

"I'm back."

"You're back."

He was leaning over, hunched, watching Soylent Green on a little black and white TV. He would have to use his imagination to visualize the dramatic color scheme of that science fiction.

"What's new?" I asked him.

"The world is grossly overpopulated and people are being

encouraged to kill themselves to make room for the people who don't feel that they should have to kill themselves."

"Oh."

I walked back by the beer, pulled a case of Riverhorse beer out of the cooler, hefted it back to the counter.

"That little bitch still out there?" he asked.

All he had to do was turn his head to look, but he would rather ask, the sound of my voice was music to him in the loneliness of his little cage.

I knew how it was, being in the tollbooth. Sometimes it made you hate people so much you didn't want to hear them speak and then at other times you wished that you had more than the ten seconds it took or less to serve them.

"Why would she be hanging out in front of the liquor store?"

"Busiest place in town," he said, yawning, "the way that this place drinks, bunch of heathens."

"Heh."

"She's got a nice ass," he said.

"Bad attitude, though," I said.

"Yeah, she does have a bad attitude," he agreed.

I looked out the window, the girl was on the phone. I paid that latest development no extra attention.

"Anything else?" the clerk asked.

"Naw, just a time machine so that I could go back and never ask my wife out on that first date."

But, he like me, would marry anyone who would have him and learn to regret it later. Those who have nothing don't understand the plight of those with shit that they don't want but lack the power to dispose of it.

As I went outside, a police cruiser pulled up. The girl went to the window with her backpack on tightly, her change cup already packed away. This fundraiser was over.

She was heatedly discussing something with the cop and pointing right at me. What could it be? Perhaps how great I looked in my black polo shirt and my blue work pants that I'd never done an ounce of work in.

The officer motioned for me to come over. He didn't recognize me, but I knew him, how could I forget him? It was my old friend Ray Casey.

"Officer, I'd like to report a robbery," I said, leaning in close, "you stole my heart."

"Excuse me," he was pissed, ready to use all of those martial arts maneuvers. Look out! But look out for me too officer, I might just take your gun out of your hip holster and hold it to you temple ask you why things are how they are and if I don't get the right kind of answer, well, fuck, I might just have to shoot you, the girl here, Sarah, the unborn baby, the clerk, one legged hair cut beauty queen Kimmy Simmons, Gale, José, Ted, Gena, all the little kids I can round up, and then myself. I'd let Kid with Clownhead live.

Ray said, "Jim?"

"Yeah."

"What happened to you?"

"What happened to you?"

We got old and things fell apart. We'd been friends in elementary school and then high school. We'd gone our separate ways after that. Now there we were again.

Reality came back, because the pink bitch with the pigtails was tapping her foot angrily.

"Oh shit," Ray said, conscious again. "This girl called 911."

"Yeah," she said. "He harassed me, and I'm underage."

"Didn't happen," I said. "Ray—she wanted me to buy her whisky, I said no."

"You trying to get drunk?" he asked her.

"No."

"Then why are you hanging outside of a liquor store?"

"I was trying to . . ."

"Save your energy, get in the car."

He stepped out, opened up the door. "Get in," he boomed sternly. The girl ducked in the vehicle, not wanting to cause any waves with a shark so near. My long lost friend winked at me, said, "You too, Jim."

I climbed into the front seat, set my beer on the floor.

We drove toward where the power lines netted together springing from a matrix of steel generator towers. Endless pebbles, endless clay. The sand pits, beneath our looming sea green water tower with the typo on it, 'SCREMING EAGLES' not 'SCREAMING EAGLES' like it should have been. Our local high school football team.

Ray stopped the cruiser, turned to the girl, said, "I didn't want to bring you right in, to headquarters. I thought I might give you a fair chance to explain yourself."

The ominous undertone seemed to suggest that not many people are given a fair chance in life to explain themselves, let alone at the scene of the crime, real or imagined.

She didn't get it.

"What's to explain?" she said snottily.

"Well for starters, why were you soliciting prostitution to a police officer?"

"I was not!" Her cheeks suddenly flushed, I could feel her heartbeat leaving the cruiser, echoing off of the water tower and coming back as a terrible ricochet. My back teeth hurt for her. Her bottom lip shuddered.

"She is obviously on PCP," Ray said gravely.

"Yeah, dusted to oblivion," I added.

This is how it was back in high school. Ray was always fucking with somebody. His father was the chief of police back then. Ray has never had a chance to be afraid of anybody even though he is short and could easily be stomped on. It has always been the shelter of power that his family name carries in the small town that has saved him from the beating he had coming his way.

And he grinned something sinister with his back teeth like little pointed daggers. The sun fell and the sky threw around drama: oranges and browns and pinks. Like some kind of sky apocalypse on the way as soon as the moon manifested itself for full devastation.

"How old are you?"

"Nineteen," she said.

"You have anything on you, and be honest, don't make us search you. We have rubber gloves."

Now the tears flowed and her makeup started to wash down her cheeks.

Oh, to be a horse in a beauty pageant.

Oh, to be a short cop in a land of long legged criminals.

Oh, to be a bridge troll yelling at the goats who pass by above without paying you any notice.

"You think things over," Ray said. "We'll be right back."

We exited our prospective doors, stepped away from the car.

"Damn," Ray said. "You didn't have to make her cry."

"Me?"

"Yeah, that was all you." Ray had taken her cellphone and was looking through it, "I wonder if this chick is single."

I just kicked the dirt and felt like I was losing my mind.

"Anyway, shit! Jimmy it's good to see you," he exclaimed, "How have things been?"

"Fine."

"You married?"

"Yeah."

"Good, kids?"

"One on the way."

"Good for you, the family man!"

He stared at me, I didn't say anything.

"How's Ted?"

"Good, too."

"Cool! Oh, OK . . . well, I thought we might as well read this girl her rights, put a bullet in her head and bury her at the base of the water tower. For old times sake . . . haha."

Since junior high, that was where I buried my valuables, just in case some of the dirt bikers came out of the pine scrub to raid our stuff while we weren't around. I'd put my dirty magazines, my unopened beer and liquor into the ground—whatever other contraband I was able to smuggle away from the sleeping supervisors of those days of adolescence. I'd dig it back up when I was good and ready, most of the time having completely forgotten what was even below the surface, just recalling subliminally that something was there wanting to be felt again.

I said, "I think that killing this girl would be a little too much."

"Then we let her go," he said, "eventually."

We walked back to the car. Back inside he asked her, "So what is it going to be? Are you going to cooperate or are you going to interfere with a police investigation?"

"I'll cooperate."

He told her ever so gently to get out of the car, motioned for me to grab the beer. We walked to the base of the water tower, sitting there between two concrete walls was an enclosure that resembled a baseball dugout. In red paint it said, "BEWARE THE SKULLFUCKERS!"

Someone had created a swastika long ago in neon spray paint that had since faded, someone else had come along and made it into four sterilized boxes in blue paint, but we could all plain as day see what it really was beneath the thinly veiled deception. Somebody had painted a peace symbol on another wall, somebody else had crossed that out, made a pentagram in what looked like blood or shit—it didn't matter.

All that really mattered was that we were still up there.

J.S. WUZ HERE '93

SO WUZ TED!

SO WUZ R.F.K IV

All of us. Me. Ray. Ted. Nobody had dared to cross us out for whatever reason. We were still etched on that wall and as long as that wall was still standing and we were still etched on it, we would live forever.

"Ha!"

"Ha yourself," Ray said.

"No, look at this." I said, tapping the wall.

He peered at our names, "Damn . . . We're immortal."

90

We sat on milk crates. I opened a beer for myself, another for Ray.

"You drink, Pink" he asked her.

"No."

"Sure you do," Ray replied. He gently handed her a beer. It was rapidly warming, something needed to be done about it soon. "You are not under arrest . . . unless you refuse to drink that beer, in which case you will most definitely be completely and totally under arrest."

The girl looked down at the beer in despair.

"I hate beer."

Inanimate objects were always getting all of this importance tacked onto them.

In a reformed moment of charity, Ray stood up, said, "You don't have to drink the beer if you don't want to." He smiled at her. "Come on, pick something better out."

They walked to the cruiser, he popped the trunk.

I wondered where I was, how I ever got there, what was next, who had caused it, when was it gonna end, where was the next breath gonna be drawn from, and what for? My head hurt.

They came back from the car; she was carrying a bottle of coconut rum like a trophy that she didn't want.

I briefly thought that that was what Sarah was going to look like carrying around that baby when it finally came.

Ray had two cans of pineapple juice. I knew just how danger-ous pineapples could be and didn't want any part of that sweet nectar and pulp.

Officer Ray switched on the red and blues. The sun was falling on us and the vampire bats were coming around in wide-arched dive bombs.

It felt sickly, like a disco.

"There was a party on the bay," Ray said. "We broke it up. I've got too much treasure to even mention. You should've seen the coke that these kids had, and two kegs! Two kegs! I've got one in my basement. HA!"

He was setting the empty beer bottles on the top of the wall. We were knocking them back like lunatics. The stars got blurry as they should have gotten clearer.

"Then I find some girl puking her brains out in the jacuzzi. I didn't think a little thing like that could puke so much. Looked like she was gonna die. And naked! Lawdy lawd."

"That'd be Gena Parker," Pink said, lowering the spiked pine-apple jug from her thin peach lips. "I went to school with her."

"Oh?" I said, intrigued.

"She had to have her stomach pumped."

"And you know this how, Nancy Drew?" Ray placed another beer bottle on the wall.

"She's popular," Pink said distantly. "I know everything that there is to know about her."

"Why," Ray asked, drunk and in love with the sound of his own voice.

"She's prettier than me."

"Girls," I said.

"I'm not really on the soccer team," Pink confessed as if she'd started the Great Chicago Fire.

"If it makes you feel any better, neither one of us was on the soccer team either," I said.

"I'm collecting money for plastic surgery," she admitted. "I want to be beautiful." Pink tried to stand but she'd drank just enough to not be able to stand.

She waddled to the side of the cruiser to piss, lowered her soc-cer shorts, ordered us not to look.

Ray stepped out from the dugout and illuminated her with his police-order flashlight.

"Looks good," he shouted to her. She came back, embarrassed and with glassy eyes. One of her pigtails had unraveled; she had lost the hair tie in her disheveled stumbling. Her left shoe was wet with piss.

She started to talk about how life was hard when you weren't as pretty as some of the other girls—girls like Gena, who got all of the attention. She said, "Technically, we aren't friends or anything. If anybody asks me, I'm her friend. Do you think she would say the same thing about me? No. I don't think so. She's such a bitch, and like I used to talk to Greg in study hall sometimes before graduation. I wanted him so bad. One time, he showed up at a party my friend threw. He said he wanted to ask me something. I was so freaking out. You know what he asks me . . . "

"What?"

"If I'm friends with Gena Parker! 'Yeah,' I tell him, 'I'm friends with her. Best friends! We have sleepovers all the time and pillow fights in our underwear and we compare out naked breast to each other. It's real scandalous; we should be outlawed.' I say all kinds of things . . . I mean, this boy is so hot, and I am so nervous to be talking to him. Then he looks me dead in the eye, and do you know what he says? 'Well if you're good friends with Gena, do you think you could find out from her if she would want to do something with me next Friday or Saturday or Sunday? . . . even tomorrow. Any day, really. All the days, I think—"

Ray fired his gun up at the water tower. Pink screamed. I didn't expect any of it, I fell off of my milk crate. My beer bottle broke, and I cut my wedding ring finger on a shard of glass.

Boom. Pop. BLANG! BLANG! BLANG!

Ray fired his gun at the beer bottles on top of the wall. He had some powerful firepower, but his aim was scattered. For all of those shots, only five of the beer bottles shattered.

"ENOUGH WITH THE YIPP YAPPP BULLSHIT," Ray screamed at her. "SO WHAT, A GIRL IN SCHOOL IS PRETTIER THAN YOU?! GET USED TO IT! THAT'S LIFE!"

"FUCK YOU," Pink yelled back.

I backed up against the wall, got out of their way. But the gun was already put away, so it wasn't as bad as it could have been. I slipped on a shell casing and almost went down onto more broken beer bottle glass. The party was going downhill.

"I don't have to take this crap from you," she said.

"Get outta here," Ray ordered.

She started to walk away from us, out of the flashing lights—into the darkness beyond.

"GET HOME SAFE," Ray screamed.

She started to run at the sound of his voice.

"You're the worst cop in the world," I said.

As we sat in the flash of the cruiser's lights, we passed a bottle of gin that I'd bought at Dinosaur Liquor for Gena's party. I wanted a cigarette but had no more. "I've got an idea," I said.

Ray started to clap.

I kicked up the sand around the foot of the tower until I found it, and then, having found it, I said, "HOLY SHIT, I FOUND IT!"

"Found what, you asshole?"

"My time capsule." It was a plastic canister I'd stolen from the bank back when Ted worked as a teller. It used to be fun to come and steal his canister. It would still be fun. I reached down into the clay, held it up like a trophy.

Inside was an unopened pack of cigarettes, Marlboro reds; a pack of matches; a few baseball cards, including a Ken Griffy Jr. rookie card that Ray scooped up as soon as he could. Then, oh shit, there in the bottom, under a PayDay bar was the old note written in purple glitter pen:

Jim,

I know that you probably think that that I'm just a ditzy cheer leader, and if you think that, it's okay. But I just want you to know that I'm not (well, I may be, but that isn't all I am). Yeah, I'm on the squad and yeah, I dated Kevin Sloan but you should know that I broke up with him and one of the main reasons is because everyday I would see you walking across the field outside earth science all by yourself. It made me real curious.

Even though everybody tells me that you're weird, I can't get you out of my ditzy cheerleader head. You always were head ed off alone and there I was surrounded by people I didn't feel like I belonged to. It made me feel stupid to walk with Kevin in the middle of some pointless crowd, when there you were getting away from all of them. Letter jacket? Ha! You didn't even have a backpack. Plus, I'm a sucker for anything orange. I like your car, reminds me of Florida someplace I always wanted to go. The Kiss Me state.

I might be crazy, but I said to myself, this kid has everything all figured out. Maybe I'm not your type, but don't write me off before you stop to see who I really am on the inside. Peo ple seem to think that my outside is the only extraordinary part about me. I want to try to show you otherwise, that my inside is good too, no matter what you have heard from these asshole gossips and followers. Also: do you like basketball? Or Mazzy Star? Maybe we could hang sometime, alone. You think that's possible?

~Hearts
Sarah

That note was from Feb. seventh 1993. I remembered show-ing it to Ray and Ted that night after Sarah found me in the hall-way, came up to me (much to my horror/shock/surprise), and stuffed it in my hand. I vividly remembered sitting under the wa-ter tower, drunk on Natty Ice, trying to decide if I wanted to call her or not, and asking for advice from my only friends.

Ray said, "Bang her."

Ted offered, "She wants to show you her insides. You better call her before I call her; then she'll have to show me those in-sides."

On their counsel, I called her that night, and then disappeared into her spiderweb, never to return to that place of our friendship.

But look! There I was again, many years later . . . drunk, look-ing down at a PayDay. The cigarette tasted almost fine, almost. I opened up the candy bar; broke it with a deadly snap. I offered half to my long lost friend, who looked down skeptically. Fine. I took it back, ready to eat the whole thing.

I bit.

There was a horrid crack.

Nostalgia had broken my wisdom tooth.

89

We drove slowly back towards town, red and blue lights shimmying and shaking above us. I liked being in a squad car. "Can you deputize me?"

"You are hereby deputized."

"Where's my silver star?"

"Check the glove box," he said.

I noticed for the first time that Ray was sitting on a booster seat because he was so short.

We rolled through town; it was about three miles from the sandpit into the neighborhood, so our ride it didn't take long. We passed Great Wok of China, Fried Paradise, Food Universe, Mattress Mayhem. Ray asked, "You hungry?"

"Yes but no."

"Suit yourself."

We turned into my development from the highway, and there, in our headlights, what did we see: Pink running scared, and we were on her tail. She turned—frightened—the police cruiser lights flashing in the shadowy trees. Her shadow was thrown a mile in front of her. The maniac cop was back.

"It's HER," he screamed. My ear buzzed.

"Let me out of this car," I said.

"Easy does it. WE GOT HER NOW!!"

But as if on cue, as we came within striking distance, Pink cut into the woods. We couldn't follow her any farther; she hopped a fence into a backyard. What an athlete!

"Doesn't matter. Sooner or later—she's ours. We've got her address."

"You have it. Leave me out of this."

I pointed at Ted's house, which was unlit. He was practically the girl's immediate neighbor. It was quite a night for darkness and in the light were hallucinations that wavered fearfully.

We were going about fifty miles too fast for the residential zone. "Left here," I said. He cut the wheel; the hub caps shot off, and the cruiser went up on two wheels . . . my side. The car slammed down. A garbage can went flying into outer space.

I said, "Last house on the left."

"Dead end, huh?"

"They call it a circle."

I got out of the car, said goodbye. As Ray drove away, my neighbor, who is always walking his dog, came out of the house with his dog on the dog leash. He came over before I could get in the front door. Sarah's minivan was not there. I was having trouble getting my key in the keyhole.

"Is everything OK," the neighbor asked.

I finally opened the door, ducking inside, not warranting his further intrusion with any kind of an answer. I walked into my backyard, turned on the garden hose. When he came back down the block, I soaked him and that motherfucking dog for an obscene count to eight. Then, I went inside my house, took off my pants, fell into bed with my shoes and my shirt still on. I hadn't the faintest clue where my lovely wife could possibly be. There was the lingering smell of perfume though. She hadn't worn that for me since Florida. Wherever she was, she smelled good.

88

The next day, I went and saw Ted at the DMV. He was working late. I sat with him at his desk, which was stuck in the corner of the office even though he didn't share the office with anybody else. They'd all been replaced by machines and computer programs that Ted struggled with. He was by the water cooler that'd been empty for three weeks.

"When that thing had water in it, I used to be able to make oatmeal at my desk. Those were the salad days. Oatmeal and tea."

"How did you make oatmeal and tea?"

He laughed, "Hot water used to come out of the red handle."

"You should fill the water cooler with margarita mix and tequila. Then you could really enjoy yourself." I started leafing through a Hustler magazine and said, "Come on, we gotta go."

"Go where?"

"On an adventure unparalleled. Seriously, come on."

I knocked the papers off his desk. *Whoosh.*

"You dipshit, do you know how long it's gonna take me to reorganize all that!"

"Don't care. Come on, let's go."

"I've gotta get this done."

"Why? So that they can give you more to do tomorrow?"

"Well . . ." he frowned, "yeah."

"So, then just do this tomorrow."

"Dude, I have a quota."

"A quota of pointless struggles," I said.

Ted stood from his desk. "Have you even looked for a therapist yet? You need help. Mental help." Ted sighed as he walked across the office to the bathroom.

I gathered all of the papers scattered on the floor and stuffed them, three and four at a time, into the paper shredder. Then I went into Ted's desk and got out his scissors. I cut the cord to his mouse. I cut the cord to his keyboard. I sat back down in the chair. I began to read a pornographic letter that someone had sent into the magazine. I made a mental note to write a pornographic letter to those editors.

Ted came out of the bathroom. I had my feet up on his desk. "What did you do with those papers?"

"I put them in the paper shredder."

"Oh, FUCK YOU!"

"You're turning red again. Relax."

So we went out into the parking lot.

"Leave your car here. I want to take you somewhere."

"OK."

We drove through the town, into the pines, closer and closer towards the cranberry bog. When I turned down one specific dirt road, he knew there was no other reason for me to be going down it other than—

"Are you going to my father's house?"

"Yeah."

"Why?"

When we pulled up, the wrecker was waiting. I parked; Ted had his answer without me saying a word. The driver side door on the tow truck opened, and he stepped out. I did the natural thing and stepped out too, smiled and walked towards him to shake his hand.

He worked for the state too and was doing me a favor. "Sam you're a lifesaver. Sam you're such a pal. Free tolls for a year, no problem!"

He laughed.

I pointed at the green shed in the back of the property and told Sam, "Back down the driveway, hug the elm tree. Should be plenty of clearance. But if you whack that clothesline, don't even worry about it. The guy who lives here hasn't used that clothesline since Ted here was a kid."

"You are a real piece of work," Ted said as I pulled out my wallet. "Save your money. It was your car."

The tow truck began to back up.

I pulled the grey tarp off of the Volkswagen, my first love. My little rabbit. My car. Flat tires, dead battery, ancient tree crash damage.

"To save her from the junkyard after all of these years saves me too," I muttered.

My car, Diesel Cottontail—mostly powder blue, orange beneath showing through from ancient impact.

83

Sarah was directing an annoying neighborhood boy who was putting new boxes in the garage.

"What's going on," I asked.

"Cleaning the closets," she said. I recognized the kid. He was the one who would come by the house every time the grass got a centimeter too high, asking if I needed the grass cut. He sure was a go-getter.

He was putting boxes in the garage. I couldn't believe it. "Look, kid, take these boxes right out to the curb. Put them all with the other boxes."

Annoyed, Sarah said, "There's too much stuff out there Jim! The township isn't gonna take any of it."

"Big deal. That shit can rot out there. I could care less."

The tow truck pulled in front of the house with Diesel Cottontail. I told Sam to maneuver Diesel Cottontail between the mountain of boxes by the seashell mailbox and park it in the driveway.

"Why is that car here?" Sarah shuddered.

"I bought it back from Ted."

"No you didn't!"

"Yup."

The neighborhood kid was standing there with me, looking at the tow truck. I said, "You're gonna have to help me push this car into the garage."

"No," Sarah shouted.

"Sarah, go inside," I said. But she didn't go. After Sam let the vehicle down ever so gently, me and the kid shoved it, with much effort, into position. I gave him the twenty bucks Sarah had negotiated and sent him home.

Sarah wouldn't talk to me. Big surprise.

I went into the garage and sat in the car, drinking a beer and smoking a cigarette. It was good to have her back. All I could think about were the great times I'd had in that car. Flashes went through my mind of undeniable fun, whizzing along country roads, music screaming from blown speakers. Those were good times: king's days.

After a while, the door to the house opened, and Sarah came in. She sat down on the steps, looking at me in the driver's seat.

"What are you gonna do with this car?"

"Nothing," I said.

"Are you gonna fix it up?"

"No," I said.

"Then what?"

"I'm just gonna sit in it."

She stood up off of the steps, walked to the passenger side. "Just sit in it?"

"Yup."

"That's boring."

I reached over and unlocked the passenger side door, faced her again. "Climb in."

"No, thanks."

"Come on," I said. "What's the big deal?"

She shrugged, walked around reluctantly. When she pulled on the door handle, it fell off. I shoved the door open, and she peaked in. "This thing is just as much of a piece of shit as I remember it."

"Well I like it."

She sat down and dust flew all around. She rolled the window down, let some of that dust out, coughed once or twice.

I sipped my beer, took a drag from my cigarette.

"You've been smoking a lot more."

"Drinking more too," I said, "but all in good fun."

"I want a beer," she said. "I wish I could have one."

"Go ahead."

She slapped my arm, "You're awful."

"When the baby comes, do you think you are gonna be happier?"

"Well, I hope when the baby comes that you're happier."

"Hope is a good word. I hope. I hope. They hope. He hopes. They all hoped. Hope, hope, hope! Don't give up HOPE."

"Talk about melodrama," my Sarah said.

All this waiting to talk it out seemed stupid all of a sudden.

"I told you I wanted kids," she finally muttered.

"I figured that you would be happy with a dog, but that didn't work."

Sarah slammed the door as she got out, walked into the house.

I'd brought a dog home from the pound two years prior, Sandy. The next day, while I was at work, she brought the dog back to the pound. Told them it didn't work out. When they said they wouldn't take the dog back, that adoptions were permanent, she lied and said that the dog had tried to bite her (our) son, Norton.

When I came home from work, Sarah was crying. I didn't even realize that the dog was nowhere to be found. That was the furthest thing from my mind, because there was my wife, crying on the couch.

"Why are you so upset?"

"I told you I wanted kids, and you brought home a dog."

"Take it easy. So what? So I brought home a dog? I thought you would like a dog."

"YOU DON'T WANT KIDS!"

"Hey!"

She was burying her face.

"YOU LIED TO ME. YOU DON'T WANT KIDS."

And yeah, I guess I had lied to her about that. I was really happy with Sarah and I wanted to marry Sarah. I really did want to spend the rest of my life with her. We had a lot of fun together. I could ignore the fact that she was prone to being nutso and paranoid from time to time. I never thought that there would be another girl as good for me as Sarah.

I still don't.

"Sarah, I want to have kids one day. I wouldn't have asked you to marry me if I didn't want kids."

"Sure you would have," she said.

"Where is Sandy?"

"Huh?"

"The dog."

Silence. Lots of silence.

"I took her back to the pound."

"You took Sandy back to the pound?"

"Yeah, I took Sandy back to the pound."

"I had a special connection with that dog!"

"We only had her one day!"

"BUT AT THE POUND, SHE JUMPED RIGHT INTO MY ARMS!!"

I'd shown Sarah the trick that Sandy did; she was possibly the daughter of highly tutored circus dogs. Sandy not only jumped into my arms, but she did back flips when she saw me at the shelter. Back flips.

"Call and get her back," Sarah said, apologetic. "They keep them thirty days before . . ."

"You aren't gonna freak out," I ask.

"No. I'm sorry I took her back. It was stupid."

I went to the other room, used the phone, called the pound, could not believe what they told me. When I came back into the living room, Sarah was breathless, flat on her back, waiting.

"What did they say?"

"Hold up, I'm confused," I said. "The woman on the phone apologized, apologized, and apologized, asked if Norton was OK."

Oh, silence from my Sarah!

"I asked, 'Norton?' She said he was our toddler, Norton the toddler, who was bitten by Sandy, the toddler-biting baby-eater. Sandy, who'd been euthanized. The lady at the shelter was very delicate in explaining all of this to me, so I very delicately put the receiver down, because ummm, because I didn't want to SCREAM AT HER!!!"

Sarah jumped, exploded in tears again. She kept saying, "I'm sorry! I'm sorry! I'm sorry!"

I got in the car, left the house, and went to the abandoned sand pit with a case of beer, where I drank alone—very sure I was going to divorce Sarah but trying to figure it all out.

When I came home, she was gone. She stayed gone for three weeks, living with her sister in Jackson, sleeping on the living room couch and whatever else. I got a phone call one day at work. It was Sarah. She wanted to come home.

"Yeah, come home," I said.

"You want me home?"

"Yeah, come home."

And then she came home.

The garage stunk like antifreeze: sweet but poisonous if guzzled.

"I can't believe you brought this goddamned car back," Sarah said from the doorway. She couldn't just let me be. She had to argue about this. "It's pathetic."

"I like it," I said, "despite the implications it brings." I motioned for her to come back in.

"You don't respect me . . . at all." she said, shutting the door, coming down the little set of steps

"Here we go."

"I thought you wanted to talk," she said, hurt.

"No, I wanted to sit in peace. I thought maybe you could sit in peace too."

"It ruined you when said I was pregnant."

I put my hand on my head, sighed.

"But it happened." She turned to me. "I thought you might leave or do something crazy. And I was right. Because every time I turn around, here you are doing something else whacked out."

"Look who is talking about whacked out."

"Fuck you."

"Don't say that to me. You know what I mean, and you owe me an apology."

"For what."

"Bullshit, you know."

"I don't."

"I didn't get you pregnant," I say.

"Yeah you did."

"You got yourself pregnant."

"OH, WHAT AN ASSHOLE!!"

"BECAUSE YOU'RE FUCKING COMPLETELY NUTS!"

"DON'T YELL AT ME!"

"DON'T PRETEND ANYMORE!!"

She swung her arm at me, but I grabbed it at the elbow, leaned in.

"I know you stopped taking your birth control."

And I knew it was true. Sarah pushed open the door, went in

the house, locked herself in our bedroom.

I sat in the garage, with the door open because it was kind of stuffy. After half an hour, a car pulled in the driveway. The front door opened, and Sarah trotted down the front steps to the car.

I walked out onto the driveway.

Some jackass with a red beard was behind the wheel. Somebody else tricked by the tricky Sarah. I imagined he was some special ed. teacher who she worked with, and I found out awhile later that I was right.

"Don't fall for her pokerface!" I yelled at him.

Walking closer to the car as it started to pull away, I shouted, "SHE'S A LUNATIC!"

He rolled down the window and flipped me the bird. I did the natural thing anybody would have done: I launched my beer bottle at the windshield. It hit, broke, but caused no damage.

"YOU MOTHERFUCKER!!"

"YOU MOTHERFUCKER!!"

Sarah was crying in the front seat, her face hidden. They continued to pull away, but I got a burst of energy, adrenaline. I ran after the car, attempting to jump kick it. I succeeded, in mid air, struck like a dragon ninja. You should have seen me!

I fell away from the car as it jetted up the road—receding towards the ground in what seemed like slow motion, as I saw the last years with Sarah dissolve into something that I could hardly believe had ever happened. I expected to hit the ground—but landed instead into my wall of cardboard boxes. A great crack was heard. I expected the crack to be a bone in my body but didn't feel any pain.

I laid there a moment. The box I'd landed on contained the chicken lamp; that crack had been the chicken lamp.

Well fuck it, I kicked the seashell mailbox and almost broke my foot.

Did some red-bearded knight in shining armor really just take a pregnant lunatic off of my hands? Lucky day, lucky day. When I swung back around, glancing down the block, I saw ten sets of curtains all close in unison. Voyeurs.

I went inside the garage.

Sometime around seven, the police came and took me briefly to the station. Charges of assault and charges of damage to property. Ray let me sit in his office rather than put me in a cell. When

Ted came and bailed me out, he found me happy, benevolent, easy going.

Good ol' Ted.

82

The next morning I sat in Diesel Cottontail, drinking, listening to that Squeeze 8 track. The garage door opened behind me, sunlight flooded my shady hideout.

Before I could react, a kid made of matchsticks stood outside of the Volkswagen window, peering in.

"I don't need the lawn mowed," I said to the kid. "Go away."

"Grass is pretty high."

"Listen, I know my wife was into throwing all kinds of money away. I'm just not into throwing money away."

He grinned.

"She couldn't spend our paychecks fast enough," I explained, "I was drawing up a blueprint. I was in the pre-plan stages of constructing a fire pit in the backyard to make her life easier."

"How so?"

"I figured that she'd be able to burn the money in the fire pit. Then she wouldn't have to be troubled with finding new and imaginative ways of spending it all."

"So you're gonna cut the grass yourself?"

"No, I'm never going to cut the grass ever again. I'm going to let it thicken out. Then, I'm gonna put vipers in it."

"Come on, Mr. Jimmy, one more cut for old times sake?"

"Forget it. You work too hard anyway. Why do you work so hard? A kid like you should be out there getting drunk and high and burning down his high school."

"I was over there last night, at your wife's new place."

I took the beer bottle from my lips.

"And why were you there?"

"Filming," he said.

"Filming . . . fuck you."

"You don't recognize me without my clown make up, heh?"

He snickered wildly. I felt sick.

"You know," I said, "I'm gonna break all of the bones in your face and chest and back and spine."

"Show, don't tell."

I opened the door, he backed away, laughing harder.

"You won't hurt me," he said. "You like me. I know you like me. And the only reason I was filming over there was because it was his birthday. I wasn't invited, so I had to lean by the back window and shoot through the hedges. He's a big Yankees fan. Sarah got him a glove that was autographed by the whole team. Very nice. He would have loved it, but I unwrapped it last week, when it was hidden in the back of her closet, and I kinda sorta took a massive three-coffee, bran muffin SHIT in the box . . . then I sold the glove on eBay. So when he opened the box, he didn't find a beautiful birthday gift. He found a soggy pile of rancid shit. The look on his face was almost as great as the look on her face!" Brian, Kid with Clownhead, was beaming. "Unbelievable footage! Do you want to see it?"

I was completely without words. How do you have words to something like that? Where do you go with the dialogue? What kind of comeback do you have to someone who has gone out of his way to infiltrate your life and seek revenge for you! An enemy? A friend? Where does anybody stand on these shifting tectonic plates?

I finished my beer, opened the passenger side door for him. Kid with Clownhead was that asshole kid who mowed my lawn. I knew I hated that lawnmower kid for a reason.

"I'm gonna sit down. No objections, right?'

"Climb in," I said, patting the seat. Dust exploded out.

There was an extra beer waiting for me to get to it in the cup holder.

"You want a beer?"

"Jim, I'm underage."

"Oh, of course."

"Nice car."

"It was my first car."

"Sarah's gone," he said, seeming upset too.

"For good," I said.

"For certain? You didn't love your wife anyway."

"You kidding me? I loved her so bad it fucking hurts. Things just get all fucked up. Sideways. Being married is like getting in a car crash—you can't always control what happens."

"She was a hot wife. Man, oh man, what a hot wife."

"Spare me," I pleaded.

"I started mowing your lawn 'cause I wanted to get in good with her. I wasn't interested in the ten bucks a week for the service. I was interested in getting a blowjob. Sadly, it never happened. Sadly, it probably never will happen."

"You really missed out on a great suck job, kid, let me tell you."

"Oh, I'm sure! Actually, I'm positive." He looked at me funny, tilting his head to the side. "I never understood how a young guy with such an unbelievably hot wife, a nice house and a seashell mailbox could be so devastatingly miserable."

"You'll get there. If you're lucky," I offered.

"The wife's out there on the patio, half naked, covered in suntan lotion, watching lawnmower boy sweat, and where are you? You're off in the fucking woods building a tree fort so that you can jerk off to some skank slut whore. No wonder Sarah got herself a new dick to slide on top of. Not that I'm happy about it either. I didn't want to see the two of you split up. I was rooting for you miserable shipwrecks!"

"So it goes," I said. "But there's more to it then you know. When you grow up, you'll understand how hard it is to grow up. You'll see how un-fun it is to settle."

"Sob, sob, sob." He shrugged. "I was gonna rig the voting at my senior prom, I was gonna get you two to be the king and queen of my prom. You guys would have swept up. It would have been beautiful."

"You've got a broken brain," I said.

"Yeah, you made me real nervous when you started to clean out your garage."

"Just making some room."

"I thought the attic was next. When was the last time you were up there?"

Brian was really starting to creep me out. My mouth was suddenly very dry.

"I don't go up there; it's too full of garbage. I'm surprised the ceiling can hold it."

"It was a wreck up there; Sarah sure was a pack rat."

"Why the fuck were you in my attic?"

"Don't yell at me, pal. I'll frame you for a murder suicide . . . kidding, just kidding. But I could."

"You like to go up there and whack off? Listen to Sarah moan as I pound her? You sick dweeb."

"Sick dweeb?! And your wife never moaned when you pounded her." Kid put his hands up, realizing that he deserved to be hit right in his kisser. I didn't even acknowledge him. What was the sense of destroying a piss-ant? Plus, I got the impression that he really wanted me to hit him, it would bring him great joy to be bloodied.

"It's sad, isn't it? All I know about you, and how little you know about me," he said, fidgeting in his seat. "I like you. You're seriously, the best pet project I've ever had. Your life in your fishbowl makes my own fishbowl existence seem limitless and explosive."

"I should be strangling you right now. Can you tell me why I'm not?"

He held up his index finger, "One sec."

Kid reached in his jeans, pulled out a crumpled piece of paper, handed it to me.

It was a note written in pink sparkle pen.
It said:

> Brian,
> I'll do it.
> Gena

"Do what," I asked.

"Participate in a little film."

"Oh . . ."

"She's got a college exam; if she fails, she's out."

"But you have the answers to the exam."

"Of course I do."

"And you will give her the answers if she vandalizes some boats in the marina or goes to the zoo and feeds a monkey to a lion or if she . . ."

"Fuck us on camera."

"Us?"

"Yeah, why not?"

"I don't think I'd be interested."

"Oh no, you would definitely be interested."

The tape was over, the music paused, then the tape flipped itself. The kid looked at it, baffled.

"What the fuck is that?"

"8-track," I said, "You never saw one?"

"Once, at a museum I think."

The youth love to make their predecessors feel even more ancient than they are; it's their birthright.

"Well you won't be young forever either," I said.

"I'll make a bet with you."

"Oh yeah, what is that?"

"That we will live forever."

"We? How did I get so wrapped up in your little spiderweb?"

"You don't want to be part of something great?"

"No. I've finally got my garage all set up. Perhaps I'll just sit here for a while, start the engine up, breathe in some unfriendly fumes."

"You know, I'm not a bad guy," Brian said. "I try to help people out."

"Like that kid who set his uncle's boat on fire at the marina?"

"For your information, Mr. Jim. That kid is one of my good friends. His uncle used to molest him on that boat when he was younger. That boat got what it had coming."

"You're warped. You need help."

I felt like I was echoing Ted's words back at the kid.

"Well Gena is ready, and Gena is waiting."

"She's all about this on-camera orgy? Kids today are so fucked up."

"Sluts be slutting."

Brian left, and I was sitting in the garage, thinking: what the fuck was he doing in my attic?

So I did what any good detective would've done: I walked down the hallway, pulled the cord to the attic steps.

"Hello," I called.

I heard movement up there. I climbed the stairs, slightly

afraid.

When I got to the top, I saw a body climbing through the attic window and out onto a tree branch. I'd never noticed, but anybody with enough incentive could climb the tree in my neighbor's yard and get into my attic. Why would they want to get in my attic?

I leaned out the window. That one-armed kid from Officetown was climbing down the tree and onto the lawn of my neighbor.

"YO! WHAT WERE YOU DOING IN MY ATTIC?"

He had a black bag slung over his shoulder.

"WHAT'S IN THAT BAG!"

He didn't say anything.

"WHAT'S IN THE FUCKING BAG!!"

I came down out of the attic and left the house, creeped out. I walked the three blocks to where Brian lived with his parents and knocked on the door. Brian answered.

"Your mom and dad home? I want to talk to them."

"I butchered them years ago."

He was wearing a bathrobe with King Kong on it.

"What the fuck were you kids doing in my attic?"

"It doesn't matter now. We're done."

"Done?! I bet. I caught your crony, the one-armed bandit, climbing out with a big black bag."

"One of many," he said. "Don't sweat it. And be advised, I keep a cyanide tablet under my tongue. If you try to beat the answer out of me, you will never know the truth. I would rather die than disclose that information. Art is something I believe is worth dying for."

"Art in my attic?"

"Lighten up."

"I thought I heard squirrels up there!"

"Listen, I have to go. I'm in the middle of making a ransom note. I have the mayor's parakeet."

He closed the door sharply. I went home, to what was left of it anyway. There was no use pursuing answers. I thought I'd be dead by the morning.

81

Years before, when me and Sarah were trying to save money to buy our house, a man in a cowboy hat came to a dead halt in my booth's lane and asked, "You interested in any side work?"

"Side work?"

He handed me his business card. It was tan and had a brown cowboy hat. In lime green lettering, it read, "PAL'S PARKING."

The cowboy was chewing a toothpick. His sideburns were monstrous.

"Call me," he said. "We have comfortable chairs in our booths." He gave me a ten spot, said, "Keep the change, Chief."

Comfortable chairs in the booths?

On my break, I dialed the number at the payphone, nervously cupping the receiver so Larry couldn't hear.

"This is Chief," I said.

"Oh hello, Chief," the cowboy said, "that was quick."

We talked about the specifics of the gig.

"Come tonight. Atlantic City. Parking garage across from Caesar's Palace. When does your shift end?"

"In an hour."

"Relieve me. I'll be in the booth waiting. The last boothy couldn't hack it, but you look seasoned, poised, full of grace and antifreeze."

"I do?"

"I'd say," he coughed. "People talk, ya know . . . I've heard a lot about you. They say you're the best. Are you the best?"

"At what? At tollboothing? Holy shit, uh, I dunno . . . "

"Listen, sky's the limit for a man with talent." His voice was scratchy, shaky. It sounded like it was rolling over a dusty mesa to find me. "By dawn you'll be able to name your own price."

"I'll be there."

"Knew you would."

I set the receiver down.

I was good. So good. The best. They needed me.

At Pal's Parking, the cowboy was sitting in the most comfortable chair I'd ever seen in my life, teetering on the threshold of sleep. I had to clear my throat and stamp my feet three times to break his spell.

He woke with a jolt, went for a gun at his hip that wasn't there.

"WHAT," he exclaimed, hostile.

He caught himself, his face softening in a flash of recognition.

"Oh you! Good. I'm so goddamned glad that you showed up."

"Yeah, I'm here." Outside, I saw the neon of the A.C. strip flickering down the ramp from the street. The cowboy motioned to the chair.

"Have a seat."

I sat.

"Well, I'm sure you're familiar with this setup: cars come, you take their ticket, you take their money, you open the metal arm, they go away—easy as pie."

"OK, got it."

"I've got a hot date. Inside the casino. Pretty lady. Black jack dealer. 36-24-36, whoa!" He winked at me.

"OK."

"If, by some strange insanity, my boss comes around, tell him I'm in the hospital. Tell him I'm dead. Say the goddamn viewing is on Wednesday in Absecon, closed casket. Tell him to donate to the Red Cross in lieu of flowers."

"OK."

Then the cowboy was gone, limping towards the elevators that'd hoist him into the casino as if it was Heaven itself.

First, there was nothing: no cars or anything. The lot was full, and there was a sign out front that read: LOT FULL, DO NOT ENTER.

As a matter of fact, it was an automatic sign; I had nothing to do with it. That feeling was comforting. I looked up from my shoes that I'd been staring at—a yellow pickup truck with a large bumblebee graphic on the hood came down the ramp. The woman inside had not noticed the huge neon sign: LOT FULL, DO NOT ENTER.

The truck made passes down each lane and then went up the ramp to the next level, where I could hear it screech its tires turning the corners. The sound of the truck grew even farther away as it entered the third level, finding nothing there either. No one leaves the casino, would ever leave the casino.

I leaned back in the most comfortable chair of my life, and closed my eyes for the briefest period of time. The squeal of the bumblebee truck came back down the ramp woke me from my doze. I'd nearly fallen asleep.

So I stood, stretched.

The bumblebee truck rolled to my booth window, poised in front of the metal arm. The woman inside said, "Hey, all of the spots are taken."

"There was a sign. Do you remember the sign?"

"I didn't see the sign."

"There are actually two of them. Each one blinking on the side of the entrance. They are something like five feet tall, blinking in hot pink and orange. They say, LOT FULL, DO NOT ENTER."

"I highly doubt that there are signs out there that say that. I would've seen them."

"Oh, but they are there, and you didn't see them."

"So what? Open the gate."

"I can't open the gate until you give me six dollars."

"I didn't park."

"Yeah, I get the argument, I understand your position, but you have to understand one thing in this scenario: I'm a professional (the best), and it's my duty, my only duty to man this gate. I refuse to cater to people who won't pay the toll. No offense."

"Fuck you."

"That isn't gonna get the gate opened."

"Yeah, only six bucks is gonna get the gate open. Well what if I ram your stupid gate, mister toll man!"

"You can try. It'll mess your grill up, probably puncture your radiator. And there is a camera recording all of this right now. We got your license plate."

"OK, please open the gate? Pretty please."

"Begging won't save you."

"Well, SCREW YOU!"

"You already said that. So are you going to give me the toll, or are we are we having a fun little standoff?"

She threw the truck into reverse and almost smashed directly into a concrete pillar. She drove back up to the second level. I put the window down in my booth, turned the air conditioning up and leaned back in the chair.

Just then, a little fat man and his wife walked out of the elevator and climbed inside a Cadillac. They drove to my booth, gave me the six dollars, went upwards to the street. The automatic neon sign switched to PARKING AVAILABLE. There was a smiley face. Up above me, I could hear the squeal of the bumblebee truck coming down from the third level.

A red Honda zipped in from the outside world, as bumblebee truck appeared on the far side of the bottom level. The Honda took the parking spot by the elevator. A beautiful girl was in the car, a caveman in the passenger seat, draped with gold chains and a tight, blue dress shirt. The woman in the yellow truck pulled beside them.

"Excuse me, that's my spot. I was here first."

"If you were here first, how did we get in your spot before you?"

"Ask the toll guy, he'll tell you. I was waiting for that spot."

I stuck my head out of the booth.

"If you aren't gonna park, please stop harassing our customers."

I smiled at the beautiful girl, "Enjoy your experience at our adjoining casino."

The caveman boyfriend gave me a dirty look, but I didn't care. The booth had deadbolts on it and was fitted with shatterproof plexiglass. It could withstand multiple bullet fractures before allowing entry by mad-dog booth attackers.

The yellow truck was still hanging out on the lower level. She certainly wasn't going to let another car get out that gate without taking their spot.

A green van came down the ramp from the outside world. I shook my head in dismay. Bumblebee shook her head in frustration. I had a PA system. I hit the little button, said, "Make it easy on yourself. You'll never win."

This garnered no response from the woman.

When the green van came to me, wanting out of the garage 'cause there were no spots, I said, "I'll tell you the same thing that I told that yellow truck: six dollars to exit the garage."

"I didn't park."

"Uh huh."

"Still six dollars?"

"Yeah."

"Let me out."

"Six dollars."

"I'll rip that metal gate off and shove it up your asshole," the guy said.

"You and everyone else."

A cold stare ensued. "Good luck," I said, closing my window and sitting in the comfortable chair. Then another car came down the ramp, and I closed my eyes. Just for a second, I closed my eyes.

80

I was on TV once. 7:30, right before CRAZIEST POLICE CHASES EVER. The show I was on was called, WORKPLACE WHOOPS! To be honest, I thought the police chases were more engaging. Criminals evading law enforcement have a special place in my heart.

I was sitting on the couch with Sarah. She had the remote. I was rubbing her shoulders, trying to get laid that night. It didn't look like it was going to happen, but I tried . . . oh, I tried. She was pissed at me about something, but I can't recall what. I'm sure she could tell you. She kept a record of everything that ever pissed her off about me: a little red notebook in a shoebox under the bed, with dates and times noted next to the offense and how I made it up to her.

> 10/2/98—Forgot my birthday (cunnilingus)
> 10/6/98—Called me a bitch (sapphire ring)
> 11/18/98—Didn't want to go to my mother's
> for Thanksgiving
> (cunnilingus. made him go anyway)
> 11/25/98—Got drunk at dinner (bracelet)
> 11/26/98—Didn't want to give me cunnilingus
> (new dress)

I found the notebook when she left me for that red-bearded freak.

But on the backrub night, we were watching TV: an attendant was at a gas pump giving change to a driver, which the driver took and proceeded to drive away, taking the gas pump handle with him . . . Thankfully, the check valve stopped a fountain of gas from covering the attendant, who just stood there dumbfounded. All of this was caught on surveillance cameras. In the show, wacky music was playing while the host made stupid comments via voiceover: "CHEAP GAS TUESDAYS: BUY A TANK, AND YOU GET TO KEEP THE PUMP HANDLE. WHAT A BARGAIN!"

Sarah was laughing, asking me to rub a little more pointedly. It seemed that I was distracted.

A few more clips followed in similar suit. People at desk jobs had their computer chairs slip out from under them, they tripped carrying coffee cups, bike messengers hit potholes and slingshotted onto sidewalks. Everyone owns a camera phone, and everyone was filming: postal carriers getting hit in the nuts by stray tennis balls, janitors slipping on wet floors, a construction worker on a ladder getting hit by a stray football in the nuts; a man at a podium giving a business speech at a convention who was hit in the balls by the microphone when the podium collapsed. Everyone laughed madcap at nut injuries. The clever host really knew how to tear into these people, make their pain be our great joke. I laughed too, until . . . "OK, now wait 'til you see this: have you ever heard the term, 'asleep at the wheel?' Well what about 'asleep at the gate?'"

And there I was, on TV, asleep in the booth at Pal's Parking. The black and white shot was too grainy to completely make out my features, but there I was, wearing my New Jersey parkway hat, leaning back in the chair. There was no audio; my mouth was agape, the producers dubbed in the sound effect of sawing wood to simulate my snores.

"Look familiar," Sarah said, nudging me.

"Ha!" She didn't know that it really was me, and I couldn't believe what I was watching. I kept my mouth shut and we continued to watch: she laughed, and I pretended to not be going completely out of my mind.

The host said, "When this guy decided to catch some Z's on the clock, it rubbed a lot of people the wrong way."

The camera changed to outside the booth, another surveillance camera. There was a long line of cars and trucks, people who were trapped by the gate. They were pounding on the window of the booth, but their efforts were useless: the chair was far too comfortable for their clamor to do any good.

"Hello in there! OPEN UP," the host said in funny voices. "Mister! Wakey wakey."

The audience roared with laughter as the sound effect of the wood being sawed was rolled again. The camera cut back to me with my head fallen forward now, somewhere in dreamland, drool rolling down my chin.

"OK, now watch closely what this guy decided to do when Sleeping Beauty wouldn't wake up!"

The outside surveillance camera captured a view of the caveman in the blue shirt, who just so happened to be unbolting the metal gate at its hinges. Apparently he was some kind of mechanic, and carried his tools everywhere. The gate came off, the woman threw it into the back of her yellow pickup truck.

"AND THEY TOOK THE GATE! THAT'LL SHOW EM!"

The caravan pushed relentlessly out of view. The camera cuts inside the booth again, the sawing sound still playing. There's a fast forward time lapse effect and all of a sudden the police are there knocking on the window. That wakes me up.

"They informed the man what has just happened and even reattach the metal gate, which was found three blocks away."

The camera cut back to the host standing in front of the studio audience, rolling with laughter.

He says, "DUH," then swings his hands at his side and concludes, "Well thanks for watching. I hope you had as much fun laughing at these jokers as I did!"

The credits roll, and then a commercial for Pizza Hut comes on. I sit there stunned. Sarah goes into the kitchen and gets us a diet Pepsi to share. I get off the couch and get a beer.

"I don't see why you need that."

"Need what?"

"You know what. Here we are, having a nice night, and you have to go and get a beer."

"So what, I'm drinking a beer."

"Well now you aren't getting any sex."

"I figured I wasn't anyway."

"You were."

"Uh-huh." I sip the beer.

"After the backrub, we were squared away. But now, because you are such a miserable guy amidst all of our TV fun, yeah, no sex."

I shrugged, drank more. She moved to the other couch.

"Get off your cloud," I said.

Her father was an alcoholic and died too young, but so what? How did that concern me?

I found this later.
6/3/2005—Told me to get off my cloud
(No sex for a month)
6/18/2005—I told him I wanted a baby
He brought home a dog
(I stopped taking my birth control)

I called up the TV station, said that I wanted to order a copy of that program. "Are you serious? That show was real stupid. Funny, but stupid," said the woman who answered, just some secretary cracking bubblegum.

"Yeah. I was on it. Uncredited, but I was on it."

"Oh, in that case . . . Were you one of the people who got smashed in the nuts?"

"Yeah. I was the pizza delivery guy who got hit in the nuts by the doorknob."

"Are you OK?"

"No, I can't have kids as a result."

"Oh my God, I'm sorry."

"Yeah, I know it seemed funny on TV, but sometimes when people get smashed in the genitals, it isn't without lasting repercussions in reality. So think about that the next time you see one of those shows on TV."

"I will," she said, "I'm sorry I laughed when I saw it."

"Can I get a free copy of the tape?"

"It doesn't work like that."

She transferred me. I had to pay fifty bucks, but it was worth it to see myself in the limelight, on the most comfortable chair in the world, sawing wood.

77

The phone rang. It was Sarah.

"Where are you now," I asked.

"Nevermind. I'm in a campground, but nevermind, with Josh, but nevermind."

"Are you trying to make me jealous? It's not gonna work"

"What do you know? I know that Josh has a better respect for me and a better outlook on the future."

"But can he hand out change inside a tollbooth?"

"I wouldn't know, and neither would he, as he would never be caught dead inside a tollbooth."

"He sounds like a grade A sucker, a real champion in the gullibility ranks."

"I didn't call you up to argue like grade schoolers. I wanted to work some things out."

"Nothing to work out."

"We aren't getting back together," she said. "That's not what I meant. I want to come home and pick up some of my stuff that I left behind."

"Too late for that."

"You can't keep me from getting my things."

"No, I'm not trying."

"I fucked Ted once. I just wanted you to know that."

"Already knew. It happened senior year when we broke up for the first time."

While extremely drunk during my bachelor trip to the strip

club with Ted, I had told him about the video of me in the Atlantic City parking garage, and he confessed that he slept with Sarah back in the twelfth grade, said he didn't think he could be my best man. I told him that he could be my best man if he let me break a beer bottle over his head. He agreed, so we went out back. I broke the bottle, and that is why Ted was wearing a wide brimmed hat during the entire wedding. I also confessed to him that I was the one who stole his Spiderman #13. I gave that back, and he confessed that he was the one who took my BB gun. I admitted that I had once french-kissed his mother. It was a lie, but male friendships are all about lies and forgiveness.

"I've been thinking about some things . . . for real," she said quietly.

"Like?"

"You seeing a doctor."

"Me seeing a doctor? Oh that's great."

"Will you think about going over to the Mayweather?"

That was where she'd done her stint back in the day. Paper gowns and checkers. Group therapy.

"Ted said the same thing, ya know," I admitted.

"Well, you should listen to your friend. If you won't listen to me, you should listen to him."

"You're really worried about me, huh?"

"I was worried that you wouldn't answer the phone."

"You still love me."

"Enough that I don't wanna see you dead."

"I'd never kill myself."

In front of me, on the end table, was Ted's father's turkey hunting gun.

"Will you go see someone over there?"

"No," I said. "I won't."

She was very quiet, "Then, goodbye."

74

I went to Officetown. Gena was leaning against the copy machine in tight pants, looking better than ever. I walked down the notebook aisle, peeked around the end cap at her.

I muttered, "You beauty queen, are you ready for my werewolf curse? I'm going to rip you to shreds with it. I'm gonna sink the spiderfangs right into your heart! Oh my god, it's gonna rip me apart too. It really is."

I took one of the notebooks, opened one of the pen packs. On the first line of the notebook, I wrote, "I'm gonna fuck Gena today."

Then on the second line I wrote:
"I'm gonna fuck Gena today"
Then:
"I'm gonna fuck Gena today"

It was for certain. I set the notebook down, walked out of the store. In the parking lot, I got superstitious. So I walked back to the notebook aisle and bought the notebook and the pen I'd used. My ears rung like the sound of the ocean in a seashell. The gun was in my pocket.

69

Kid with Clownhead showed up at my house on a dirt bike. He wanted me to ride on the back of it, but I wouldn't. Instead, I followed in the Subaru on the back roads, away from the strip malls, into the pines.

I knew where we were going. It'd be the Shamrock Motel, where they rented rooms by the hour. It was the only place within a fifty mile radius that was sleazy enough for what was about to happen.

The previous night, a package arrived: a cardboard box with a devil costume, pitch fork, pencil thin mustache, and goatee. There was a note that said, "Jim, obviously, be wearing this Satan costume when I show up tomorrow night at eight thirty. Then you can hop on the back of my dirt bike and it will look wild for the other motorists, a crazed kid with a clown head and the devil clutching onto him."

But, I wasn't his bitch, and I wasn't gonna ride bitch on the back of his dirt bike. As I turned my Subaru off the highway, I glanced over at my pitchfork on the passenger seat and wondered if I was making the wrong choices in my life.

67

There was a strobe light and a fog machine in the bathroom. When the kid opened the motel door, smoke billowed out. Inside, there was a bed, a small TV, a dirty orange shag rug. Pieces of the wall were missing. James Brown played on the clock radio: "Funky Drummer." Somebody cut their initials into the ceiling. Someone wrote in black magic marker, "TIM SMOKED CRACK IN HERE WIT DEZI 9-11-01." An employee of the Shamrock Motel tried to cover the message with one coat of primer, but the primer clung like a ghost skin over the declaration of the crack smoking.

There was a red velour blanket with cigarette burns, a plaid green, teal, and yellow secondary blanket, pink sheets, pink pillow cases, a rose stitched on the center of each pillow. The air conditioner screamed ineffectively.

Gena sat on the bathroom sink, her face hidden behind a tiger masquerade mask. Likewise, my face was hidden. We were strangers there. Most of the tiles were missing from the bathroom wall. She was drinking a beer. In the bathtub, there was melted ice and seven remaining Natty Ice cans, floating.

She had the mask on the whole time, because she didn't want to show her face in a porno. She had this crazy idea that she was gonna transfer to an Ivy League college despite her middle road grade point average. She sipped and looked at me, said to the kid, "Brian, you brought the devil with you? This oughta be fun."

Brian was dangerously charismatic as he took her hand,

kissed it, said, "My pet! I would like to introduce you to Lucifer."

"Hi, Lucy!" she said.

"Gena, are you of legal age to take part in a pornographic film?"

"You know I am," she said, pretending to slap his clown face, "I'm nineteen."

"Oh goody," he said. "I would hate for anything to happen with Lucifer right here to condemn us to an eternity in Hell."

"I wouldn't dream of it," Gena said, blowing me a kiss.

"Hell is what you make of it," I offer.

63

There were a few ground rules. The kid got to fuck her first, all of this was his deal. I got sloppy seconds, which I wasn't too excited about. Beggars can't be choosers.

God bless our hearts, even when we are dressed up like the devil.

Gena said that she was for all intents and purposes a virgin, saving herself for her wedding day. Kid with Clownhead said, "Out of bounds. There has to be penetration, or no exam answers."

"I'll let you do my mouth," she counter offered.

"Yes, I will fuck your mouth, but without non-oral penetration, this whole thing's a joke. This film needs coitus."

"I give the best blow jobs, just ask the football team . . . or the soccer team."

"I will not stoop so low as to associate with those heathens," he said.

"Come on, Brian," she said, smirking.

"Give up the pussy, or give up on college."

"Fine then." She folded her arms, tilted back her beer, and then gave a pouty face after lifting up the tiger mask. "I'm gonna wear a white dress down that aisle one day. And I'm not going to do it without being a virgin. So, no pussy. End of argument."

Kid with Clownhead reached down into the bathtub, pulled out two beers, tossed one in my direction. I was staring at Gena's tits, so I don't see it coming. The can hit the edge of the counter-top, got a pinhole in it. Beer foam sprayed out. Without comment,

Brian got me a new beer. He was beginning to be my good friend.

"You're a liar anyway. I know you aren't a virgin. You fucked Kyle Rind," he said.

"No, I didn't. That was a rumor."

"And you fucked Frank Lasterinno."

"I did not, also a rumor."

"Mr. Higgins?"

"I sucked him off, and he still gave me a B on that test."

"You didn't fuck Bobby Gent?"

"I did fuck him, but . . ."

"But what?"

"That doesn't count."

"Why not?"

"I went out with him for three months, and he pressured me, got me drunk."

"So? You're drunk now, right?"

"Kinda."

"Perfect."

"And I wouldn't have sex with him anyway. I did it the other way, kept my virginity."

"Other way?" I laughed.

"Yeah, in the ass. That doesn't count."

"Huh?"

"I still got my hymen," she said with pride. "I'll still pop my cherry for my husband on our honeymoon."

"So you'll do anal?"

"No, I won't do anal," she said. "Forget it."

"I got a small dick," the kid said. "You won't feel a thing."

"It feels four times bigger in there."

He unzipped, she looked at it. "Well, that actually is really tiny."

"See, no big deal," he said, proudly shaking it.

She shrugged, considering.

I unzipped and showed her mine. She was satisfied. "Oh good, you guys are hung like toddlers! This won't hurt at all."

For once in my life, it was paying off to be way below average.

58

I wasn't happy about holding the camera while Gena sucked the kid until he got hard. Her face was concealed by the tiger mask, but her white teeth were so bright in the blacklight. They were like horrible ghosts that had met center stage in some other-world sex show, and here I was, in my costume, sweating and itching.

As she was getting into it, Gena said, "You like that? Oh yeah, I like this cock!"

Then she sucked on it like a lollipop for a little while, and he groaned. Turning and facing the camera, Kid asked, "How's she doing? All of this carrying off well from a cinematographic standpoint?"

"Maybe too much fog machine," I said.

He tapped her on the head. "Hey, can you go turn the fog machine down?"

"Right now?"

"Yeah."

She stopped, turned to me.

"Cut," he said.

Gena looked upset, huffed and puffed for a moment, but then got up off of the floor, off of her knees, walked into the bathroom, turned down the fog machine, and came out with a beer.

"This is actually kinda fun," she said.

I gave her a dirty wink, she didn't wink back. We had no chemistry, no animal magnetism: that'd been me and Sarah in our youth, two perfect animals for each other. I was useless to Gena.

"The next scene has to be really hot," our director said.

"Oral for me," Gena asked.

"No way," he said, "I'm not gonna lick you."

"No fair."

"If I can't stick my dick in it, I am by no means gonna lick it."

"You are so fucked up," she said.

"Look, I am doing you a favor here. Ten minutes after I bust my nut I'm gonna need more. My dick isn't gonna remember this. You, however, will benefit from this night for a lifetime."

"Lifetime? We'll see," she uttered, doubtful. But I could tell that behind that mask she really believed it.

Belief: that's what drives people towards the tiger trap, catching them by the toe, dragging them to the gallows. Belief laughs when the noose drops.

52

Kid with Clownhead took off Gena's pink thong with his teeth, while I filmed. Then, he spit on his dick, asked her, "Are you ready?"

"Uh-huh."

And then he pushed into her and she let out a horrible shriek, "OHHHHHH FUCK!!"

He pumped then pumped again, grabbing onto her shoulders. She shrieked again and again, and I wanted to leave the hotel room. Suddenly, the shriek became a moan of pleasure, rising, contorting pitch, morphing into something less dangerous.

"OHHHH FUCK FUCK, FUCK ME, BRIAN!"

And he did, while she screamed, "YES, YES, YES!"

My cellphone started to ring. I ignored it, but the person called back again and again while Brian fucked Gena's ass. Three minutes like that seemed like ten years. I grew so angry at the ringing phone that I finally took it out of my pocket, lowering the camera. On the screen was a text message from Sarah's sister: SARAH N LBR COME 2 THE HOSPTL N PRETND 2 B A MAN

"Oh shit," I said out loud. My world spiraled through a tunnel.

Kid with Clownhead was oblivious. He was sweating, the drops running down his back as he pulled out from Gena and then stuck his cock back in.

"GET OUT OF MY PUSSY, YOU FUCKING ASSHOLE!"

"Oh, sorry."

"It's alright. Don't let it happen again." He stuck it back in her ass. "Oh . . . better."

I lost it. I kicked the green chair over. I punched the wall, making a new hole in the sheetrock. I made my way quickly through the smoke, like a figure in a hallucination; opening up that door, and almost knocking over three old men who were standing on the balcony with one ears each to the door. I went down the steps as they watched the show inside.

"Hey, Satan, where are you going?" one man called as I climbed into my Subaru.

The last time I saw Kid with Clownhead, he was out on that balcony, screaming at me—naked. But I had the radio up and was pulling out of that motel parking lot, racing as fast as I could towards the hospital.

50

As I drove down the parkway, I couldn't concentrate on a single thing. Hot flashes of terrible darkness snapped through my skull. The lines of the highway meant nothing. I swerved around other cars, onto the shoulder, wherever I could. The tollbooth ahead grew in size until it was everything.

I had no change in the Subaru, so I opened up the video camera, took out the VHS. Nearing the booth, I slowed down briefly as if I was going to stop. I lowered the window and screamed as the wind came in at me, pushing the latex mask even tighter against my face. It must've been something of a vision to my replacement in the booth. My war cry was dangerous, nearly shredded my vocal chords. Later, I'd cough blood. My scream was a call for the world to end. For anyone who dared to be sleeping through what was left, I wanted them to know: I was gonna eat their faces while they slept.

Fuck the past and all of the chains it wrapped around my heart and the webs the spiders spun around me while I was idle. Fuck what the werewolf moon did to my brain as I laid in wait for it to rise again so that I could head oblong towards oblivion. Fuck all of the yawns of suburbia, the myths, the legends—the folklore of eternal life. Instead, war cry into the wind, we're all gonna die. There's no excuse for not kicking up the icing on birthday cakes while dark angels traced my life in doomed flight. Fuck the future, it meant nothing. I say bomb blasts to anybody who denies me. I say: I'm ripped apart down my spinal column anyway, I'm a thousand shards of ribs, I'm wayward planets thrown out of orbit—lost of magic. I'm on my way down.

Timing it just right, I released the videotape from my fingertips. It exploded against the side of the tollbooth: streams of film marked a black passage behind me, shards of plastic landed in the basket, loops of magnetic tape and sticker decal rapped against the toll window. I screamed in the face of some poor substitute girl. She lost her breath, falling over in tears.

I was four miles up the highway by the time she closed the booth, walked into the building, told Larry she needed to go home. She couldn't explain what it was she'd seen; it was too horrible.

48

I pulled up. The valet parking attendant laughed at me in my devil suit, so I gave him my car keys, pointed back at him, laughed too.

"What're you laughing at?" he asked.

"Everything."

I ran towards the revolving door, where a man was pushing an elderly woman in a wheelchair. I was trying to beat them through the door. I succeeded. He saw me coming, saw my cape and my pitchfork, stopped dead in his tracks.

"Yeah, that's what I thought," I yell.

The security guard leaned on the wall, opened his eyes, and turned his head. Thinking he was still dreaming, he closed his eyes again.

I told the front desk woman to give me a visitor pass.

"I'm not really the devil. I'm a new father."

"Oh, good," she said, writing the pass. "Congratulations. Leave the pitchfork, though."

I gift it to the woman next to her with a Lilly of the Valley pin. I run down the hallway. In the elevator, a male nurse in sea foam OR scrubs smirked at me. He thought he was clever. When I looked at him, he looked away.

"Costume party," he asks, cracking up.

"Porn set."

He is silent after that.

"You're costume is no better," I said.

The elevator doors opened, and I rushed out into the fluorescent light—leaving the nurse behind with no chance for a comeback.

44

Sarah was in room 502—so I ran blind past all of the screaming and all of the comas in the surrounding rooms. My sneakers screeched as I ripped around corners.

Red beard was in a chair facing her. My Sarah was under the blanket. She looked sick or dying or recovering, or all that. When I appeared in the room, she gasped.

There was no baby.

The baby had come three weeks premature and was in an incubator, struggling.

"Jim, what are you doing?"

"Nothing." I stood there with my shoulders slumped. The way she looked at me, I felt embarrassed to be alive.

"Why are you dressed like that?"

"Long story," I said. "Your sister called me, said you were in labor."

"I was, you missed it."

"It was real nice, pal," Red Beard said. "I got plenty of pictures." He held the disposable camera up.

"Shit."

Sarah put her head back on the pillow, let out a deep sigh. We were all silent for a good long time after that. There was a bicycle race happening on the TV in the corner. I turned my head to that.

A nurse stopped in the hallway, stared into the room.

"Is everything OK in here?"

At the sound of the nurse's question, Sarah began crying hysterically. "I want this monster out of the room," she said between the tears.

And it was no confusion who the monster was, as I was in the monster suit and all.

The nurse asked sternly, "Can you please leave?"

I un-slumped my shoulders, stood up straight—prepared to put up a fight, but Sarah started to wail twice as hard. So I left, walking into the hallway, into the elevator, into the strange night.

41

The next morning, I awoke naked, with a headache, but that was to be expected considering how much poison I guzzled from such a strange bottle. I went into the bathroom, puked, looked in the mirror. I didn't shave, but I did brush the puke from my mouth with Sarah's old toothbrush, which I put back into the holder just in case she ever came back for it . . . or for me. There was no outrunning fate.

My teeth had sharpened and yellowed significantly. My eyes were pink; the one on the right was actually more of a shade of red. I'd slipped and hit my face on the coffee table somewhere in the middle of an episode of Cheers. The bruise looked nasty, but what kind of mouse would miss a day of work over a lousy bruise? I wanted to kill myself in the garage but couldn't get Diesel Cottontail to start. If I'd been a better mechanic, I would've just gone to sleep in the passenger seat after starting the engine and let the grim reaper drive me a couple thousand victory laps around an afterlife track.

Instead, I put on a collared shirt, pulled my khaki pants up, tightened my belt. Then, I went back in the bathroom. *Look at these stupid yellow teeth . . .* I threw Sarah's toothbrush away, threw mine away, opened up the cabinet, pulled out one of the new ones that she had in reserve for the day our old ones got too old to work anymore. I popped the brush out of the packaging and squirted five times the needed amount. I brushed until I saw blood rush from every section of my gum line.

I reached to the shelf above the toilet where my baseball cap sat and looked at it for a moment: ABOLISH NJ TOLLS. I threw it in the wastebasket. What a dumb idea for a hat. Sucking in the gut I really didn't have anyway and standing up as straight as I could, I pushed back my shoulders and growled.

In the mirror, I didn't look too good, but at least I had one thing going for me:

My hair was growing back on the sides; the last three hairs I had were sprouting up. Since Sarah had left, I hadn't been shaving my head. I twirled those three fellows together. It made me feel a tingle in my lower left leg. The tingle spread, as if the leg was waking up, and traveled up to my hips. I felt a burning there. In my gut, I thought this was something important—some awakening, but the pain in my stomach wasn't that at all. I curled over, got sick on the goddamned floor.

40

Dawn widened over us all. Something slow and drenched in doom was on its way. The ringing in my ears got worse. I feared retaliation for everything I'd done.

I studied every face as it approached, but they were all blank. No clues. The last traces of fog swept away; the sun lit us all. With no hiding places left, I had a change of heart. I'd be alright. The faces brought no dread or revenge, they just asked, "How much for the toll?"

"Thirty-five Cents."

"How much for the toll?"

"Thirty-five Cents."

"Can I have a receipt?"

"Can I have a receipt?"

"Can I have a receipt?"

"Can I have a receipt?"

I smirked at a man in a tan business suit. I said, "You cannot have a receipt, you pathetic motherfucker."

He just sat there, as if he didn't hear me, numb. He squinted although there was no sun that could be reflecting in his eyes.

"No, seriously, can I have a receipt?"

I went back in the booth, handed him an entire arm full of receipts.

"Whoa," he exclaimed, his eyes brightening. "Thanks!"

As he sped away, I knew he was dreaming about tax write-offs as a rebirth.

Coins and bills. Fumes and splintered windshields. Radios not turned down. Fuzzy dice. Dogs at back windows, their noses pressed. Personalized plates—CATLUVR, GODZGUD, SANTOS3, XTREM69, people eating, people with messy hair, people who were lost, "Which way to . . ."

"To heaven," I asked.

"To Passaic."

"Onward and upward," I said. "Exit 153."

"You're a saint."

A sinister cloud appeared above the pine barrens from the direction of my old fortress. The cloud was as big as an entire city. For the better part of an hour I thought it was a city in the sky full of assassins. Then the wind changed, and the cloud became a rabid monkey head before it finally broke apart, pushed towards the ocean without even offering me a ride.

Rush hour ended, and I sat there staring into my hands as if they had mirrors embedded in the palms.

I heard my name, "Jim?"

Looking up, I recognized the woman but couldn't remember anything about her.

"Hey, Jim," she said again. As she spoke, the sunshine grew to dizzying power. I stopped gnawing on my inner cheek. I stood, recharged.

"It's me, BEE!"

"Oh, hey," I said, leaning out. "What's going on? You're back?"

She was twirling her long blonde hair, smiling. There was a cardboard cutout of Jimmy Cagney in the passenger seat. "Back," she asked, confused. "I never left! But I am leaving."

"Oh, good," I said, realizing that sounded wrong. "Well, not good that you are leaving, good that you're getting away. That make sense?"

She nodded, "I feel you." Bee tilted her head, considering me. "The toll man . . . OK, well I don't have any money," she confessed, "but I'll pay you when I get back."

"Alright . . . really, it doesn't matter," I offered. I was getting a hard on. It was awkward. It touched the gun in my pocket. "This is my last day here, too," I confessed.

She smiled, started to roll forward. Without realizing, I screamed, "WAIT!"

Bee slammed on the brakes, backed up the three feet, faced

me again.

"I was hoping you'd scream!"

"Where are you going?"

"Iceland."

"Iceland," I said as if the word was magic.

"Get in the car," she commanded.

"Can't."

"Come on."

"Sorry, too many . . ."

"Come on!" She was beaming at me. "Pretty Please?"

I opened up the back door of the booth, ran around the side, and yanked Jimmy Cagney out. I set him in the booth, set the revolver on the tollbooth seat, climbed back in her shitbox car. I pleaded, "Go, go, go, go, go, go, go, go, go, go," slapping the dashboard with my palms 'til they were red and throbbing.

She laughed wildly, drumming the steering wheel.

We made tracks, lunatic tracks forward—go, go, go, go!

38

A man pulled up in a blue Dodge pickup. He asked cardboard Jimmy Cagney, "How much for the toll?"

The cardboard cutout said nothing.

"You deaf? How much for the toll?"

Cars flooded in behind, laying on their horns. Desperate, the man in the pickup shouted louder at the cutout, "Hey, buddy, how much for the fucking toll?"

Eventually, making no progress in establishing a line of communication, he stomped the gas and blew through the red light. The next car appeared; a man shook a dollar at the cardboard cutout and asked, "Can I get my change in dimes nickels and a quarter? Oh, and can I please have a receipt."

No response. Well, that's rude.

"Ehhhh hemmmpph—excuse me, bucko . . . can I please have a receipt and some change? Not getting any younger over here."

That infinite line grew eternal: never dying, extending through earth, overflowing into the netherworlds, out into the vast void of space and the dark and final whoosh of the great beyond. But we go go go go go go go go go go go go go go go go go go go go go go go go go go go go go go go go go go go go!

Iceland

einn

I was on our futon looking through an Icelandic magazine, which I couldn't understand. There were beautiful pictures at least. A glacier called Eyjafjallajökull. Try to say that ten times fast. Other photos of interest: beautiful models in hot springs eating oatmeal with neon spoons, vapor floating around like ghosts. In another spread, a small blonde boy flew a kite in a green field that went on forever. The kite had a picture of a protestor setting himself on fire. I couldn't make out the captions. Art.

Bee was sitting, Indian style, on the bare wood floor of our flat. She was surrounded by photographs of dead animals. A white fox, flattened. An elk ripped in half. Mountain goats, eviscerated. She was sorting through them, trying to complete her masterpiece— a roadkill calendar. "There's art in here somewhere," she said, batting the blonde dreadlocks out of her face while holding up a picture of a squashed beaver. "Mr. February," she asked—stone cold serious.

I looked up from my glossy Scandinavian magazine but couldn't bring myself to comment. Things were becoming tense between me and Bee. Reykjavic was not the mecca that we'd hoped. It'd been two years, and the money was almost gone. My desperation in New Jersey was a distant memory. My boredom here was white hot and easy. I'd begun to masturbate, strangely, to the thought of Sarah at the kitchen table eating orange slices topless.

Bee was not Sarah. She didn't watch TV or movies, and she

didn't understand what a joke was either. She just laughed even though she didn't get it.

"I like this squashed goose," she said, shaking another photo at me.

"That's nice."

"It's down to a skunk ripped into five pieces and a moose hanging over a highway railing."

I thought the same thing that the moose had probably thought right before getting struck, *why did I think this trip out of the wilderness would solve all my loneliness?*

I considered Bee's pretty face; the high cheekbones; the laugh lines; her fair skin, freckled; her pronounced goodness. It wasn't enough either. She never once called me a motherfucker. She had no guts. There was no animal magnetism.

At any moment, the landlord was gonna show up and kick us out of the decaying flat that we called home. Bee had been having reoccurring nightmares about us being forced to live in a tent on the fjord, being eaten by wolves as the hail came down. I began to think that it was my fault, that I gave my women reoccurring nightmares. Neither one of us were smart enough to realize that there were no wolves that lived in Iceland.

At night, I clutched onto her while she figured out where she was. The bed was small. She ran her fingers through my beard. I had a haircut that made me look like Jack Nicholson from The Shining: long on the sides, bald up top. She smelled like Ivory soap. I would sing her back to sleep with *Ruby Tuesday* or *I Guess the Lord Must Be In New York City.*

We were quite a long way from home, but, we didn't talk about America—not even once. Whenever a McDonald's commercial came on the TV though, our souls started shouting the Star-Spangled Banner. That's what living abroad is all about.

There are no tollbooths in Iceland either, enhancing my homesickness. I fantasized about building my own booth from sticks I could gather from the banks of rivers that rushed through the hills.

"Please forget the calendar for awhile," I said. "Let's go down to the café and get some wine and sandwiches."

"No," Bee said, "I've got to finish this today."

She'd been fucking around all week. It was on the tip of my tongue to tell her to beg her parents for more money. They were loaded. That'd been our M.O. in Iceland, to keep sucking cash from them, but Bee took a stand. Her roadkill calendar was gonna make her rich. At 36, she was cutting the cords from her pipeline of coin.

I'd confessed my disdain for her art project.

"The idea's already taken," I criticized. "I saw it in a mall back in the states. There was a calendar stand near the embroidery kiosk. I remember 'cause I had the hots for the embroidery woman."

Bee just said, "Nobody ever has their own ideas anyway; we all get our ideas form telepathy."

"Who telepathically told you about this idea?"

She just shrugged, smiled. The way she looked at me never contained pain. Our common bond seemed to be that we were both really wonderful shruggers. Technically, I was still married. Technically, I was a father. She didn't care about any of that. We didn't talk about her past either. It was a great shroud of mystery, the lives we'd occupied before our current day dream.

I stood up from the futon and walked next to her. She looked up at me. Her eyes were so blue that I never worried about the grey skies over Iceland that seemed like they would never leave. I extended my hand to her. She took it.

"Let's go get stoned and drive around the island."

tveir

No one knew where I was. I didn't know where they were. We raced our little car through golden fields, soggy with sweeping rain. The wind whipped, the car slid. Volcanoes in the distance waited silently to spill magma across us all. Bee drove, 10 and 2, mouthing along to her Peter Gabriel tape—not the one with *Sledgehammer*, the other one. The way she squinted, looking far off ahead, I knew she needed glasses—but try to tell her that.

"You're crazy," she'd say. "Plus, I live by sense of taste, smell, and touch anyway."

"I think there is something down there in the road," I concluded.

She laid on the gas and we zipped along. I held a Nikon camera on my lap as if I was bouncing a baby on my knee. It was probably just as heavy. I wondered if Sarah had named the kid, Nikon. Then I wondered why I had wondered that.

Bee was OK with my sloth, my laziness, laying there on the futon like Han Solo encased in carbonite. She'd never had a job—ever. Ever: in the history of forever. I'd worked for most of my past life, so it only made sense that I take a break from overworking myself. I'd pet the Nikon as we drove, as if it was a small lap dog. My fingertips grazed the cold steel of its housing. I thought about the silliness with Ted's gun. I wanted a PayDay bar like you wouldn't believe.

Bee's family was in the elastic band business. She came from old elastic band money. Her real name was Beverly. I saw it on her passport. I wanted to call her Beverly while she rode on top of me, but she would get so angry. I once called her Beverly at a vegetable market near Leif Erickson's house, and she hit me in the face with a rhubarb then left the market. That was one of only two times I saw her cry with anger against me.

Bee worshiped the full moon. She had a hardcover copy of Linda Goodman's Love Signs that she carried everywhere. She loved me for reasons that Sarah did not. I felt a kinship with her, not a love. There was no infatuation. The lunatic, can't-shut-them-off-fireworks I'd shared for a time with Sarah never went off with me and this artist.

Both women had come from different holes in the earth. Bee was built with poetry, Woody Allen film references. She asked me what I thought about rain and wind and coral reefs and death. Sarah lived a life of cigarettes and Bruce Springsteen on the juke-box, tight ripped jeans, writing our names on walls with a gold Sharpie, whispering in my ringing ear underneath neon signs as the night hummed. The earth must have been collapsing in on itself; I missed her.

"Oh this is gonna be good," Bee said.

Enthusiasm coursed through her veins, but didn't reach me. I wanted to shake the shit out of her say, "LOOK, NOTHING IMPORTANT IS GONNA COME OUT OF THIS SLAUGHTER-HOUSE EXPEDITION!" Roadkill just didn't do it for me.

Down there in the road there was a small object.

"Oh! I hope it's a wolf!"She was obsessed with finding an arc-tic wolf for the calendar. "Hand me the Nikon, love."

I passed it over. That was my only function.

We stopped fifty feet in front of the object in the road. Bee leapt out, photographed it. Generally, I didn't get out of the ve-hicle. After a few moments, she came back, frowning, huffing and puffing. She tossed her camera in the back and slammed the door.

"Well, do you want to know what it was?"

"Yeah, OK. What was it?"

"IT WAS A CHILD'S DOLL!"

We drove thirty miles one way and thirty miles back. We were out of petrol when we got back to the flat, and she still didn't have a fitting candidate for Miss or Mr. April. Where the hell were all of the dead animal celebrities?

"I think you are going to have to get a job if this project is ever going to get off of the ground."

"A job?"

Just a day later, Bee met a woman at that goddamned vegetable stand who was the wife of a boat captain, a man named Kjern who looked exactly like Ahab except he wore Ray Ban sunglasses.

"Found you a job," Bee said as I studied another magazine on the futon.

"Porn star?" I asked.

"Commercial fisherman," she said

Þrír

The ship was called Sága. On a chilly, pre-dawn morning, I walked up the ramp with a bounce in my step, whistling the theme to The Andy Griffith Show. For the first time in my life, I was excited about the idea of work. It was a strange sensation. I'd really put a groove into the futon. My blood felt like glue. My muscles like jello pudding. It was good for me to get the glue moving.

Bee was out of money. She was being a prideful fool, refusing to ask her ma and pa, the elastic waistband industrial tycoons, for more. Kronors, we had no kronors. Dinero. Clams. Guacamole. Smackers. Cashola. Greenbacks. None of that.

On the dock, headlights on, Bee honked the horn, yelled, "Good luck! Catch some big ones, Jimmy!" As she drove away, I wondered if they were gonna pay me by the fish. In fish? Both those things? The crew glared down at me in their knit caps and high-visibility jackets. I stopped whistling.

It was three hours before dawn. I helped two other crewmates hoist the anchor, then they disappeared into bunks below deck. I watched the sun coming over the water as we embarked through tides and ripping currents. My next order of business was trying to show the captain that I was all right.

But he didn't say much, or anything at all really. I stood by his side, watching him steer. He looked good at steering. Twenty minutes went by, and he still hadn't said a word. The clouds were dark spots on a sky that was growing lighter. It appeared as if we were headed into a storm, I thought.

"It looks like we are headed into a storm," I said.

The captain shrugged, said nothing. The wind picked up. It almost blew me off the boat, but I tripped on a net and was wrapped up, didn't go over. The captain saw all of this, said nothing. He had a cooler at his feet, he opened the cooler and retrieved a beer from murky water. A star fish was stuck to the side of the can. He added a cigarette to his lips, and the cooler water splashed up and over the side. The wind pulled the cigarette out over the dark water. I went below deck.

The two other members of the crew were Halldor and Fjalar. Both of them were lying on the floor: one was reading a biology textbook, the other was trying to sleep. As I came down the stairs, Halldor put down his textbook and said, "It's gonna be bad."

"Today?" I asked.

"No, tomorrow and the following days."

"Well, then we just don't go out."

He looked at me like I was an idiot, "We're already out. Too late."

I sat down on a box. Halldor said that my section of the floor, being that I was new, was the stairs. "You'll have to sleep on the stairs."

"I'm not going to be doing much sleeping," I said. "I don't like to sleep on the job."

"No sleep?"

"Nope, I'm good."

"For 31 days?"

"31 days?!" I was stunned.

It was the first I had heard of that. I assumed it was an eight hour shift, and that we would arrive at the dock sometime before dinner.

"The captain never said anything about 31 days!"

"He can't speak," Fjalar said, opening one eye. "Take it easy or you'll wind up like the last deckie."

The last deckie had gotten in an altercation with the captain and had gotten himself fired . . . right in the middle of the Atlantic Ocean and luckily not too close to the Arctic Circle. He was sent off the Sága in a life raft. He was still missing.

"I'll have to ask the captain about all of this."

"I wouldn't," Fjalar warned.

"Besides, he don't speak," Halldor said. "Throat cancer, and they had to remove his throat. He don't speak."

"They have those little voice box mechanisms now. Why doesn't he get one of those?"

"Why don't you ask him?"

fjórir

Until that first night as a commercial fisherman, I'd enjoyed my stay in Iceland very much. I found the country to be beyond beautiful. In Iceland, I was as free as I'd been in junior high school. Everyday, I woke up feeling as if I had just been born. I had pins and needles in all my fingertips. I could almost slam dunk a basketball. Wine went down and never came back up. Dogs in the street smiled at me. There were no lonely nights, no wounded days, no pain. I had nothing to do, nowhere to go. I had started to paint pictures. I had carved a chair out of old wood. My parents were both dead. My wife, estranged, visited me like a spirit, but did me no harm. I didn't know my child's name. Or sex. I timed myself, to see how long I could hold my breath; I was impressed: 52 seconds.

Sometimes in the black night, I'd wink at the shine of the moon, knowing that Sarah was under it. I didn't care if she was doing the same for me. But Bee wouldn't wash my chest in the shower. She didn't like oranges. She'd never been to Graceland or Florida. All that felt important.

I couldn't sleep that first night on the stairs of the ship. All I could do was think back in blurred disbelief on the two previous years I had spent on my international adventure. The volcanoes glowing, the smoke drifting across the road, cities shimmering in the distance as Bee drove and I sat there with the Nikon on my lap. I wondered what her reaction to finding me in the road would be. My throat ripped out. My ribcage exposed.

Would she be surprised to see that I had no heart?
Would Beverly take my photo? Would I be Mr. November?

fimm

I opened my eyes. Fjalar kicked my shoe. Halldor scratched his nuts. They wanted me to come up on deck. Both of them were in bright yellow slickers. I sat up, followed them without a slicker—apparently I was supposed to bring my own.

It was raining heavily and had rained heavily for twelve days. Our schedule in that harsh rain was as follows: wake up, throw out the nets, go downstairs to get out of the rain, drink, clean fish, cook fish, walk upstairs, pull the nets in, drink, clean and cook more fish, entertain ourselves however possible—card games, talking about how crazy the captain was. They seemed to think I was a very adept cartoonist. As I drew, at their request, they egged me on:

"OK, make Minny Mouse a little sexier."

"Make her ass firmer."

"Yes, make Elmer Fudd's cock longer."

Once, hearing gunshots, I went up and saw the captain shooting into the sea. Although it was dark, he was wearing Ray-Bans. No explanation was given; none was sought. Knowing for certain that the captain had a gun, I slept less soundly on my stairs.

I told my crewmates how I used to work in a tollbooth. After ten minutes of stories, they begged me to tell them no more stories. I didn't even get to the interesting parts about me rescuing Wanda and her daughter Allison Lewis from the car fire; my mental breakdown; Kid with Clownhead; the pineapple; Gena's sweet titties; my hatred of José; my hatred of the neighbor and his crappy dog; Sarah's amazing silver dollar pancakes; Bee's roadkill calendar.

Halldor said, "America . . . who fuh-king cares?"

On the fourteenth day, I began to rot in my clothing. I hadn't brought any spares. Halldor ordered me to go away from them.

"The smell of fish is bad enough . . ."

I laughed.

"I was on the TV once," I said. Halldor gave me the evil eye. We all knew what came after the evil eye. He kept a knife in his boot that he sharpened often. Also, Halldor was much larger than me. So, when he interrupted my story, raising one hand, point-ing—

"Go into the engine room. And take your stench with you, or we will have to kill you."

"I didn't know we were going to be at sea for this long . . ."

"Sssshh. Go talk to the engine."

I went into the engine room, laying next to the screaming en-gine, I closed my eyes. I couldn't sleep, so I opened my eyes, look around in there. Just a boring, loud engine room. But, I did find an old notebook. On the inside cover, it said *Property of Lyrghrn Fjlryn*. The rest of the notebook was empty.

I had a pen in my pocket because I always had a pen in my pocket. What is the use of being penless? After another three at-tempts to fall asleep, I began to fill the notebook with everything that happened since Sarah's pregnancy. I didn't leave the engine room until Halldor came there a day and a half later.

"You're still in here?" He left momentarily, coming back with a set of clean clothes. "Jesus Christ, I was just kidding with you, man. I guess you Americans never heard of sarcasm."

I left the engine room for a while but found myself missing it for some odd reason. Maybe just because I knew my place in it, similar to how inmates feel comfort in their cells. As we hoisted the net, random silver fish flopped in its confines. We dumped them on the deck; it's obvious that most aren't happy to be trapped but the majority of the fish who've been plucked out of the vast poten-tial of the deep blue sea just lay there, like, "I'm bored."

It occurred to me then why I liked the engine room, why it somehow reminded me of home. It was the same size as the coat closet where I used to jerk off when I was a little kid, the same size as the downstairs bathroom in my house with Sarah. It was the same dimensions as the inside of the tollbooth.

sex

And this is how it went for quite a number of days: pull the fish in, throw the fish in the hold—a disgusting saltwater tank in the center of the vessel, go down into the cabin, sit with Halldor as he reads his biology book and watch Fjalar as he slept. They played no cards, they told no stories. This made me miss my good friend Ted, who would have played cards, told stories. I started to feel bad about not even letting Ted know that I was alive.

From up top, we heard more gunshots.

Halldor flipped a coin, said, "Heads you go up; tails, I go."

It landed against me, but we all saw that coming.

Something was strange up top, a new sound: the sound of the rain having stopped. The captain stood at the edge of the vessel, again firing into the black sea.

"You sonofabitch," he snarled at the water, smoke rising from the barrel of the gun, "I GOT YOU!"

I stood benignly in the moonlight, not sure if I was about to get shot too or if something wonderful was happening instead. The man looked reborn. Drunk, proud of his aim, whatever that aim had found.

"LOOK AT THIS," he shouted.

I stepped to the edge, saw nothing other than the black and the reflection of the moon on the black. There were no stars.

"THERE," he yelled, as a whale breached. My stomach sunk. We were on such a small boat.

"It's just a killer whale," he said. "Don't worry, those things are harmless."

I gulp.

"Then why call it killer?"

"Same reason we call it Iceland, dumbass." He leans over the rail, spits into the water. "It's been following us, so I've been shooting it."

"Why?"

"I don't like being followed."

"Oh . . ."

"Stupid thing wants our fish."

I didn't see how that was so stupid.

After checking the barrel with his wet fingers and deciding that it'd cooled enough, he placed it in his pocket.

"I thought you didn't talk. They said you had your larynx removed."

"A man supposes that his ship is the world. The world has everything, and so does the ship. There is the leader, the dreamer, the clown, and the fool."

"Oh."

"Don't listen to Halldor. He has something wrong with his brain. That's why is he's always reading that Biology book. He's trying to find a way to fix his broken brain."

I went back to the engine room . . . for safety's sake.

Sometime later, there was a ghostly call on the water. I imagined it was the killer whale slowly bleeding to death, drawing sharks. What I didn't know, was that it was Sarah's mother. She had finally found me. Her two years of searching were over. She came through the wall of the engine room. She did not smile, but sat down calmly on the chugging machine. She opened her mouth and began to speak.

sjö

There was an afternoon, quite a few months before the fishing trip, where Bee and I laid around the flat drinking Spanish wine and watching the snow fall. She kept grabbing my hands delicately, saying they were so soft and pink, that she had never seen hands so soft and pink.

"The lines on your palms are as vivid as a baby's. They look like brand new Michelin tire treads."

"Keep drinking," I said.

She brought the bottle to her lips, laughed.

"I wish I was a fortune teller," she said.

"Who doesn't?"

"I'd read your palms and see the future," she said seriously. "Then we'd know what to do, also what not to do."

I explained, "Ya know, my dear, these are the perfect kind of hands for collecting tolls, but sadly . . . nothing else."

She was serious when she asked, "Do you miss it?" As if it was a great calling. Toll collecting: a mission from God.

"Nawwww," I said, pulling my hands away in case she could actually read something from the lines. Why were all the women in my life mystics? Sarah, her mother Dolly, Bee. Mystics. Even my own mother predicted her own death.

"I'm not so sure. You seem like you miss it. I've seen your eyes when clerks give you back change of a Kronor."

"Ha! Change of a kronor, you made a funny."

She smirked, "I remember your hands, when you first gave

me change."

"Oh?"

"I knew you were married. Even though you never mentioned it."

"It wasn't a secret or anything."

"Just never came up? You didn't wear your ring, why?"

"I took it off when she killed my dog."

"Sad."

"It doesn't matter. She left me," I said. "Well, it was complicated. We were both shitheads. It was kind of a contest to see who could be the biggest shithead."

"It doesn't matter," Bee said. She looked away from me, out the window, her dreads hid her entire face. The fun was almost over.

"Come on, don't get weird," I said.

"Do you still love her?"

"No."

"So what do you love?"

"Nothing," I say. "Maybe Ted. Maybe I love Ted."

"Who's he?"

"The only person who gave me good advice when I was out on the ledge, I'd have killed myself if it wasn't for him. Ah, nothing. I love nothing. Final answer."

"Nothing?" She took it, took my ring finger, squeezed. "This little piggy used to belong to somebody who loved you and whom you loved."

"You ever belong to anybody?"

"No. Not yet."

"Keep yourself. Don't give yourself to anybody, all the way anyway. Save a little hiding spot."

"We're still strangers," she said.

"I didn't want to get to know you."

"I didn't want to get to know you. You belong to her? Does she belong to you?"

"No more. We're strangers too." I said.

"Familiarity is a passing glance between two pedestrians heading in opposite directions on a busy sidewalk."

"Yes it is."

"What happened between you and your wife."

"She was mauled by a tiger in the middle of the Philadelphia zoo."

"Get out!"

"It was horrible."

"I'm so sorry . . ."

"It's OK. You couldn't have known." I sigh, "Besides, I can't blame you for being jealous. Before the tiger ripped her head off, she was a very beautiful woman."

"I bet she was."

"Not that you're not."

"I'm also stupid though, very stupid."

"You?"

"What kind of prick says some bullshit about a tiger eating his wife?"

"A guy trying to lighten the mood with humor."

"You wish she was really dead?"

"No, I don't wish anybody dead."

"What happened between you and her?'

"People go through a metamorphosis."

"Bullshit."

"They do," I said flatly.

She had my ring finger tightly in her grasp. Her mouth was open; all her teeth were sharp. She had a mouth to be feared.

"Do you want me to bite it off? Maybe you'll grow a new finger. You can try again."

"I'm not a worm," I said, which was maybe a lie.

"I'm missing a part. You can miss a part too." Bee had a prosthetic foot. I didn't realize that until we'd already been together for a year. That says a lot about the both of us, doesn't it?

"Sarah wanted a baby," I told Bee. "I didn't want to give her a baby."

"Sarah," she said. "Her name was Sarah?"

"Is Sarah. Why?"

Suddenly paler than usual, Bee said, "I had a dream, a few dreams, and I was afraid that you were going to say that her name is Sarah."

"Why?"

"In the dream, there was a woman looking for you. She's old, wears black, horn-rimmed glasses, has a high pitched voice. She said that she was Sarah's mother."

"Dolly."

"Yeah, that's her name. That's what she said."

"Oh fuck," I remarked. "All you women are goddamned mystics."

"She said she was looking for you but that she couldn't find you."

"What did you say?"

"In those dreams, I never say anything. I would never rat you out."

"You have a lot of honor."

"I think it's attachment."

"That's OK."

We pulled the covers up, making a nest around ourselves.

átta

The engine room of the Sága was a loud, horrible place . . . that is, until the ghost of Sarah's mother began to materialize. As she came into focus, everything suddenly got quiet and calm, as if I had cotton balls stuffed in my ears. Dolly got in my face.

"Jimmy, you're a real piece of shit."

I had no response. I just glanced at her in her favorite white smock with the tire track, floral pants, only a little bloody. Lilies. She'd died in spring.

Dolly said it again as I sat there like an emotionless hunk of stone, "A real piece of shit!"

"Look, Dolly, I'm sorry," I muttered, looking anywhere but her. Wherever I looked, she moved to stay in my line of sight.

"I've been looking for you for two fucking years! Look at me when I talk to you."

"Well, you found me."

"What kind of man deserts his wife and child like that?"

"Hey, you told me I was no good the first time that I came over. You should be happy! You were right! Doesn't that make you . . . eh . . ."

"I'd smack you, dummy, if I was on your plane of existence."

Sometimes when she spoke, her voice morphed into strange animalistic sounds reverberating into tinny echoes. She had a blue tint to her. I thought she looked really good for a dead woman. I wanted to kiss her.

"So, is it a girl?"

"Yeah."

"Name?"

"Gena."

I flinched, hearing that. Why had Sarah listened to me?

"I like it. Despite its origin, I like it," Dolly remarked. "Grandmas love unconditionally, even from beyond the grave, but Dolly would have been a much nicer name if you ask me."

"Middle name?"

"I didn't get the honor of the middle name either," she shrugged. "Sarah never liked me but girls usually have that problem: hating their mothers."

"I loved my Mother."

"Congratulations, asshole," she shrieked. "Man loved his mother, wants a fucking medal for it. What are you doing on this rotting boat? You're no fisherman."

"It was a mistake," I said. "Now I'm stuck."

She howled with laughter. "Stuck?! He's Stuck!" Then, in my face like a nightmare, "You ever heard of limbo?"

"Look, Dolly, I'm sorry you're in limbo. What do you want me to do about it?"

"Get back together with Sarah. Be a decent human being . . ."

"And that'd get you out of limbo? I'm a little unclear on all of the technical mumbo jumbo."

"No, it wouldn't get me anywhere, but at least I could sleep at night. I'm always worrying about her."

"I won't do that."

"You won't do it for me? As a favor?"

"You can't take blood from a stone."

"A very wise cliché from a very unwise peon."

"Where do you get off insulting me about living life? What the fuck did you ever do? Every time I was around, you would be sitting at the kitchen table, knitting."

"Knitting is not a crime."

"Get out of here. Stop harassing me for trying to live a life full of adventure."

She laughed so hard, she slammed into the wall, disappeared through it. I could still hear her out there, laughing.

"Laugh it up!!!"

"JIM! Listen to me," she came back through, "Sarah's not doing so well. Believe it or not, she needs your help. End this fiasco."

"I didn't start it. She left me."

"First of all, you didn't try very hard to get her back. SECOND, I AM NOT EVEN REFERRING TO THAT FIASCO! I am referring to the one that got me crushed on that basketball court. You should've never let her drive that car!"

"I was trying to be nice."

"BACKFIRED," she screamed. I jumped. She crossed her arms, huffing and puffing. "And if you don't go back to her, I'll keep haunting you," she said. "I will always be bothering you."

"Rewind. You said Sarah isn't happy?"

"Duh," she snickered. "Destroy the car."

"She doesn't like the kid?" I shook my head. "I told her that she wouldn't like the kid. I told her so."

"Destroy the car."

"I'M NOT GONNA DESTROY MY CAR, DOLLY!"

Fjalar opened the door.

"Will you shut up! I never heard somebody write in a diary so LOUD!"

I looked down at the yellow notebook. I'd drawn a topless picture of Sarah sucking on an orange slice.

"It's not a diary," I shouted. That word was embarrassing.

The next day, all I could think about was getting off the boat. No matter how hard I tried to not think about it, it was all I could think about.

"How many more days," I asked Halldor.

He shrugged, "Fourteen."

"Fourteen more days?" I can't take fourteen more days here."

Halldor studied my eyes. He stunk like garlic. I wondered where he had gotten garlic. What other luxuries did they have that I don't know about?

"What," I asked, annoyed.

He kept studying. I bobbed and weaved. He bobbed along, weaved along, all the while studying. "Yup, just as I thought," he finally concluded.

"What is it," Fjalar interjected.

"He's gone mad."

"Shit. Sea madness," Fjalar said, "I suspected it last night! He woke me up from a great dream, ranting and raving to himself in the engine room."

They tried to get a hold of me and they had little trouble; they were powerful Scandinavian fishermen and I was a meager American tollbooth operator. They brought me to the captain.

"Captain, he's mad."

"Mad about what?"

"No, mad in general, as in madness," Fjalar clarified.

"Oh . . . coo coo, over the rainbow . . ."

"Gone fishing . . ." they all said in unison.

The captain let go of the wheel, revealed that silver revolver, said, "No room on this vessel for wackos."

They led me to the back of the ship, where I hadn't noticed— the plank.

"You know what to do," the captain said, cocking his gun.

Reluctantly, I jumped into the dark water. The captain lazily shot his weapon at me, but it didn't matter. Halldor chucked the notebook I'd been drawing pictures of Sarah in towards me; it was in a Ziploc bag.

"Don't forget your diary," he shouted.

They threw a lifesaver, a ring of hope to cling to in the dark water.

As I bobbed on the ring, all I could think about was the killer whale. I prayed it was imagined and not somewhere near.

And then I called out, "Dolly, where are you?"

I was worried. I wanted someone to talk to until the worrying was over. The boat went cruising away. As the sun fell, I was all alone in the sea.

níu

Nearly frozen, nearly dead, I drifted on the icy ocean expecting death. I wasn't surprised when I began to see and feel a glow all around me. I'd heard about that. The peace that overtakes the dying. There was even the sound of an orchestra. Angels, I thought. I looked up at the lights, my eyes almost sealed shut by ice. "H-h-h-heaven . . . " I muttered.

I heard the massive horn of a ship hovering above me. A spot light lit me up in the water. Voices. Shouts. Someone threw a net and scooped me up as if I were just another fish.

On the deck, shivering and stuttering, they brought me blankets as I tried to pantomime my plight explaining to the crew what had happened. They took me inside to thaw out. When my teeth stopped chattering, someone brought me a satellite phone and I called Bee on her cell.

"Where have you been?" Bee asked on the other end of the line.

"At s-s-sea," I said, "baby—on the S-s-s-Sága . . . they k-k-k-kicked me off."

"Where are you now?"

"At sea," I said, chugging hot tea. My internals melting.

"At sea? Are you insane?"

"They made me w-w-w-walk the plank."

"Who?"

"The captain, and I thought I was going to die, because there were k-k-killer whales . . . "

"Look, I don't need this. If you wanted to break up that's fine. I never even knew we were really together, but you don't have to go faking some sea voyage to get out of it."

"I'm not faking it."

"No?"

"I'm on another ship. They picked me up. I almost froze!"

"Froze?" she was silent, all I heard was wind. "Do you love me now?"

"Where are you? Y-y-yeah, I love you n-now," I was shivering and I was hallucinating. I noticed for the first time that the whole crew was in tuxedos even though they were fishermen.

"I went to see where Leif Erickson lived," Bee said.

"Hold on, I'll find out where we're going."

The crew told me they were from Norway. I yelled, "I CAN'T GO TO NORWAY!"

They told me to calm down. I refused to calm down.

"They're taking me to Norway!" I yelled into the phone.

"I heard, I heard . . . Jesus," Beverly said.

Then, a man who spoke pretty good English came over and grabbed my wrist. He took the phone from me and informed Bee that I'd be in Reykjavik in four days.

"Baby, can you wait four more days for me?"

"Take as long as you want," Bee said. The line went dead.

I found out later that it wasn't a fishing boat, it was a cruise. I'd interrupted a wedding. During the champagne toast, the captain had seen me directly in the line of his travel. They thought I was a dead seal. When someone began hoisting me out of the water, it had really enhanced the good feelings involved in two souls being bonded. The bride and groom thought it was good luck. The groom himself hoisted a dying man from the freezing clutches of the endless sea.

tíu

It's strange how quickly life returns back to normal. Just a week later, I was back at our flat. Bee was leafing through photos of dead animals. I was watching television. There was a news report and they were interviewing a hospitalized man. I didn't recognize him at first, but it was Halldor. His head was bandaged and they'd shaved his beard. He talked very weak, saying, "Then the whale attacked the ship, and the ship went down . . . "

"I KNOW THAT GUY!" I shouted.

Bee shut the TV off. I glared at her. "I missed my period," she said.

"Don't say that."

"Last month too."

"Not this again," I said.

We went down to the corner store and bought a pregnancy test. Bee was very upset and started to cry at the register. I had to pay the clerk while she just stood there bawling. Outside, I pulled her into an alley.

"I think that if I'm pregnant, I'm just gonna have to kill myself," she threatened.

"Don't do that," I said. "You do that, I'll do the same thing. It won't be good for either of us."

"Yeah, so, you at least have the decency to murder me first?" she said. "I need a drink."

So we walked down the alley into the bar across from the hotel where we lived. It was quiet in there. The bartender regarded

Bee's crying and he leaned in real close said, "The world is real beautiful, and if you don't believe it, here is proof . . . "He slid her an upside down plastic cup, a free drink.

The rest of us without tears, we would have to pay dearly for our drinks.

I took Bee over to the jukebox and together we picked some songs even though most of them were Icelandic pop songs. I kept looking for Bruce Springsteen, remembering Sarah dumping untold fortunes of quarters into the jukebox at the Spider bar, playing "There's a Darkness on the Edge of Town" and "Thunder Road". There were diamonds among the Icelandic jukebox though, we plucked them out with whatever coins we could drop into the slot. Then we sat down again in the dimness around an unused dart board. I guess everybody knew that bullseyes no longer existed how they once had.

"I don't think you're pregnant," I admitted.

"I don't want to be."

"So remain positive."

"Positivity can't solve everything."

"You should go into the bathroom and just take it now."

"Not in a pub," she said.

"Why not?"

"If I'm pregnant I am just gonna have to drink Drano."

"No you won't."

"Why?"

"Because I won't let you."

"That's sweet."

She went into the bathroom for a minute, came out. "I can't bring myself to do it now," she said.

There was a buzz in the bar, the few customers that were there gathered by the window. "There's a fire," someone said.

Firetrucks were dumping a million gallons of water on the blaze. We stood beside the window too. It was our apartment. I could see the fire in our window. I'd left rice cooking on the stove.

"The night just keeps on getting better," I confirmed.

Our things were burnt. Everything we owned, which wasn't much anyway.

We took the car north, both of us feeling free and shot out of cannons even though the test said that Bee was in fact, pregnant.

ellefu

Having no home, we drove. Bee told me of the beauty out there. We pretended that everything would be alright. Water drawn up from the hot springs was stored in the hills, naturally heating the homes, running through pipes in the walls.

The mountains that lined the rim of everything threatened that they might turn into volcanos at any point and burn us and this section of earth away for our carelessness and sin.

I opened the glove box and gave Bee some tissues to blow her nose.

It'd been decided: we were going to see waterfalls and then she was going to get an abortion. She didn't want to keep the baby and I didn't want her to keep the baby. On a lonely highway on the brink of utter breathlessness we stopped in a little store. They sold shirts and things there. *I (heart) Iceland.* I bought us some food and went out to the car. The attendant came over, at first I thought he was gonna yell at me for pumping my own petrol but then I remembered we weren't in New Jersey. Instead, he told me there was a problem, Bee was in the bathroom and wouldn't come out.

I knocked and she didn't say anything. The man spoke loud and fast. He wanted the door opened, or he was calling the police. "I saw her go in there with razors. Is she sick? She might be dead."

"Are you dead?" I asked the door.

No response, the man went to get the key to the bathroom

from under the counter and I started to break the door down. Bee screamed from inside. I stopped smashing and the man ran over with the key but she opened the door on her own.

Her eyes were puffy and red, her dreadlocks were gone. She'd hacked them off. They laid in piles on the floor, in the sink and on the toilet seat. The severed dreads looked like large dead caterpillars waiting for crows to come and get fat on their leftovers.

We left there quickly, headed for the hot springs and the waterfalls.

I held her hand for the last time as we drove upward.

tólf

There were good times with her, just like there'd been good times with Sarah. We'd walk hand in hand like probiotic fiends exchanging life support through each other's palms through the streets. We would see things with our eyes and feel things with our hearts and our brains would coo with satisfaction at the impulses and chemicals we were releasing into its wet tank.

We still had money then, not that I think money had anything to do with our happiness.

"It's really stupid for us to live in Iceland and not be able to speak Icelandic," she said.

"It is," I agreed.

And so we'd go and meet with an instructor and he would show us how to place our tongues in our mouth to say certain words such as cat and dog and grass and sun and moon and please and hello and thank you and expressions such as I love you. But we were bad students and could never do it right, so he would go to the sink in the corner of the room and he would wash his hands and then he would come sit in front of us. We would open our mouths and slowly pronounce the word over and over again, his hand in our mouth, moving the tongue for us. It was very hard and very expensive.

Bee hated animals so very much. That had a great effect on how much love I could give back to her. I said, "Not all dogs are bad. My friend has this Rottweiler that will eat anything. A very useful dog."

"One ran away with my foot."

"What?"

She said it'd been taken away by a stray dog who lived behind the building where her car crash had happened. The Silver City, she said. I had no idea where the Silver City was. The doctor had said it wouldn't have mattered, even if they had found the foot immediately the nerve damage was in such a way that they would not have been able to reattach it. Regardless, she hated dogs, I suppose sometimes people are allowed their hatred as a crutch that even they get no joy in leaning on, but do so anyway.

Bee walked fine, you'd never know.

Sarah lost a mother and limped for the rest of her life.

After Bee's procedure . . . our procedure, the baby gone . . . the car died. We took the train east into the sprawl of lakes and hot springs that boil and mist in the night. For endless days the sun refused to disappear. In our last hours together, we walked single file down a trail through woods that looked like they were filled with things from fairy tale books. I wanted a sword to slay orcs if they jumped out. There was a waterfall, its torrent like something from beyond. Godafoss, it was called. Bee had hash that we smoked on an outcropping of rocks, watching the water fall forever, wondering where it was going in such a hurry.

"Why do glaciers bother to form? Just to melt?"

She frowned behind me, I could feel it, as she massaged the knots from my shoulder. I cracked her knuckles for her because she wanted them cracked but didn't like to crack her own. It made her stomach hurt to cause herself pain. But she would willingly allow others to do it for her.

She began to pull the moss in thick chunks from the wall. Padding the rocks with it. We layed down next to the waterfall, hovering right on the edge of sleep, soft and strange and parting ways.

þrettán

I have a scar on my hand to remember those days. That's fine. Some relationships leave physical scars. Some are mental. They're all there.

We were staying at a small inn about a mile from the waterfall. That evening we had our last meal together. Her eyes looked devoid of feeling for me. I'd worn her down. That was all I could think. I'd finally done it. I was not proud.

"Tell me more about your wife?"

"Sarah? What's there to say? She drugged me once and shaved my head in my sleep."

She laughed so hard at that.

"Did you deserve it?"

"Probably, and it made her feel better."

"Hmmm," she said, sipping the last of her wine.

While I was asleep, Bee put a piece of metal into the fire, waited until it was white hot, then she put it on my hand. A human being has never screamed that loud before. There I was rolling around on the carpet, grasping onto my hand. She gathered her things. There were not many things.

"Goodbye," she said at the door of our room.

"AWWWWWWWHHHHHH."

"I am not happy about this . . . "

"AWWWWWWWWWWHHHHHHHHHH."

"I don't want you to forget me, that's why . . . "

"AAAAWWWWWWWWWHHHHHHHHHHHHHHHHHH."

"I loved you."

"AWWWWWWWWWWWWWHHHHHHHHHHHH"

I will never forget you, you evil demented roadkill wacko.

By the time I was down the stairs. Bee was already pulling away in the car sent from mom and pop. I stuck my hand into the snow. Much steam went up.

The inn keeper was at the kitchen table in his robe. He was sipping a cup of tea, spooning hot cereal into his mouth.

"She's gone," I said.

"I saw," he said. "What was that screaming?"

I showed him my hand.

"Been there, done that," he assured me. "Don't let it happen again." It was fine advice.

fjórtán

Dear Ted,

I don't know if you remember me or not. Five years . . .whoa. Time just erases people and places and things—poof! They're gone.

I still have a good picture in my mind of all of those that I left behind in New Jersey that come running up to me in the darkness of dreams, saying things that they would have said if they had never changed. But, time changes people. Even me.

How so? I now wear European underwear and I can say fifty words in Icelandic. Dog. Cat. Bathroom. Sex. Yes. No. Taco is the same here. So is burrito.

All joking aside, as you can see from this letter, I'm still alive, and I have learned how to type. Very impressive.

But, I'm stranded here at the gates of oblivion, and it's rain ing out. I'm friendless and directionless in Scandinavia and need your help. I was with a woman for the last five years, I met at the tollbooth. Yes, can you believe it? She took me to Reykjavik. Can you believe that either?

Bee, her name was. I won't say anything bad about her, be cause you think there is good in everyone and wouldn't listen to my complaints anyway. My hand is melted though. The skin is gone. She burnt me in my sleep. Nice girl. Real cute. She set me on fire.

Life is fucked up and confusing. Every time I think I've stum bled upon some cypher to unlock the truth, I find that the truth is just another code that nothing can descramble. It's all just a bunch of inside jokes that nobody outside ever un derstands. God must sit around his living room, looking at his crystal ball saying, "Look at these nut cases! THEY THINK EVERYTHING IS IMPORTANT, THAT EVERY THING IS LIFE AND DEATH!"

I got this tollbooth woman pregnant too. It happened here. Not in the tollbooth. The baby is gone now, only it never even got to be a baby. I don't know whether to feel bad about that or to feel like a hero for saving the world the burden of an other unloved creature who would be starving and vengeful all through its life at the very idea of being alive.

We didn't love each other. Bee, had gravity boots. She'd sleep upside down suspended from a bar. She'd snapped her back when she was a child in a car crash in Silver City. Even lost a foot. I missed holding Sarah from behind and watching the Simpsons, smelling her hair: that coconut shampoo she uses. You were right.

There are no tollbooths in this country, I have no money and the innkeeper has told me that I have until the end of the week to get out and then I will have to go find some other stray dogs to belong to.

Any ideas? Any money? Any rescue ropes that you could low er? Huh? Well?

Remember the times when we were in sandpits and couldn't even stand up straight? Good nights. I do love you, Ted. I should have listened to you. I should have gotten help. I should have voluntarily committed myself to the Mayweath er. Group therapy. Meds. Word association games with ink blots. All that crap.

I stole your turkey hunting gun, ya know. I'm sorry about that too. I met a man named Halldor on a fishing vessel called the Sága who said it was extremely hard to shoot a turkey with a pistol. I don't know, maybe he was right.

My happiest memory was my wedding night with Sarah. You and Kelly looked so happy dancing to that Zombies song. I held Sarah tight across the dance floor. I remember you giv ing me the thumbs up. I should have kept things positive with her. 100 percent thumbs up. We should have moved to Florida. We were looking into Clearwater. I could have taken a job with her cousin cleaning saltwater tanks at the aquari um.

I was happy with her until she was pregnant. I may have been a stupid motherfucker who deserved a bullet in his head for what happened, but sometimes life just seems to slip out from under a person. It's like watching a magician pull a ta ble cloth out from under so many glasses and plates and ran dom piles of silverware. It takes skill. Or maybe they're all trick glasses and plates and forks and knives made of lead, who knows . . . I'm not a magician.

Please, help an old friend out. Lower some rescue rope, and quick! I need to get on a plane. I need to get out of here. I need to get back to America. I've never felt so consumed with national pride. Everywhere I go, I think I hear the Star Spangled Banner playing. I can't sleep. I can't eat. Save my life, man. I beg you.

Your friend on the iceberg,
Jimmy Tollbooth

36

I got off the airplane with wobbly knees and a spinning head. We'd flashed across vast oceans through undulating darkness existing above and below. I'd eaten my peanuts greedily. The stewardesses were hardened slabs of steel. Our pilot hadn't even said hello.

At the gate, Ted was standing there with a sign that said, "BALD TOLLBOOTH COWARD." He was smiling at me, until I got closer and then the smile vanished and he whipped the giant yellow sign at me like a massive Chinese star. It hit me and cracked into shards that scattered across the waxed floor.

Ted lowered his head, charged at me, tackling me into an empty row of chairs. A fist flew into my chin, I bit down on my lip. A knee drove into my stomach. Ted was unleashing on me, like he hoped to kill me. His hands closed around my throat. His full weight pressed against my lungs. I floundered around to no avail. Something popped.

"STOP!" an airport worker screamed.

This broke Ted's spell, "STOP! STOP!" The world began to go black around the edges of my vision. Bright stars. Muffled sounds. He let go, stopped strangling me. I was relieved when the air rushed back into my lungs. I rolled over coughing and dry heaving.

Ted stood, tears in his eyes.

"You FUCK!" he yelled.

" . . . me?" I coughed, falling on my side.

"Yeah you," he said, booting me in the ribs. I was squashed.

Airport security came at that point. Two big guys, Ted's dude speaking rapidly in French, zip tying his hands.

"It's OK!" I shouted, "We're from New Jersey! That's how we say hello."

I caught my breath, struggled to my feet.

"We're fine! We're fine! Let him go."

They released Ted's hands. I kept my distance from him, just in case.

30

The parking lot was too big, it was snowing and my nose stung. The punch in between my eyes caused a headache. I followed Ted, noticing that he was dressed a lot nicer than he used to dress.

"Fancy shoes," I said.

"Thanks."

"You hit the lottery?"

"I got a promotion."

"At the DMV?"

"Uh huh." He faced me, "Keep up with the class Jim, we have an appointment in Montreal."

"Oh, I bet we do. Why Montreal?"

"You'll see," he said, stone faced.

"Something sinister?"

"I'm not sure, but if it is, it won't be my doing."

"Anybody who punches you in the face that hard must be out to get you," I said, my nose still bleeding. I was using my shirt sleeve to stop it. Very classy.

"The car is around here somewhere."

"What letter did you park it in?"

"I think C."

"We're in E."

"We have to walk through E and D to get to C, remember the alphabet?"

"Yeah."

"I got a kid now. Noah," he said.

"Oh . . ."

"Say congratulations, you leech," Ted instructed.

"Congratulations," I said, shaking his hand.

"It's a lot better than you made it out to be. Kids are alright, I mean . . ." he furrowed his brow, "nothing to run away to Greenland over."

"Iceland, fuck off."

"What? The abandoner is sensitive?"

"When did you become a bleeding heart?"

"I'm not a bleeding heart, I just have a heart, unlike my friend Jimmy who used to work in the tollbooth, who has no heart."

We stepped around an orange van and there was Ted's car—only I kinda couldn't believe what I was looking at because it was a car with rich history. It was my car, Diesel Cottontail. It had been fixed up. All the rust and dents removed. It'd been given a second chance.

He unlocked my car door as if he was my prom date, "Pretty sweet, right?" he said.

We climbed inside. The interior was completely restored, smelling like new leather. He turned the key, the engine rumbled. What a sound! What a growl! Diesel Cottontail was alive again!

"Sarah sold it to me," he informed.

"Shit."

"She was having this big sale. She sold all kinds of things out on the front lawn, then she sold the house."

"Oh."

"They tore it down and the woods behind your house, put up a 7-11." A convenience store. Lottery tickets. Coffee. Soda. Ice. Hot dogs on metal rollers.

"A 7-11! That fast?"

"The world is fast."

"Man, it is."

"So I hope you didn't have any treasure chests buried in your backyard or anything. It's been paved."

I didn't know what to say.

"That tree that you had the tire swing on . . . that's where the dumpsters are now."

"So the moral of this story is, do not abandon your wife and your new child, or God rips all of your old memories from the surface of the earth and puts up a convenience store."

"That's the message, yes."

"That's a hard message to take."

He put the car into gear and it moved fluidly. Diesel Cottontail seemed to love Ted much more than it'd ever loved me.

"I've got a secretary now," he said.

"Oh yeah, she hot?"

"Very hot."

"Congratulations."

"Now I look forward to doing paperwork."

"I should have just gotten a secretary, then I wouldn't have had to leave."

"Yeah, that would have fixed everything, you stupid asshole."

We left the airport and headed in some direction, what direction it was, I didn't know. I was just along for the ride. I asked him a few times where we were headed but he kept saying he didn't want to ruin the surprise. We climbed a steep hill and I was amazed at the power of the car. When it used to be mine, I would fear every hill. I would dread ascending them because I was always sure that the drive shaft was going to crack and I was going to be sent on a spiraling descent backwards where I would greet whatever the earth really had in store for me.

"I couldn't let this thing go to the junkyard," he said.

"Thank you."

"It would be too much like sending you to the morgue."

"Thanks for not sending me to the morgue."

Ted turned the car down a narrow road that swept downhill. The sky was just darkened enough. The streetlights came on. Snow began to fall and he pointed to the sign, Centre Cinema.

"A movie before we leave town," he said, drumming on the steering wheel, pulling into the lot.

"I don't think I'm in the mood for a movie."

"Let me take you anyway, I had a long drive here and I'm not looking forward to hitting the road just yet."

"Whatever you say."

There was a kid at the counter who sold us each a ticket. I decided to buy some popcorn. Another kid was leaning on the glass counter, it was a slow night in the movie house. When I came to him he looked at me as if he suspected he was in the middle of an odd dream, or losing his mind. I asked him for popcorn and a cherry Coke. He gave it to me for free with a strange look of recognition in his eyes, as if he wanted to shake my hand in appreciation and awe.

I figured he was stoned.

29

The theatre was about 3/4 of the way full. "This movie is pretty big here," Ted said, "It won the Montreal film fest, best documentary."

"Boring."

"They're trying to get distribution in America."

I shoved popcorn in my mouth as we took our seats in the middle, saying to Ted, "I should have eaten on the plane . . . but, free popcorn? That kid was a weirdo." He just shrugged.

The previews flickered off. Momentarily, the screen was blank.

"Where we going after this?" I asked.

"I'm going home."

"And me?"

"I was gonna drop you off at home."

"I don't have one," I muttered.

"No? What about the 7-11?"

The screen flickered, the lights went down to darkness and the images began to creep across the screen. "This better be good," I warned.

"People love this movie," he said. "It's pretty inspiring."

"I don't like real life," I said. "Let's leave."

"The director is making a lot of waves. People are freaking out about him. He's from our neck of the woods."

"So what, come on, let's go."

But he wouldn't let me leave.

It was a three part film that captured the lives of three people.

The first segment was about a woman who worked in one of the world trade center buildings that'd toppled on 9/11. It started out as a retelling of the events of September 11th, showing stock footage of the attacks and of New York City in horrible turmoil. After a few moments of that horror show, it centered on one woman in particular, Laura Mooreski. She was the mother of two, wife to a plumber who lived at the Jersey Shore in Seaside Heights. She'd been a secretary in NYC and made the commute every day.

Her kids got on camera, in tears. The plumber husband was with them too, crying. He said he wished for closure in her death. He said he wished that he could have seen her one last time, even if it had to be at her funeral. Her body was vaporized. They had an empty casket. Her carpool was interviewed, they all cried, saying what a great addition to the carpool she had been.

To make it all the absolute worse, as a close friend confided, someone had stolen the family dog off the clothesline. The screen went black.

"Then . . ." The narrator said, "In California, a woman was receiving a routine physical, the physical prompted further exams, which eventually diagnosed kidney cancer. She needed a kidney or she was going to die. The woman? Laura Mooreski."

The camera cuts back to a close up of Mike Mooreski, her plumber husband. It's some years from the original footage, he has put on a lot of weight and he is now wearing glasses. He looks coldly at the camera for a second, then gulps, says, "So . . . on a Thursday morning, I stop back at the house after dropping the kids off at school—my routine on a usual work day. I'm grabbing a quick cup of coffee before I go pick up my helper on the other side of town, and the phone starts to ring. I pick it up. Who's there? Whoddya think is there?"

"How did it feel to hear she was alive?" A voice off-screen asks.

"How did it feel? I don't even want to know how to begin answering that." Mike was getting angry, his face becoming red, "I mean, you can only have your heart ripped out once and then after that what are you then . . . heartless, right? And here she is, the mother of both my kids, my wife, the woman who I always loved—she's on the phone . . . "He starts to break down, "and she's not dead, and she didn't fucking die on that day or any other day, and she needs my help, because she wants to live . . . "

"What did you say?"

"What would you say? And don't judge me."

"Nobody's judging."

"I told her to go fuck herself and I hung up the phone."

The next scene was a hand held shot done by a camcorder. It passed down a long hospital hallway. The camera stopped at a door, "This is it." A hand turned a doorknob and the shot continued inward, coming to rest on a woman who was flat on her back in the hospital bed.

It was Laura Mooreski.

The film cut to a steady shot of her face, breathing tubes in her nostrils. "Well, things don't look good," she said, "and that is not, ehhhhh . . . any kind of an understatement . . ." Her face puffy, corpse-like, her eyes have bags under them that hold the weight of all the world.

"I received the second transplant last week and it looks like my body isn't accepting this one either. There's an infection, it's not good. I'm dying."

"For real this time?"

She managed to laugh, "Yeah, I guess for real this time." It's quiet for a few seconds, all we hear are machines beeping along with some heartbeat. Laura coughs.

"Have you heard from anybody? Your husband, your kids?"

"They are too little to know better, you know? It's not right for their father to not let them talk to me. I made mistakes," she said. "I made a lot of mistakes, but life is hard."

More silence.

"I would like to talk to them before I die. The only person that talks to me is Beth, my neighbor in Arizona, after I left. After September 11th and well, everyone assumed I was, ya know, dead."

"Yeah, dead," a voice says. "Do you regret faking your own death?"

"I was suicidal," she says. "If you can believe it, September eleventh was a very good day for me. It gave me a chance to leave my old life behind. I was very unhappy, unhappy about everything, even though my family loved me very much. I was sick."

"Now you are sick."

"In the desert for seven years I felt really alive."

"And you would do it again?"

"Sadly, yes. I would."

The screen fades out, white letters appeared that read Laura Mooreski born 1/13/74 died 5/2/08.

From that blackness the voice of the husband can be heard lightly sobbing, he says, "How the fuck could you do that to your family?"

As I sat there, I couldn't figure out if he was talking about what Laura did to them, or what they did to Laura by not forgiving her, by letting her die in that hospital bed all alone.

25

The second feature in the film was about a man named Tom who lived in a motel room also on the Jersey shore. It looked like the Shamrock Motel. Tom seemed halfway crazy, halfway drugged. He talked into the camera and told a story that took about twenty minutes all together to get across, the other ten minutes were scattered clips of him almost killing himself on a skateboard. It all would happen randomly throughout the narration, apparently he was a pretty decent skateboarder and the filmmaker thought it might be good to catch him doing some really crazy stunts in the midst of the unbelievable story he was explaining to the audience. The filming had a feeling that a lot of hallucinatory drugs were being consumed by both the filmmaker and this Tom character.

According to him, his wife and daughter had died in a car crash on the NJ parkway not too far from my tollbooth. After their death, he'd received a piece of mail from Hell offering him an opportunity to lease his soul to the forces of evil for two years. At the end of that lease, he was supposed to get whatever wish he wanted. His wish, well, he wanted his wife and daughter back from the great beyond, as he loved them very very much, according to his testimony.

"They set me up in a tiny apartment and during the day I had a desk job as a telemarketer. I would call people on Earth and try to get them to sell their souls to the devil in exchange for prizes and supernatural rewards, most of the time people just cursed at me and hung up. It was a hard job."

The filmmaker was laughing, laughing, laughing.

"Dude, don't laugh at me, that's messed up."

"I'll laugh if I want, you're so burnt out."

"Not as much as you. I'm not the one in a clown mask," Tom said.

Then Tom stood off the dirty motel bedspread and came at the camera angrily. The camera cuts to Tom skateboarding, he does a daredevil jump over three desks, they all have telephones and computer chairs. The camera cuts to a sword fight between a one armed figure dressed in a devil costume and Tom.

The camera cuts back to the motel room.

"I bought the costume at a yard sale just down the block from me. Two bucks," the director says.

"Too fucking funny." Tom was smoking a cigarette, appearing to be as drunk as his limit would allow. He said, "And then when I was in Hell, I had this other phone on my desk, a red one. It'd ring and . . . oh, get this, it'd be people calling a suicide hotline only it was my job to insult them and tell them that they deserved to die and would be happier dead and so forth. If they killed themselves as a result of my insults and threats and laughs, the boss of the Hell office would come by and pat me on the back and say, 'good job!'"

"Sounds like a great job."

"We were in a competition for a free trip to Hawaii. You have no idea how broken my heart is from that job."

"I can guess."

20

The grand finale was my favorite part of the documentary. It was about a guy who worked in a Garden State Parkway tollbooth. He was bald—resembled a zombie; appearing miserable in countless shots skillfully captured by the award winning film maker.

Jimmy Tollbooth slowly ate a PayDay on the hood of his car, the green Subaru that he also hated, thinking, *Help me I am trapped in this spiderweb of a tollbooth . . .*

Kid with Clownhead, Brian Castner, really knew how to catch truth on film.

The camera focused on his face, he must have been fifteen years old. He said, "Today I realized that my neighbor is the most miserable person in the entire world, so I decided to make a movie, catch all of that misery on film. I want the world to not be so miserable."

It was an ambitious attempt.

Shot after shot, there I was—misery personified.

There were interviews with people who had known me before I'd disappeared; Ted, Billy Booth, Larry, burnt up Wanda Lewis, her daughter Allison . . . Kimmy Simmons, the mayor, my annoying neighbor with that goddamned dog.

Sarah was'nt included. It was probably better that way. Who knows what she would have said.

My part of the film was a character study, and it was told if you can believe it, in my defense. Kid with Clownhead made point after point on why it was a good idea for me to get out of the life that had made me that miserable. He told the story with pride.

And then for a good laugh, there was the TV special of me falling asleep at Pal's Parking covering for that damn cowboy. The kid had bought the VHS at Sarah's garage sale, along with a chicken lamp and my devil costume.

The film ended on a high note, it was a slow motion shot of me with love in my eyes, the cause of that love unapparent. A voice said, "I'm through with all of you spider heart motherfuckers, I am getting the fuck out, and well . . . I would love to say that it was nice while it lasted, but the truth is that it was never nice to begin with so . . ." Then a phone clicked. It was some drunken answering machine message that I'd left to someone . . . who? I don't know, we'll have to ask Kid with Clownhead.

The credits rolled, we both sat there, saying nothing.

At the end, the last line held on the screen for about fifty heartbeats before fading away, it said, "This film is dedicated to the unwavering virginity of Gena Parker, class of 2007."

Ted and I didn't have anything to say, I felt almost sick with fever and he must have felt something similar. Somewhere deep inside he must have loved me twice as much as ever, because I had been the catalyst to place him inside a movie, even if it was just a low budget art house documentary.

In the film, Ted had said, "Jim is a really good guy, don't get me wrong, he is fucked up and well, actually really fucked up, but he is a really good guy." I wanted to hug him now for saying good things about me when it would have been so easy to feed me to the wolves.

So, there in the movie house I hugged him from the side and he tried to break free, but I wouldn't release. When I did let go, I was also thankful that nobody had been watching.

I opened up the doors to the lobby. I expected people to ask for autographs, but no one did. They were dumb asses and totally blowing their chance. Jimmy Tollbooth and Ted, the DMV god, were right there.

We went across the street to a bar, sat down by the window. Ted bought us drinks as the snow fell. Scotch and water after scotch and water for myself and like six beers for Ted, which is four beers over his limit.

When he stood up and grabbed his keys, I couldn't believe it.

The snow was really coming down heavy. We hadn't even noticed.

"Let's go, Hollywood," he said. I was a star.

17

Well, a lesson to all of you, do not drink to ease yourself into oblivion and then act surprised when oblivion's eyes come barreling out of control in your direction.

That road was slick and no sane human being should have been driving on it the way we were driving on it, concerned with escape or not. My head was sideways as I said to Ted, "I missed you while I was in Iceland. I was gonna send you a postcard but I was worried that Sarah would have sent an assassin."

"It was wise of you to not give up your location. She would have definitely sent an assassin."

"Ha!"

"And it probably would have been me, I would have come to your glacier and knocked. I would have had a whole box of Pay-Day bars and a case of Guinness, and when you opened your glacier door I would have ripped the machine gun out of the candy bar box and ripped you apart with millions of bullets."

"Hey, watch the road!"

"I'm watching the road," he said.

"Back there, where we almost went over, that's all the way down the mountain."

"You got nothing to live for anymore anyway, what do you care?"

"Knock it off."

"OK, I was just screwing around, don't soil your diaper."

I played with the radio, I don't know where Ted had gotten a brand new cassette player, but there it was. I pushed the tape inside the glowing tape head, wondering what joys the speaker had in store for us. It was Rod Stewart.

"Fucking Rod Stewart? Are you insane?"

"It's the only tape I could find. They don't make tapes anymore."

"Well, no tape would have been better than Rod Stewart!"

"I know that now," he said shamefully, "I guess I should have just installed a CD player, but I wanted . . . "

"I know, I know. To live peacefully in the soft down comforter of the past."

"Yeah!"

"Well in retrospect, most of the past was not comfortable."

"I noticed that too." He ejected the tape, searching through the radio stations, most of them were talk radio in French. The windshield wipers were in overdrive but barely doing anything. I started to get the notion that as long as we had good music on, it'd all be okay, we would find a way out of the snow storm and into safety.

You know what static sounds like?

That's what you get most of the time.

Finally, a Credence Clearwater song came on.

I turned it up.

Ted turned it up, too.

We started to sing along.

It reminded me of when we used to sit around in the sandpits, young and drunk, huddled around a boom box with Ray.

Memories . . . Ted never was a very good driver, I remembered that. All of these memories, as a matter of fact, Ted had been the worst driver. And Ted was never a very good drinker either. Look at the way that Ted was drinking and driving so well in Canada!

Just then, we hit an extra icy patch of road and the car began to slip end over end. We did a 360 degree spin at 20 miles per hour, the whole time both of us as cool as cucumbers. We were too inebriated to understand that that was not how a car was supposed to react in Canada. We straightened and I saw a sign coming our way, Ted was going to strike the sign, "YOU SONOFABITCH!!"

The sign fell over, the car stopped. Thick wooden posts folding the front bumper and the grill of the vehicle punched inward. The hood was cinched and bent sharply upward on the passenger side. We got out to see the damage, cursing. The snow was sticking, there was about an inch. It fell on our clothes like seeds from a dandelion.

"Car looks OK," I said.

"Yeah, but no, yeah."

Laying in the snow like a person that had fallen over backwards with no bend in the knee was a large wooden sign that said, "WELCOME TO AMERICA."

We hadn't even noticed the border facility, as we had been doing a giant out of control spin passed its glowing lights. They wanted us out of their country, didn't care how we did it, drunken road spins, bicycle, hitchhiking, taxi cab, parachute, genie's third wish from the magic lamp.

"WHAT AN ENTRY!" I yelled.

"YEAH!"

We climbed back inside the car. Ted backed out onto the highway, "Thank god this is a high performance machine with armor plating or we would both be dead," I noted.

I didn't bother asking him if he was OK to drive, I knew the answer. We were only nine hours or so away, so—no sweat. As we sped away, the snow answered our enthusiasm and optimism with a double rate attack.

"Are we in a snow globe now?"

"Don't worry," Ted said, "I put on the all weather traction tires, they were fifty dollars more for the set, but worth it for safety."

"Ted, we are about to reap eternal rewards regarding traction, I can feel it!"

Diesel Cottontail seemed to have enjoyed its little crash. It was handling the road better now that it was ugly again. It is too difficult to handle the ugliness of the world when you yourself are a beautiful thing. It's better to be scarred and stinking of garbage so that you can perform without the high expectations of the king and queen of the prom slapped on your ass like a toe tag fifty years too soon.

The highway was dark and lead nowhere but home. We passed signs that were simply blurs. I couldn't even read these signs, I tried to squint and see what they had to say, I didn't see anything, just smudges.

Lit up like a ghost, hovering like a specter in our headlights over the highway came a sign for the next town, it said, "SARAH-VILLE."

"AAAHHHHHH!" I yelled.

"What?"

"Nothing."

Another sign came at us, it said, "REST AREA, NEXT REST AREA 27 MILES."

"Hey pull over," I told him.

"No, I want to get home to Kelly and little Noah."

Then, a cool white specter of a roadside sign appeared, "SAR-AHTOWN KEEP LEFT" it read.

"OH MY GOD!"

"Hey, relax," he said.

"Did you see that sign?"

"Yeah, I saw it. Sarahtown. You want to go there?"

"NO, I DO NOT WANT TO GO TO MOTHERFUCKING SAR-AHTOWN!"

"OK, so we won't go to Sarahtown, take it easy."

"IF I HEAR YOU SAY TAKE IT EASY ONE MORE TIME . . . "

"You'll jump out of this moving car and bury yourself in the snow?"

"FUCK FUCK FUCK!"

I was getting a little too hysterical for my own good.

The next sign said, "Mercer 5 Miles."

Then a sign said, "Poplar Keep Right."

I was starting to nod off, beginning to feel the effects of lunacy that had been smashing against me as if I was a boat lashed to a darkened pier receiving the brunt of every wave with nothing to do about it but wait for low tide.

"I think we should pull over at the next town."

"You paying for the motel?"

"Sure."

Ted was always the one who would bail me out. Even in the times that we had betrayed each other we were still there for each other, to fall into our old roles the second the universe allowed those old roles to be tangible again. A hundred thousand years after our deaths, the spectral ghosts of our old lives would be acting out those motions of him saving my ass.

"I'll pull over, but just an advanced warning, I'm still not gonna give it up. You'll be sleeping on the floor."

"Floor? Go to hell. What about a blanket layer and reverse head to foot?" I compromised

"You got clean feet?"

"Yeah."

"We'll have to have an independent party sniff your feet to see if they are clean enough to initiate a blanket layer reverse head to foot same bed heterosexual sleeping arrangement."

"Or I could just wash them."

"OK, Jimmy Tollbooth . . . "

The sign for the next town said this, "SARAH"

"AAAAAAAAAAAGGGGGHHHHHH."

The following sign for the following town said,

"SOUTH SARAH"

"AAAAAAAAAAAAARRRRGGGGHHHHH!"

I was clawing at my own eyes.

The following sign for the following town after that said, "NEW SARAH" and then "SARAH RIVER" and then, "OLD SAR-AH"

I screamed and screamed, Ted just laughed and laughed, as if he had never seen anything funnier in his whole life. We were both going insane, just insane in different directions.

Then, I heard Dolly in the backseat—the shrill doom of her long island laughter. I turned, could not see her back there. But, I heard her voice, as she cooly said, "Relax, Jimmy. If you tense up, it'll cause more damage."

I turned forward, there it was—the eyes of oblivion headed right at us from the opposing lane. A large truck, its headlights consuming all.

In a flash, everything blinked out. Death.

13

I woke in a flimsy chair. I scanned left, scanned right. There was nothing and nobody, just empty chairs. A TV in the corner played a talk show. A man who had lost his legs was proposing to an extremely tall women. A pro basketball player, a power forward.

She accepted. They embraced.

Love is so ridiculous and confrontational that nobody ever gets away from it, whatever shape or size, we all get scissor locked by it and forced to make difficult decisions. Pretty soon around a new corner is going to come the most preposterous scene of your life, and trust me, it's going to be draped in the horrible robes of love.

I heard a sound, the receptionist was back from wherever receptionists go when you don't see them.

"It's almost your turn," she said.

She was a very plain woman with strong perfume. I nodded at her and sat back down in my chair. There were magazines scattered across a table. I leafed through a few of them.

"Nice day today," she said.

"Is it?"

"Yeah." She was also looking through a magazine.

"What am I waiting for?"

She looked uncomfortable at the question, she skated around it, "Do you want a cup of coffee or anything like that?"

"No, I'm fine." But, I wasn't. I was in the waiting room to enter into the afterlife. I was dead. The accident had killed me and I was simply waiting to be assigned some position in Heaven or Hell. Of course, I had no doubt about where I was going.

Heaven.

"I hate waiting," I said.

A door opened and a person walked down the hallway, the receptionist said, "OK, well my shift is over, good luck."

"Thanks."

She took her bag and she took her jean jacket off the coat hook, waved goodbye, walked down the hallway. The new figure, the relief secretary walked down a different hallway. She got herself a cup of coffee. Then, after a few minutes of me just looking at the potted plant, she came and sat down at the desk. I got a good look. It was Sarah.

"Oh hey," she said, winking.

"You've got to be kidding me," I said.

"Not kidding."

"Sonofabitch," I said, punching the chair next to me. It didn't hurt. I was dead.

"Anyway . . ." Sarah remarked curtly, blowing on her hot coffee. "Someone will see you very shortly."

"Is this what I think it is?"

"It's the waiting room for the afterlife."

"And I'm dead?"

"Dead."

"That sucks."

"You didn't like being alive anyway," Sarah said.

"I DISAGREE!"

"Look, it's not in my job description to be yelled at."

"Sorry."

"Yeah be sweet, it might work out in your favor."

"I bet," I scoffed.

She looked pretty good again. Thin. Her hair was longer. She'd bleached it, which was something she had never done in my lifetime. It'd figure that once I was dead, she'd look her best.

"How is everything going?" I asked diplomatically.

"Pretty good," she admitted, filing her nails, which were long and french tipped. Her lips were full, her neck was begging for me to jump over the desk and bite. Regardless of my desires, I felt very weak, that whole business of being killed on the side of the snowy road had taken a lot out of me. I shifted my weight in the chair, nervously.

"How did you get this job?" I quizzed.

"They let all ex-wives sentence their ex-husbands to the fate that they deserve for eternity."

"Oh shit."

She laughed, her whole body shook. "I know! And to think that I never suspected there was justice in the universe. Turns out there's a lot of justice in the universe."

I was scrambling, "Well in my defense, I just want to say that I always loved you."

"Oh, look at him scramble!" she shouted.

"I was never unfaithful . . ." I confessed.

"Like a cockroach about to be crushed by an angry boot heel," she hissed.

"We had a wonderful life before you were pregnant."

"HA HA HA HA HA HA HA!"

"What are you laughing at, it's true!"

I knew that there was nothing I could say. I was doomed to burn forever in the pit of eternal suffering. Disgusted, I looked at the potted plant, as if it held some answer.

"It's fake," my Sarah said about the potted plant, "just like your love had been for me."

"It looks real," I argued, grabbing a plastic pedal.

"It will seem real from a distance, but trust me, it's fake, very fake."

I sighed, wanted to cry.

"Is Ted OK, did he make it?" I begged.

"I don't know any of his details."

I put my head in my hands.

"You'll have to go through one of two doors. It's up to me to pick the door. I'm sure I don't have to tell you where they go. You were always smart, and superstitious."

"This isn't fair," I whined.

"Who better to judge you than the person who you choose to make a vow with to spend the rest of your life?"

"In the modern world, I say foul. Let me go."

"Nobody knows you better than I do, Jim. Too bad for you. Why should I let you go?"

"Maybe because it isn't my time yet," I said.

"Very original! That was what the man said who gave me this job, he said, everybody who comes to this waiting room would make the claim that it's not their time yet."

"Well it isn't my time yet."

"Why not Jim, why exactly do you want to be alive?"

"I have forever to be dead, but not very long to be alive."

"That's why you went to Iceland, because you thought you were being alive?"

"B-b-b-b-bingo."

"You were no more alive there than you were in New Jersey."

"I climbed a mountain, I wrote a book, I went to a recording studio, I sailed on a ship—the m'f'n Sága . . . on which your mother haunted me! I ran like a lunatic down hills, up hills, I howled at moons . . . I burnt down a building in Reykjavik with rice!"

"You could have done all that in your own backyard, you stupid asshole."

"I'm not ready," I said.

"Get ready, or I can make the phone call, and security can throw you face first through the door. You can walk through it like a man or be tossed through it like a spoiled child."

"You better call security," I said, standing.

"Ha! I thought you'd say that."

"I have to use the bathroom."

"They have urinals in Hell."

"Do they have urinals in Heaven?" I mocked.

"Nobody ever has to piss or shit in Heaven, it's euphoria."

"Should've known."

"OK, look, if you really have to go, go down this hallway, last door on the left. But don't you dare make a mess in there, I just cleaned it last night."

"You're just asking for trouble," I said. But, I turned to the small half door separating us. I booted it as hard as I could, it splintered apart. She screamed. Then I grabbed the back of her blouse reeling her in, she was quite an angry fish.

"Let go of me!"

I bit her neck, hard. She screamed, spun her face around. I kissed her on the lips deeply and dangerously. She squirmed but was not half as strong as I was, with all of my fear and love and hate and hope coming across her like a bitter wave. She gave up trying to pull away, went slack, when I felt her dead weight I pushed her away, knowing she was preparing a return attack. I went in the opposite direction, towards the bathroom.

"NICE TRY JIM, IT'LL TAKE MORE THAN THAT!"

She picked up the phone, called security.

I locked the bathroom door behind me. I didn't have to go to the bathroom, so I just stood there shaking my head in the mirror. Nothing to do but shake.

I heard men's voices outside. Surely they were very powerful. They don't give weaklings those black security T-shirts.

I paced around the little bathroom, which was just about as big as my tollbooth. I wasn't too heartbroken however, certain there were tollbooths in Hell. That was where I was going to be spending the next section of eternity: breaking dollar bills, handing out receipts. It was just too bad that I wouldn't have the one thing that kept me from going insane while I was in the tollbooth on earth.

That thing?

Sarah.

She had saved me time and time again. Sarah, who I loved more than anything, but who had been torn away from me by the tragic circumstances of life. You should never let the world get in the way of a love that deep, you will wind up ripped apart by wolves, your blood sucked dry by spiders, your bones crushed to dust by the hooves of devils.

Now the men were knocking on the door saying very politely to come out so that they could very politely toss me into the fire and brimstone of eternal damnation. No problem. I went to the far wall, closed my eyes. So this was the end. Something was poking me in the back. A window sill, just a window sill.

A WINDOW SILL!

"OPEN THE DOOR!" they boomed in unison.

In a fever, I turned to face the window, sure it wouldn't open. But, it opened. It OPENED!

"DON'T MAKE US KICK THIS DOOR DOWN!"

"FUCK YOU!" I said, climbing through the window, sliding out onto the wet grass. On the ground, I ran, "FUCK YOUR MOTHERS!"

There was a forest shrouded in ominous fog, those same woods from Iceland when we'd walked to the waterfall. A window from the office building opened. Sarah stuck her head out.

"Come back here!"

I turned to her, blew her a kiss, "I LOVE YOU . . . YOU HEART-
LESS CUNT!"

"AHHHHHHHHHHH!" She was angry, so angry, but as I
broke into the darkness of the woods, I thought I heard her shout,
"I LOVE YOU TOO." But I couldn't linger long, there were gunshots ripping my way, the sounds of wolves howling in the woods,
the hissing of spiders falling from the trees, the chilled hand of
death seeking chase for the run I was giving it through the darkness I'd known all of my life.

It wasn't long before I broke out on the other side of that
darkness, standing in the blinding white, pain rushing to me from
places I never imagined. Coming back to life.

Dammit.

11

I jumped about three feet out of my hospital bed when I gained consciousness. A deadly pirate was giving me the eye with his only good eye remaining. A jagged scar ran over the patched hollow of his missing eye. I was hooked up to an IV, but when I had pulled my bed flip maneuver, it had disconnected, causing some life sustaining fluid to trickle uselessly all over the floor.

Life juice.

"Jim . . . JIM! It's me."

"What?"

The pirate was grabbing me on the floor, he was in my face, saying, "It's Ted."

Why was this fucker impersonating an old friend of mine who'd died in that car crash some thirty years ago?

"Jim! JIM, RELAX!!"

I knew I was in a hospital, there was no confusion concerning that part, so when a hospital orderly appeared it made common sense. I sighed with relief. Coming out of a coma was hard business. I was shaking and partially foaming at the mouth. The orderly pulled pirate Ted off my torso.

I was laid back down on the hospital bed, injected with freak-out chemicals.

The orderly was a little fat black man and his name was Jody. He said, "Hi, my name is Jody, I am here to help you."

"I don't believe you."

"Don't believe what?"

"That you're not a hallucination."

"Why?"

"What woman would name her short fat black son Jody?"

"I know that I may seem like a good candidate for a hallucinogenic episode but I assure you that I am for real and that I am here to help you."

"Why do I need help?"

"Exactly."

"Exactly what?"

"Anybody in this much trouble who not only doesn't notice that they're in trouble but also has to ask why they are in trouble, definitely needs help," Jody explained.

"I need help?"

"Exactly."

"I thought I was dead," I said.

"For certain you're not dead, I'm your proof."

Jody, smiled kindly, "I just changed your bedpan three minutes ago, your piss is still warm."

"I really am alive?"

"You're in Buffalo, New York, you were in a coma."

"I always wanted to be in a coma."

"Congratulations, you are now out of the coma."

"Officially?" I asked, things were becoming less of a blur.

"Yes, officially decomatosed," he remarked. "Welcome back. Now don't do anything stupid like going back into it."

I caught my breath, I said, "I have no intentions on going back to where I came from."

"Good, because we really like having you back. Your friend was pretty banged up too . . . Ted. He's still here, has been here for a week after discharge, just waiting to see what happens to you."

Just then, good ol' Ted came back into the room wearing the eyepatch. He saw me staring and said, "I lost the eye in the crash."

"Oh."

"It's not as bad as it looks. I'm actually glad that I lost it. I think the eye patch and the scar gives me character that I lacked before."

The sad part is that Ted hit the nail on the head with the hammer called truth.

They lifted me off the floor, placing me on the hospital bed, plugging the machine back into my highway blood system. I assured them that I was fine, they assured me that I was not fine. It's like we're playing table tennis. Bing. Bing. Bing, back and forth. I was never good at table tennis so I gave up. I'm not fine.

I rested my head back on the pillow and Ted said, "You almost died!"

"Figured."

"I almost died too," he said.

"You seem OK now."

"It took until yesterday for me to recover," he says.

"You look good now."

"But I wasn't, I was in a coma too!"

"Coma? Sounds rough, how long?"

"30 hours," he said gravely.

"Is that really long enough for it to be considered a coma?"

"YEAH!" he yelled, hurt.

"I would think a coma would have to be more than three days, thirty hours? Really?"

"I lost an eye!" he said, placing his hand on the patch.

"I can see that." My left side hurt tremendously. "Hey what is going on with me? My left side hurts."

"I don't know," he said. "Let's consult your charts." He lifted the folder at the base of my bed, "Oh, damn, you have a bunch of broken ribs."

"Damn."

"Says here you lost your dick too, and your balls."

My heart stopped, the color drained from my face.

"I'm just kidding, don't go into another long coma . . ."

"For future reference, that's not a good joke."

"We should have never been driving in that snowstorm."

"Drunk like that . . ."

"I was already in mourning before I even picked you up at the airport," Ted confessed.

"What happened?"

"Well, don't say anything to Kelly, but I was walking Rommel and Bubblegum out by your old hideout, and well, they both died."

"How?"

"Rommel bit Bubblegum, the whole thing, all of that poor cat . . . choked on her."

"Holy shit."

"Yeah, I buried them right before I got in the car to come get you in Montreal."

"I'm sorry."

"They seemed to be getting along so well."

"That's how it is, you know?"

"Words of wisdom. So . . . Kelly went to get some cake and balloons."

"Why?"

"She seems to think that you coming out of the coma is like a birthday, and that there should be cake and balloons, probably a wish. I told her that you wouldn't appreciate it."

"She better not bring back a clown."

"I didn't give her enough money for a clown," Ted said.

"Good."

"You probably already know this, but the car is demolished."

"Yeah."

"Did you know that you were thrown fifty feet through the windshield."

"No."

"Yeah, the reason you aren't dead is because you landed in a snowdrift." He reached in his pocket and pulled out a photograph, it was a picture of me lying on my back, my arms outstretched, there was some blood about the perimeter of the fresh snow, but otherwise I looked peaceful. "The police thought it was the craziest thing. You'd made a snow angel."

"That's a nice photo."

"They say it was a miracle we survived."

"I don't know what to say to that," I said.

"And according to your doctor, an even bigger miracle that you woke up from the coma."

"They probably say that to all of the people that come out of comas, it's like a pep talk to get people to come back from the ledge. Like, live a good life."

"Why not?"

"Live a good life?"

"Yeah."

"Oh shit! Did you see God or something while you were in your thirty hour mini coma?"

"No comment."

Jody came back followed by Kelly. He was carrying the cake,

she had a bundle of balloons and a box wrapped in silver foil. I acted surprised, "Oh you shouldn't have!"

I didn't know Kelly all too well but she seemed like a very good woman and I was glad that my friend had found her. What a stroke of luck it was for him to find a good one.

They say cream rises to the top. I don't know what that means, but at that moment I supposed it meant that Ted and Kelly were wonderful people and they had found each other on the top. I thought of this in its polar state: filth sinks to the bottom. Sarah and I had found each other in the grime and sludge, we were dirty for each other. I didn't know if it could be any other way. As I lay in bed, broken and burning I was happy to have at least been reunited with wonderful people in a world that was full of shitty bitches and fucked up assholes.

Jody set the cake down on the little table in front of me, lowered the lights. Kelly stuck a candle in the center of the cake. One candle, my 1st birthday all over again.

There was a momentary darkness to the room. The space between fire being set, candle ignited, where everything dropped out and I was suspended forever as if in a cradle that was rocking to the pulse of some hand that was larger than everything. I shuddered, and felt myself going backwards even though I was stationary. It was like I was crawling back into my spine and taking note on how things were and how they could be. Sometime later, after an hour or so of contemplation, in super slow motion, a dark figure in the shadow struck the flint of the lighter and set flame to the top of the wick and I began to move millimeter by millimeter from the cocoon of the cradle towards the idea of a future that was growing lighter and lighter, warmer and warmer as I approached the station it occupied on my new birthday party.

They sang off key but with love, "HAPPY BIRTHDAY TO YOU, HAPPY BIRTHDAY TO YOU, HAPPY BIRTHDAY DEAR JIMMY, HAPPY BIRTHDAY TO YOU, HAPPY BIRTHDAY TO YOU, HAPPPY BIRTHDAY TO YOU, YOU ACT LIKE A MONKEY AND YOU BELONG IN A ZOO." They clapped.

Belong in a zoo?

I wanted to hock a loogie onto the candle, extinguishing the flame with my spit, making the entire birthday cake my own. Despite the second chance that the world and my loved ones had shown me, I wanted to tear shit up. But instead, resolving that wasn't my way anymore, I just peacefully blew out the candle.

There was a moment of silence. The light came back on. In a show of good manners, Kelly cut the cake. She handed me the first slice, smiling. She handed Ted a slice. Kelly said, "Happy Birthday" again, then apologized that she couldn't be having any cake, she was diabetic. Ted sat down in the chair next to me. He forked cake into his mouth.

I smiled as I ate my birthday cake.

"We got you a present, too," Ted said.

Kelly brought over the giant box, I unwrapped it. There was nothing inside of the box. It was an empty box.

"It's supposed to represent the unlimited possibilities of the future," she said.

"Oh," I said. "Well, thank you."

"You're welcome," she said. Then she came to the side of the bed, leaned down, kissed me on the forehead. Ted shook my weak hand.

"Hate to be doing this to you, but we have to get going," Ted said, woefully.

"My mom has had the baby for . . . too long," Kelly said, "if we don't come back soon, she may never let us have Noah back."

"People get attached," Ted said. "If you can believe it."

"Even to kids, even to shitty kids?" I said.

"Our kid isn't shitty," she said. "You'll see, real soon." Ted walked Kelly to the door and kissed her, told her in a low tone that he would be right out. Then he came back to the side of my bed and said, "I'm probably coming right back up for you. But I gotta make sure everything is OK with my family first."

He threw a folded object on the bed. "This was in the trunk of the car. Thought you'd want it."

It was the hooded sweatshirt that I had given Sarah when she was in the home and was all pissed about having to wear her aunt's pink kitten sweatshirt. Three wolves howling at the moon. A secret stash pocket inside. I checked the pocket, there was nothing in there.

"I can't believe you have this thing . . ."

"You have it now," he said. "I'm leaving. Love you buddy, hang in there."

"Love you too, Ted," I said.

It made me feel pretty stupid to have not kept a family of my own in my pocket for rainy days. It made Ted feel bad too, I could see it. As good as friends as we were, we were not family and he could not place me above his own family, even though I was laying in a hospital bed.

There's a chain of command in the world.

You don't always get to be the general. Even though it breaks your heart sometimes. You wind up a lowly drummer boy more often than not.

He shook my hand again, and then he left the room and all I could do was lay there and listen to that machine go beep beep beep beep beep beep beep beep. What did it mean? Beep beep beep beep beep beep. Was it trying to get some message across?

Oh yeah. It was trying to tell me that I was still alive.

Did it have to be so annoying with how it went about telling me?

10

I was alone for the rest of the afternoon. I sat in bed watching
TV, nothing was on, so I watched an infomercial on a product
that was supposed to regrow hair. I didn't believe what I saw,
as I usually don't believe in anything.

It was a long and troublesome day.

Ted had left a movie poster hanging on the hospital wall. It
was a picture of me running down the street in that devil costume.

I was reading the bottom of the poster, smirking, KID WITH
CLOWNHEAD Productions. I wondered where that was based
out of? Where was Kid With Clownhead that night? Was it crazy
for me to wonder why he wasn't visiting me in the hospital? Was
it even crazier to wonder where Sarah was, why she wasn't here?
Why stop there, where was Gena? It didn't matter, it didn't matter at all.

Then, I heard that old familiar nasty raspy voice; that Staten
Island pain in my ass.

"You really are a miserable dick wad," Dolly hissed.

She materialized in one of the chairs in the corner. She was
not alone, there was a man with her. He didn't appear malicious
though, even though he had a pretty tough looking beard.

"Hey Dolly," I remarked, flipping the TV off.

"Jim, look at you! I'm amazed you made it through. I didn't
take you for a fighter."

"Thanks for the vote of confidence."

"You should be dead," she said. "Anyway, I figured you could
use a visitor, and I wanted to introduce you to my new boyfriend."

The ghost man in the chair waved, smiled.

"Hi, I'm Paul."

"Hi Paul, I'm Jim."

"Nice to meet you Jim."

"Likewise."

"Me and Paul are in love," she said, beaming with happiness.

"Yes we are," Paul confirmed, "big time."

"I'm very happy to see that you two found each other," I said.

"We met at the library, he sometimes haunts the nonfiction section . . . around the automobiles . . ."

"I'm an amateur mechanic," Paul said, cracking his knuckles. I was surprised that still worked.

"I was looking for information concerning my passage into the afterlife," Dolly said, "there was quite a debate for some time there."

"What debate?" I asked.

"Well . . ." she said, "that car of yours, that little trashy German junk heap was mangled beyond all recognition and I always thought that I would go to Heaven when it was . . . well, ya know. But then, there I was for a whole week after the accident, still waiting for the white light to come for me and for all of the angels to pull me up into heaven and oh . . ."

"I'm not so sure that there is a Heaven," I said.

"Nobody's sure," Paul said.

"I'm sure," Dolly remarked, "I've always been sure."

Paul and Dolly were holding hands. Their bodies were almost transparent, a faint glow with a background of wavering blue. Where their hands met, the two hands were glowing a deep pink that would sometimes rise into an orange like that seen inside a violent fire.

"Is it rude to ask how you died," I asked Paul.

"A steel beam fell and crushed his head in a power plant," Dolly offered.

"I've seen you around," Paul said, "I used to drive through your tollbooth everyday."

"Oh, I never noticed."

"I drive a silver ghost Cadillac."

"Talk about a beautiful car!" Dolly said, beaming, kissing Paul on the cheek, "talk about a beautiful man!" Then looking at me she says, "Paul's son was the boy who had his finger bitten off by the German Shepherd just around the block. I remember because

I told Sarah to stay away from dogs because of that story. She always had beautiful hands, didn't she Jimmy?"

"Yeah, very nice hands," I said to her. "Have you heard from Sarah?"

"Nope."

"Is she OK?"

"Don't know."

"You know, you're just being difficult."

"No, I'm not, you have it all wrong," Dolly said. "I came here to thank you."

"For what?"

"Duh! For getting me and Paul together!"

"Yeah Jimmy, thanks," Paul said sincerely.

"No problem."

"You know how they say something good always comes out of something bad? Well it turns out its true. Getting murdered by your car and walking the earth in limbo for the last twenty one years turned out to the be the most rewarding part of my life, because NOW I'M IN LOVE!"

"Love fixes everything," Paul said, "honest."

"Paul was waiting for the powerplant to be torn down so he could go to Heaven . . . I was waiting for the car to be demolished, and well, now that we have found each other none of that matters anyway."

"I'm happy for you," I said.

"You want to hear something even crazier?"

"Shoot."

"So anyway, the other day, they get your car in the hydraulic car crushing mechanism at the junkyard and they push the button and the thing squashes the stupid car into the tiniest little box of metal and smushed whatchamacallits . . . meanwhile, me and Paulie are like two lovebirds, oblivious, kissing and singing in Madison Square Garden watching the Knicks game when all of a sudden the roof of the stadium opens up and oh my gawd . . . all of these angels start flying down and there is this heavenly light, and it's Heaven! It's actually Heaven! The Knicks were losing, but all of a sudden they start to beat the Pacers and everybody cheers! No one else can see the angels or anything, but it was like God was intervening and well, just making the earth a better place, starting with the basketball game! A five foot seven guard slam dunked from half court, it was a miracle! I started to cry, because I always wanted to go to Heaven, and I wanted to see my mommy again and Grandma and Uncle Johnny, and Paul held me close and the angels were kissing my eyelids saying, *'you are such a pretty lady, you belong with us, you belong with us.'*"

"Wow."

"Yeah, but wow is an understatement," Paul said.

"Then, I heard the voice of the Lord!" Dolly exclaimed, "And the Lord said to me, DOLLY, IT IS TIME FOR YOU TO COME HOME! IT IS TIME FOR YOU TO COME BACK TO THE PLACE WHERE YOU HAVE ALWAYS BELONGED . . ." Then she gulped, "And you know what? I looked right at Paul, and I saw the love in his eyes for me, and I thought, going to Heaven right then would be the stupidest thing that I could ever do with my life! I have love! Right here, in eternal limbo! FUCK HEAVEN, THIS IS HEAVEN!"

"Isn't she the greatest woman in the world?" Paul asks.

I nodded in agreement. After all, Dolly does seem like she's somewhere high up on the list of the all time greatest women in the world. The two of them kissed, they kissed so long and hard that they changed many colors and caused the heat of the room to vary wildly. Sparks popped, small lightning bolts were generated from their energy fields. One of these small bolts hit the TV, the glass shattered, black smoke bloomed out of the empty shell where the information used to be transmitted. Then the two are making out and their chairs lift up off the ground and things in the room start to flop around. I have to yell, "KNOCK IT OFF!"

They looked embarrassed, but not too embarrassed. They were very proud of their new love and they were gonna flaunt it wherever they could. It was strange to them how easily their control over it got away, and how they wound up causing forest fires, hail storms, lightning strikes, and earthquakes. How they caused the sun to blink out like an extinguished lamp, or the moon to swell in volume and illumination until all the others on the earth looked up at it in wonder and in fear thinking that it was falling on them. Many people were saved and redeemed by their whirlwinds and freeze frames as they materialized and dematerialized wherever their crazy love brought them.

"Until the power plant gets torn down," Dolly said.

"Yeah," Paul said, smiling. "That'll be a happy day."

"When the bright white light of heaven closed for me over Madison Square Garden and all of the angels went back inside of the flashbulbs of the court side press, I held Paul's hand extra tight and we drank a few more seven dollar beers by taking control of two lovebirds who were in the row below us. When the game was over, we left their bodies again and floated up over New York City, looking down at all of the tiny specs as we swam up to the stars, where most ghosts hang out, on Venus. A big club scene. And classy! What a night Jim, what a night, talk about romance!"

"Very romantic," Paul remarked.

"Well, look Jim, any second now we are going to get interrupted by another human being. I've said all I have to say and since there is nothing more to say, I will say one more time, fuck you for what you did to my daughter, and thank you very much for making my life the fairy tale that it is now. You're a fucked up individual, but you can't help it. So I forgive you."

They started to fade away.

"It was nice to meet you, Jim," Paul said. "I would shake your hand if I could."

"Bye bye, kid," Dolly said. And then all that was left in the room was the stink of the burning television and the empty chairs in the corner.

Just then Jody opened up the door.

"Ewwwwwwww," He flipped on the light. "What happened?"

"The TV blew up."

He was very concerned, "Are you OK?"

"Fine."

"Sit tight."

He left the room momentarily, the door ajar, came back with a wheelchair. Then, gently he picked me up from the bed as if I was just a little baby. He placed me down in the wheelchair, there was flash of hot dull pain from my broken ribs. Jody wheeled me out of the room and down the hallway, to an empty room, where the TV had not exploded.

As he set me down in the bed, I felt about as weak and helpless as I'd ever felt.

"I gotta put on some weight," I said.

"You will," he tucked me in. "Don't worry."

9

Four days later, I got a letter from Brian.

Jim,

Congratulations on not dying in that car crash, even though you and I both know that you probably deserved to die. Oh well better luck next time. I'm kidding! Fuck, it's been a long time, where the fuck did you go?

Now I got this thing going, it's not a good thing. It's a TV show about a rock band full of ninja spies. Not exactly the thing I had in mind for my next project, but I need the money. I need the money really bad. I'm trying to scrape together enough cash so I can start a cult that will overthrow the US govern ment. But hush hush, you didn't hear that from me. So far so good, a lot of people around here in Brooklyn are starting to think that I have these ideas that are worth dying over. All I have to do is not let them find out that my next film is not a film at all, but a TV show for cable about rock 'n' roll ninja spies. Credibility is everything when you want to control peo ple's minds.

Anyway, I have been telling my followers that you died, that you died many years ago. I figure, that you have NOTHING going on for you now. I am sure your wife is no longer your wife, actually, I know that for a fact as the private investigator uncovered that little tidbit, that you have no job, that you, well. . . have nothing in the world. So, what I'm proposing is that you come and join my cult. Actually, that you help me lead my cult. I need another good leader, as the sects are get ting large enough now that I have three leaders under me al ready controlling the minions. Ha! A fourth leader, I think that is what my cult really needs. We'll tell them that you rose from the dead after being dead for five years. These people are stupid, they will do anything, we feed them drugs to make them crazy and then brainwash them and so forth, it's really great.

I think by the end of the month we are going to start having them murder people. I want to break all the old serial killer records. Anyway, you just tell me what you want to do, and I will send a limo up to your hospital. I won't bother you if you don't want in, but I can't suggest that my minions won't.

Oh, I heard from Gena the other day, she is doing real good. This guy named Gunny who works in the auto shop has her inside a 55-gallon drum. She isn't in danger or anything, she actually likes it in there, apparently it gets her off. That girl is one of the most fucked up sex slaves we've got. College didn't work out so well, but sex slavery is panning out just fine for her. If you did want to come and join us, she could be all yours, but I already know your answer, that you have grown as a person, that you're not interested in any of our horror show nonsense. I applaud you, and I love you for it. Good luck with everything.

Your pal,

Kid With Clownhead

6

I could barely walk with a cane, but even barely is something. I changed out of my paper gown, I walked out into the darkened hallway. It was two hours before dawn, the night security guard was sound asleep, the nurses were all playing cards in the lounge. They didn't hear me walking past them in the hallway. They were accustomed to only listening for screams of pain. They were not concerned with people who did not scream.

I do feel bad about one thing. I stole an ambulance with its lights flashing. It was sitting right outside the ER. The keys were in the ignition. I climbed inside, a voice from the back said, "Excuse me . . . can we get going? I'm knocking on death's door."

I turned, there was a man lying on a stretcher.

I walked around to the back of the ambulance.

I pulled the man out of the back, rolled his stretcher on the sidewalk, pushed him into the hospital. He couldn't lift his head. He was too sick.

I was having an emergency of my own. I had to get back to New Jersey right away.

I hopped in the ambulance, began to drive out of the parking lot as if nothing had ever happened.

I had the lights on in the thing, and it was truly a gift, how people got right out of my way. If only I had possessed those flashing lights earlier, a lot of my problems would have been answered. I was headed home, down highways cluttered with people who knew nothing. They'd drift from lane to lane, not sure at all where they were headed or why they were headed there. I zoomed passed all of them.

Mile after mile zipped away.

I was exhausted and tired and sometimes when I would cough there'd be stars, other times a small glob of blood, that I'd swallow, sending it back to where it belonged, inside my stupid temple.

It was snowing as I crossed into New York State, the ambulance lights still flashing. It snowed harder the farther south I drove. I was coming face to face with another storm. I wasn't too happy about it. No matter how warm I made the interior of the ambulance, it just didn't seem to be warm enough. I pulled the vehicle over and filled the gas tank. I was saved, when I discovered that Ted had slipped a hundred dollar bill into my wallet. I went inside the store, bought two PayDay bars and a cup of coffee.

I was light headed and thought briefly about lying down in the back of the ambulance for a while, where I belonged, but decided against that too. I felt out of place, and all I wanted to see, as sick as it may seem to you, was something familiar, so I carefully climbed back in the driver's seat as would any cripple on the run and I put the ambulance into gear.

It was almost sunrise when I saw the first Garden State Parkway tollbooth, my eyes welled up with water.

I was home.

I zoomed through my old tollbooth. There was some indistinguishable figure slouching in the booth. It could have been anyone. I wondered if it could still be the cardboard cutout of Jimmy Cagney?

Nah, come on. But maybe. I flew through my lane with the lights flashing wildly. Larry's car still in the lot. Most of the lanes were EZ pass then. I honked as I passed. My dreams of burning down the entire toll plaza were long abandoned.

I left the highway, the roads were not as bad down there. I'd managed to cut in front of the storm somehow. Heavy snows were on their way, though. I passed the strip plaza with Officetown, Fried Paradise, Food Universe. I passed Dinosaur Liquor. The brontosaurus's head was missing. Its body was gold instead of green.

A lot had happened in five years. Good, if a lot didn't happen, what kind of town would this be? The post office was gone, a car wash was in its old place, who fucking cares . . . Then I noticed police lights in my rearview mirror.

I pulled to the side of the road.

The cruiser just sat back there for quite a long time. I had a coughing fit and saw stars. When the officer finally got to the window, I breathed a sigh of relief, it was Ray.

I rolled down the window, "Hey . . ."

Then I see that he has his gun out.

"PUT YOUR HANDS ON YOUR HEAD!"

I put my hands on my head.

"RAY, it's me!"

"SHUT THE FUCK UP OR I'LL BLOW YOUR BRAINS OUT! STEP OUT OF THE VEHICLE, DO IT SLOWLY, I WANT TO SEE YOUR HANDS AT ALL TIMES!!"

I opened the door, both hands hanging out of the ambulance, pulling the handle from the outside of the vehicle, just so I definitely knew I wasn't going to get shot. I stepped out, almost falling. The world almost blacked out around me.

"GET AGAINST THE AMBULANCE! SPREAD EM!!"

I do as I'm told. Ray comes up behind me, knocks my head into the van. I go down on one knee, I feel the gun against my temple.

"PUT YOUR HANDS BEHIND YOUR BACK!"

He zip tied my hands and then knocked my head into the van again, "YOU THINK YOU CAN JUST COME INTO THIS TOWN . . . YOU THINK YOU CAN JUST COME FROM VERMONT YOU MOTHERFUCKER!!"

He's screaming. I'm screaming, he flips me around, then he stops beating me, having seen my face, his breath was hot and fast, but suddenly became level " . . . Jimmy?"

I cough, I almost cry. "Yeah . . ."

"Oh my god!" He pulls out his pocket knife and cuts the zip ties free, "I'm so sorry, pal."

"Uhhhhhh," I am almost completely broken.

"WHY THE FUCK ARE YOU DRIVING A STOLEN AMBU-LANCE WITH OUT OF STATE PLATES AT TWO NINETEEN IN THE MORNING?"

"Just trying to get home," I mutter.

"Dude, I could've killed you! I'm so sorry. I thought you were an out of towner."

I was trying to get off the ground, Ray was helping me.

"Jimmy, this was all a misunderstanding. Wait, Ted said that you were in a car crash . . ."

"I was."

"Jesus," he looked back at the ambulance, "where did this thing come from?"

"I stole it."

"Nice."

"I probably should have just taken a bus."

"Screw that. Well, I guess I gotta get rid of this ambulance then. But it's cool, I always wanted an ambulance." He took the keys out of his cruiser, shut his lights off, said, "you back for good?"

"I don't know."

"You should stay," he said.

"I got nowhere to go."

"Ah!" he exclaimed, "take this." He gave me his flashlight from his side hip holster and the plastic bag on the passenger seat with the last of my possessions. Then, he jumped inside the ambulance, "Jim, it's great to have you back for good, but I really need to get this ambulance inside my garage before the sun comes up. I'd hate to have to kill witnesses over a stupid ambulance that I probably have no use for anyway."

Ray put the vehicle into gear, peeled away before I could even ask him for a ride. I looked down woefully at the flashlight. He'd lost his mind, for real. I was left in front of the Food Universe, the snow really pounding down.

The neon sign above Burgerland went dark.

4

Even though I had ghost friends, the woods seemed haunted and foreboding. I walked down the trail behind Great Wok of China and all its glory. The flashlight kept illuminating furious snow. I was sure that a skeleton was going to come out into the light, hungry for sinew and cartilage.

The Skullfuckers' hideout had once looked impressive, now it was just a tiny house ready to fall over. It'd faded from its original construction. I rediscovered it, tired and sad. If the sun was up I would've seen for real all of the damage. Time had made quick work upon its walls.

The Skullfuckers had grown up, had no reason to love this hideout of the past. They were not old enough yet to have dangerous nostalgia for it. Give them a few more years, they'd begin to get seasick over that nostalgia. When they returned to that hideout, they'd find that the place was not what they'd remembered. They'd breath fire and stomp up tornados of terror in their own small lives.

The door was ajar. I walked inside, the lights no longer worked and all of the amenities had been stripped from the place. Whoever had once loved it had stopped caring. They'd left just a tiny little kid mattress. I curled up into a pathetic ball on it.

I slept lightly. When I woke, there was heavy snow all over the ground. I couldn't get the door open. I opened up the mini garage door, walked out of that. Circled on the ground all around the house were paw marks, some animal was circling the house, doing laps around it in the night. It appeared to be wolf prints.

Not that I knew what wolf prints look like, but I assumed they were wolf prints.

"HEY!" called the voices of children coming out of the white-wash. "You were in our clubhouse!"

They were small children.

That's the way things work. The past kept abandoning things that it loved and the future had to adopt its unloved shell. "STAY AWAY FROM OUR FORT, YOU ASSHOLE!"

"I'VE HEARD ALL OF THIS BEFORE!" I screamed.

They'd loosely surrounded me in their snow gear, one of them had a sled, the other had a garbage can lid. They were poised to throw themselves down hills to see how fast the hills would propel them. I would present an even more entertaining distraction for them.

"GET OUT OF HERE!"

They began to launch snowballs at me. I ducked behind a tree. Does this ever end? I should have burnt their fort down when I had the chance. Snow balls started to smack against the tree I was hiding behind. In the past I would have beaten the piss out of these little kids, but I couldn't bring myself to do that anymore.

"COME AND FIGHT, YOU PUSSY!"

I started to walk in the other direction, ignoring them, being a much better person, and time having taught me valuable lessons. Snow balls pelt me in the back, "GET OUT OF OUR WOODS!"

"THEY AREN'T JUST YOUR WOODS!" I yelled.

They kept coming and coming. When I broke the tree line, they were still following me, "GET OUT OF OUR NEIGHBOR-HOOD!"

"WHAT THE FUCK!?!"

A snowball pegged me in the back, but I was a better person then. A snowball hit me in the shoulder, but I was a better person then. A snowball hit me in the back of the head, THAT'S IT, YOU MOTHERFUCKIN' BRATS! PREPARE TO DIE!

I ducked into the nearest yard, they followed but couldn't see me hiding.

"WHERE DID HE GO?"

The new kids were much more persistent than the old kids had been. That's darwinism for you. Natural selection making a deadlier youth hungrier for the blood of the last few remaining dinosaurs.

I'm inside a carport, crouching down next to a minivan, personalized plates: CATLUVR. The children don't know where I am, they come up the street, scanning left to right, but I'm in a good spot. I could have been gathering gravel from the driveway of the carport and stuffing that gravel into snow balls. But I wasn't. I just let those kids pass. I waited ten more minutes once they were gone. There was no need to destroy them, though they had it coming.

I cut through the backyard. Through a little gate I went, despite the protest of a neighborhood dog, I growl at the dog, he growls back—a back door opens, an elderly man is standing there in his long johns, "HEY, what are you doing to that dog! I'll kick your ass! GET OFF MY FRESH SNOW!"

I move quickly away from him. It make sense that he would have a gun, being elderly, having to worry constantly of the youth coming to his door in an attempt to overthrow him.

I made wolf tracks the back way down streets that looped to where I used to live. My house was gone. A sign in front of the store said:

ANOTHER GREAT JOB COMPLETED
BY D R MASTERSON & SON BUILDERS!

Just like Ted said, it's a 7-11. I wanted a cup of coffee so I walked in through the front door, which is pretty much just where my own front door had been. There was a young kid leaning on the counter, as all young kid clerks will always do, until the end of time.

I gazed all around the store like a madman, imagining where my TV used to be, where my bed had been . . . I got myself a cup of coffee, brought it to the register. "I used to live here," I say to him.

"Oh yeah."

"They tore my house down to make this."

He looks at me fearfully. "The coffee is free, please leave."

I walked out of the store. I noticed something that makes me decidedly sick. IT'S THE SEASHELL MAILBOX! THE CHEAP BASTARDS ARE REUSING MY SEASHELL MAILBOX!

I limped away, heading farther into the labyrinth of iced over streets.

0

At the apartment building where Sarah grew up, I heard the thud like a distant heartbeat. A basketball slapping the frozen surface of the court. I came around the side of the building, there was Sarah behind the chainlink fence, standing in the center, dribbling. She had on an army coat and an aqua green scarf. Her hair looked dirty and green in contrast to the pure snow all around her. The wind whipped that hair in her face. I watched her take her hand from the basketball and pull strands from her teeth. She'd shoveled and salted from the foul line to the hoop, so she could shoot free throws to her heart's content.

She looked beautiful in a way that I forgot existed in the world.

I watched her square up and take the perfect shot. The ball released from her fingertips—sailing through the air. It would have been a swoosh, but the metal net was frozen. The ball got stuck.

She stood there looking at it for a moment.

I walked up slowly while she threw snowballs trying to dislodge it, doing no good. Her back was still to me or else I am sure that she too would have been throwing snowballs at me.

"You want help?" I asked.

She turned at the sound of my voice, her face draining of the small color that winter allowed. She didn't have anything to say, I'd snuck up on her pretty good.

I lifted my cane, knocked the basketball out of the net. It fell down and bounced four times, came to rest in the snow.

"What happened to you?" she said.

"You look good," I said.

"You don't look good," she said.

"Car crash," I said, "but I'm fine."

"Hold on—What? Why are you here?"

"No reason, just visiting."

"Get away from me," she sneered.

"Spare an injured man a little additional pain, please."

"Nice cane, it's a nice prop in your costume of pity."

"Pity? I was thrown through a windshield," I said.

"Good."

"I knew you were going to say that."

"I was thrown through a windshield too. When you left."

"You left me first," I said.

"You're being very technical. It's making me sick to my stomach."

"I didn't come here for trouble."

"I want to believe that."

"Believe it," I said, she was looking down at her shoes. Her shoes looked great, so did her legs, her arms, all of her. "You look great." I said.

"You already said that."

"Did I? Well, you look great."

"You already said that twice."

"Did I? Well you look great." I swung the plastic grocery bag at my side. She looked at it curiously. "Got something in here of yours."

I opened the plastic bag I'd carried all the way there. The Three Wolves Howling at the Moon sweatshirt. She caught it, smiling.

"Oh my god, I remember this. Where'd this come from?"

"It was in the trunk of the car." She took her coat off and pulled the old sweatshirt over her head.

"Still fits!" Her guard was down now. She was smiling at me. "Thank you. I feel like shit," she said.

"I'm with you on that."

"Are we supposed to be having this contest where the other person tries to make the other person feel like they haven't suffered as much as them?"

"I missed you like crazy," I said. "I had all these weird dreams about you sitting at the kitchen table, eating an orange."

"It's Thanksgiving," she said.

"Is it?"

"And your birthday."

"I didn't even notice. I just came out of a coma last week, I lost track of a lot of things," I said.

"Like . . ."

"Space and time for starters."

"Oh, I thought you were going to say something cheap like, I lost track with what went wrong between us," Sarah said.

"I don't read romance novels."

"Maybe you should start."

"Nawwwww."

"Because if you had said that, then I probably would want to hear the rest of what you have to say," she said.

"But I don't really have anything else to say."

"Bullshit! You're here!"

"Yeah, I'm here, but me and you don't talk. Hey, look, I was just walking down the street. I saw you needed help. I stopped to help a damsel in distress."

"Oh, that's all?"

"Yeah, is it illegal to walk down this street?"

"For you, yes."

"Restraining order?"

"I don't know why I bothered to put a restraining order on an abandoner," she laughed.

"It doesn't make sense."

She was looking at my cane, "You look nice with a cane."

"I am jealous of Ted, he lost his eye, he has an eyepatch now. He looks great."

She actually laughed at that, "You're so fucking sick."

"Then why do you laugh?"

"Because I'm sick too," Sarah said. "Same as ever, if not worse."

I looked at the building, its red bricks were not welcoming. "You live in here?"

"Right across the hallway from where I grew up."

"Oh, I was worried that you were going to say the same apartment."

"No, but almost." She fixed her hair.

"Red beard isn't gonna come down here and break my other ribs is he?"

"Red beard? Long gone," she said.

"OK."

"You cold? You're shivering."

"I'm freezing," I said.

"I would invite you in my apartment, but I don't think that it's a good idea."

"Why?"

"Because I don't want you in my apartment, or near me."

"But I'm cold," I said.

"And it's your birthday."

"You got it."

"And it's Thanksgiving," she added, looking me in the eye. Her eyes were so blue. They could kill a person. "Since we don't have anybody else, we might as well spend it together."

"Sure," I muttered.

"Look, I was having a great time shooting foul shots all by myself. I would still be having a great time shooting foul shots by myself if you'd stop trying to take me to dinner."

"Chinese?" I said.

"Absolutely," she said, looking down at the ground, blushing a little bit. I had butterflies in my stomach. I was going on a date with my wife . . . a second chance. When I looked up, her basketball hit me square in the face and broke my nose.

Stars. Dark clouds. Blood.

We drove her Nissan to the Great Wok of China. I held the tissues against my nostrils. "The blood looks like it's stopping," I said. "Who cares," Sarah said, but I could tell from her eyes, that she did care.

The people in the restaurant treated us lovingly, as people often treat stray dogs during a snowstorm. They brought noodles and tea, we looked at the menu and ordered too much food for four people. The waiter was a tall Chinese man, very unordinary, also clumsy. He kept spilling things but none of it landed on us. The disasters would crash to the floor and he would apologize, rushing off, coming back with new items, half of which he would spill.

He was very nervous around us. We were intimidators on that day, our eyes were the eyes of wolves, of spiders, of sharks. We felt clumsy too, she didn't know how to look at me, I didn't know how to look at her. We kept spilling out odd phrases that we both knew were blown out of proportion due to the gravity of the dinner, what it meant and what it was going to mean.

"This doesn't mean anything," she said.

"I agree."

"As far as anything."

"Yeah, definitely."

"You can't just show up."

"Nope, won't," I said.

"Thinking to, whatever . . ."

"Not even attempting it," I said.

"Because it's over."

"I'd be the first to tell you that," I said.

"Would you?" she asked suspiciously. "You can't just buy me dinner and think I will take you back,"

"We're divorced you know."

"Yeah, people are stupid, they remarry," she said.

"I'm not that stupid," I offered.

"Neither am I."

"You are really stupid."

"I know, so are you."

"And you are really fucking crazy. I mean like, as crazy as people get without being permanently locked up," I said to her.

"You too."

"Only a matter of time before one of us gets locked up."

"Or kills the other one," Sarah said, slurping her green tea.

"This restaurant might get burnt down in the crossfire."

"Whole town."

"Better we part."

"That was the plan, after dinner."

"Yeah, agreed."

I munched on my egg roll, "How is your egg roll?" She asked, and she couldn't even do it with a straight face.

"My egg roll is so perfect, it's all I ever wanted in the world from an egg roll."

"Even though it's full of things that'll kill you."

"Yeah, choke my heart and my veins and all of that."

"But you love it anyway?"

"I have a death wish," I said gravely. "They tore our house

down," I said.

"No shit, Jim, where you been?"

"Iceland."

"Should have stayed there."

"I never liked our house."

"The truth is, I never liked it either."

"It was too ordinary. It looked just like all of the other houses," I said.

"I felt great the day they tore it down," my Sarah said.

"It's always good when things get torn down."

She was eating brown rice with a chopstick, very delicately. She said to the waiter, "I think we could all use a drink, all of us."

Quickly, he disappeared, coming back with a very cheap bottle of champagne that must have been left over from the previous New Year. He poured three glasses. We all toasted, but as strangers will often toast, with ambiguity and hope towards a future that is unmarred by the relations of the past.

The waiter was gone again, there was still an obvious weight of terror in the air surrounding us. She pulled clove cigarettes out of her pocket, throwing one to me, "I don't smoke anymore."

"Time to start back up."

I placed it in my mouth and she lit it for me. Being that close I caught her scent, that smell that I had known for what seemed like forever.

"You didn't even ask," my Sarah said.

"About what?"

"About the obvious thing you've been skating around, our kid."

Outside the window it had started to snow again. She saw me looking out there at it, "It's the second wave, the big one. A blizzard," she said.

"Oh fuck."

"I like it, it's nice." She had always loved the snow.

"Reminds me of the time we got snowed in."

"We won't get snowed in," she said. "You have no chance of ever getting snowed in with me again."

"People don't get to choose when natural disasters make victims out of them."

I asked for the check. The man brought it quickly.

I paid it with Ted's money.

As we were getting our mints and leaving, the waiter wished us a Merry Thanksgiving and a holiday of much happiness. I wished him the same.

In the lot, I stood outside the car door. Sarah unlocked her side. "You aren't invited in," she said. "The bus still runs."

Sarah got in, shut her door, started the ignition. I stood out in the wind, pathetically jiggling the door handle. "Come on, let me in." She laughed. I noticed that she had a oiled up shirtless Chippendale model air freshener. That made me jealous. I said, "If you open the door, I'll tell you the secret to life. It was given to me by a guru on top of an erupting volcano . . . he begged that I only share this top secret info with beautiful girls from New Jersey who hate my guts."

Immediately, Sarah leaned over and unlocked my side, "OK, get in, I wouldn't want to see you freeze to death on your birthday."

"Where are you staying?" she asked.

"Nowhere," I said. "The woods."

"Oh . . . Tent City?"

"Tent City, sort of."

We said nothing and I was dismal as we passed the old things that were getting further buried.

"You could move back into the 7-11? Our beds were by where the Slurpee machine is now. That would work out. You love Slurpees."

"Tropical Mystery was always my jam."

"Gonna take your old job back?" she asked, steering with her knee, zipping her old sweatshirt up.

"I have figured one thing out and one thing only: I want absolutely nothing to do with that tollbooth. I'm through sitting inside it or anything like it. I'm gonna go get a job—carpentry, masonry . . . something. I called a place earlier, DR Masterson. They're hiring."

"Build shit? You don't know how to do that?"

"I learned my bonnie gal, I learned. I can fish too. I'm a hot shot working man now."

She glanced at my hand on the center console, the scar there. I stared at the side of her face as we drove back through town. The light had a blue grey quality to it. Everything smelled like wood fire. The streets were stained with salt. There wasn't a hint of ice on any of the avenues. I noticed that she was driving deliberately slow through traffic lights, as if hoping to catch the red ones.

Acknowledgements

So many people helped out during the creation of this book. First of all, thanks to my wife, Rae Buleri; my parents Gary and Robin Smith, my brother Will; thanks to Elaine and Ben Buleri; thanks to Mark Brunetti, Keith Baird, Bobby Fisher and Andrew "Ink" Feindt for the attention to detail that went into the editing and proofreading, book layout and design; thanks to Michael Gillan Maxwell, Aaron Dietz, Erin McParland, Chuck Howe, Anthony Thomas, Dustin Holland, Robert Vaughan, Ben Loory, Martha Grover, Meg Tuite, Misti Rainwater-Lites, Paul Corman Roberts, Stephanie Bryant Anderson, Brian Fugett, Matt Guerruckey, Gabriel Ricard, The Idiom, Kleft Jaw, Uno Kudo, Jmww, Red Fez and everyone who makes art of any kind; most of all, thank you for reading.

Bud Smith grew up in New Jersey, and currently lives in Washington Heights, NYC with a metric ton of vinyl records that he bought at Englishtown flea market for a dollar. He is the author of the short story collection Or Something Like That (2012), and Lightning Box (Kleft Jaw Press, 2013); he hosts the interview program The Unknown Show; edits at Jmww and Red Fez; works heavy construction in power plants and refineries. Currently, he's probably watching My Cousin Vinny.

www.budsmithwrites.com

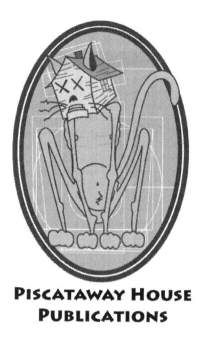

PISCATAWAY HOUSE
PUBLICATIONS

Piscataway House Publications is an independent publishing company based out of New Jersey.

Our books range from the anthologized back issues of The Idiom Magazine to a collection of Haiku from Central Jersey Poets to the collected writings from the MFA program at William Paterson University.

You can learn more about PHP and The Idiom Magazine at www.theidiommag.com

Made in the USA
Charleston, SC
23 January 2014